Buffy dropped to her knees by Pike. The first thing she noticed was that he was still breathing. A huge wave of relief swept over her.

"Pike," she whispered.

His eyes fluttered open. "Hey, Buff," he croaked. "Did you get Giles back?"

She shook her head. "But I will."

Pike nodded painfully.

"What happened to Grayhewn? Why did he leave?"

Pike smiled weakly. "Dude didn't have any reason to stay," he said simply. Then he raised his left hand, and Buffy saw what he meant, saw the long stretch of skin on Pike's right forearm that had turned to stone.

"He touched me," Pike said. "And it's spreading."

Buffy the Vampire Slayer™

Child of the Hunt
Return to Chaos
The Gatekeeper Trilogy
   Book 1: Out of the Madhouse
   Book 2: Ghost Roads
   Book 3: Sons of Entropy
Obsidian Fate
Immortal
Sins of the Father

The Watcher's Guide: The Official Companion to the Hit Show
The Postcards
The Essential Angel
The Sunnydale High Yearbook

Available from POCKET BOOKS

Buffy the Vampire Slayer young adult books

Buffy the Vampire Slayer (movie tie-in)
The Harvest
Halloween Rain
Coyote Moon
Night of the Living Rerun
The Angel Chronicles, Vol. 1
Blooded
The Angel Chronicles, Vol. 2
The Xander Years, Vol. 1
Visitors
Unnatural Selection
The Angel Chronicles, Vol. 3
Power of Persuasion

Available from ARCHWAY Paperbacks

BUFFY THE VAMPIRE SLAYER™

SINS OF THE FATHER

CHRISTOPHER GOLDEN

An original novel based on the hit TV series created by Joss Whedon

POCKET BOOKS

New York   London   Toronto   Sydney   Tokyo   Singapore

This book is a work of fiction. Names, characters, places and incidents are products of the author's imagination or are used fictitiously. Any resemblance to actual events or locales or persons, living or dead, is entirely coincidental.

An *Original* Publication of POCKET BOOKS

POCKET BOOKS, a division of Simon & Schuster Inc.
1230 Avenue of the Americas, New York, NY 10020

™ and copyright © 1999 by Twentieth Century Fox Film
Corporation. All rights reserved.

ISBN: 0-671-03928-8

First Pocket Books printing November 1999

10 9 8 7 6 5 4 3 2 1

POCKET and colophon are registered trademarks of
Simon & Schuster Inc.

Printed in the U.S.A.

For my brother, Jamie,
and my sister, Erin

Acknowledgments

Thanks, as always, to Connie and the boys, to my agent, Lori Perkins, and to Pocket Books' "Team Buffy," Lisa Clancy (the termineditor), Liz Shiflett, and Micol Ostow (go Jumbos!). Thanks, also, to Joss Whedon, Caroline Kallas, Debbie Olshan, and everyone at Fox and Mutant Enemy for working with me on this one. Finally, thanks to the crew: Jose, Tom, Jeff, Nancy, Stefan, and Bob. And a special SO to Little Willow and Labrynth.

SINS OF THE FATHER

Prologue

IN THE STREETS AND ALLEYS, THE SHADOWED CORNERS and open spaces of Sunnydale, California, the darkness stirred with horrid life. Monsters of nightmare, demons and vampires and things which defied description, prowled the night, stalking the light and life and laughter of the people of that town. And they had no one to protect them.

Behind the door of 1630 Revello Drive, Buffy Summers, the one girl in all the world gifted with the power to fight the darkness, shuddered in terror, frozen with dread, and closed her eyes, hoping it would all just go away. Hoping the horror on her doorstep would disappear into the shadows.

But he would never go away. She knew that. What he wanted was inside the walls of the Summerses' home.

Against her back, the wooden door shook slightly as he pounded on it again, and Buffy winced. *I don't think I can take this,* she thought, eyes downcast as she gnawed on her lower lip.

"Buffy?"

She glanced up to see her best friend, Willow Rosenberg, standing in the living room, arms crossed, a stern expression on her face.

"Let him in," Willow chided her.

"But Will," Buffy protested. "Don't you remember what happened last time?"

Willow looked at her with profound sympathy, but then shrugged. "You can't protect her forever," she said.

With a sigh, Buffy rolled her eyes in surrender, then turned and unlocked the door. She drew it open, a false, half-smile on her face, and saw the man standing on the front step. He wasn't half bad looking actually, for an older guy. His brown hair was a bit too long maybe, and there was some gray in it, but that was to be expected. Otherwise he was in good shape, and when he smiled, as he did now, his eyes seemed to sparkle.

"You must be Buffy," he said pleasantly, holding out his hand for her to shake. "I'm Alan Wickstrom. It's nice to meet you finally."

"Yeah," Buffy muttered. "Charmed."

She stood aside to allow Alan across the threshold just as her mother came down the stairs. Buffy thought her mom looked about as good as she ever had. Her hair was tame for once, and she wore a light cotton sleeveless dress in a burgundy floral pattern that Buffy had helped her pick out the week before. She'd been working out, mostly for confidence, and her smile showed it all.

"Joyce," Alan whispered, "you look radiant."

Mrs. Summers pretended not to be loving it. "Just looking forward to tonight," she confessed.

"Me too," Alan agreed.

He met her at the bottom of the stairs and they shared a brief, chaste kiss.

Buffy wanted to stake him.

Out on patrol later that night with Willow and their friend, Xander Harris, Buffy stopped in the middle of the street and looked at Willow imploringly. "Isn't there some kind of spell you can put on him to scare him away?" she asked.

Willow glanced around uncomfortably. "You know I don't use magick like that," she said. "Besides, Alan is of the normal, I would say. I mean, he's not a vampire. He's not a demon. Not a big honkin' evil hell beast."

"He's a man," Buffy argued.

"Well, there's that."

"Besides," Buffy went on, "he doesn't have to be a demon. Ted wasn't a demon."

"He's nothing like Ted. You said so yourself," Xander reminded her. "For starters he's, okay, run with me here . . . not a machine."

With a withering glance, Buffy silently challenged Xander to continue with that train of thought. Wisely, he didn't say another word. For at least five seconds.

"Okay, make Slayer-eyes at me, I don't care," he said, throwing his hands up. "I'll shut up now. I know when nobody wants to hear me. Nope, I can shut up when my opinion is completely disregarded. I get it, don't worry. Your mom once dated a homicidal robot—who, by the way, was an excellent cook—and you're a little skittish. We understand it, don't we Willow?"

Willow nodded and opened her mouth to respond, but Xander didn't give her the chance.

"And, okay, Mom plus dating could at some point equal sex, and that's a giant economy size wiggins. But let's face it, Joyce is a young, unattached woman, and not half a hottie for a woman of her age—"

"Xander!" Buffy snapped, eyes wide.

"I'm just *saying*. I may only be eighteen, but I'm male, after all. Despite the complete disregard with which I've been treated by the female portion of the human race, I am capable of noticing that an older woman is a babe."

"A *babe?* My mother is *not* a babe!"

"So you think your mom's not attractive?" Xander demanded, as if Buffy were on the witness stand.

"That's not what I meant," she replied, her head beginning to ache. "Of course I think she's—"

"My point," Xander concluded. "My work here is done."

"I thought you were shutting up?" Buffy said, moving toward him, eyes narrowed.

"I am. I'm shutting up. Totally. I know when to shut up. But you should give the guy a chance before you—"

"Shut up shuttin' up!" Buffy shouted.

Eyes wide, Xander looked at her, a hurt expression beginning to spread over his features. This time he lasted ten seconds.

"Just trying to help," he said.

Buffy buried her face in her hands and a deep sigh escaped her lips. Then she turned her back on Xander and Willow, and set off through the gate at the entrance to Hammersmith Park.

"Come on," she said sharply as she started along a paved path that wound through the trees and lawns of the park. "I need to kill something."

Dutifully, her two best friends followed. Buffy reached inside the bag slung over her shoulder and re-

moved a solid, tapered wooden stake. She handed the
bag back to Willow, who took one for herself and another for Xander.

In the daylight, Hammersmith Park was glorious.
The trees were beautiful and the landscaped gardens at
the far end of the park drew visitors year round. There
were food vendors and merchants with flower carts,
street musicians and dancers, jugglers and magicians.

The beauty of the place and the sheer energy and life
of it made it one of the most popular spots in town. On
weekends and in the summer, local kids sprawled on the
grass sunbathing or tossed Frisbees, but mostly just hung
out in order to see and be seen. When the sun was up.

At dusk everything changed. Sunnydale had been
built over what its original Spanish settlers called *Boca
del Infierno:* the Hellmouth. It was a kind of supernatural magnet drawing all manner of horrible creatures
inside the town limits. Though the populace turned a
blind eye most of the time, a great many of them, Buffy
had reasoned, must realize that *something* was rotten in
Sunnydale.

As a result, people rarely walked around alone at
night. Certainly, given the job the mayor and the police
department did putting spin control on the bizarre and
horrific things that happened in town, the townspeople
weren't frightened enough to stay in entirely. But it was
California. Most people drove. Those with the ambition
to walk usually did so in the company of others.

And there were, admittedly, places people tended to
shy away from after dark. Weatherly Park, for instance.
Bad things tended to happen there after nightfall. And,
of late, Hammersmith Park had begun to get the same
reputation. Buffy had noticed a sharp increase in the
past week of vampire activity in Sunnydale, and Ham-

mersmith Park seemed to be the focal point. As she walked along the empty path, passing benches devoid even of the homeless, Buffy hoped people had gotten the message.

But she was prepared to be disappointed. After all, there were a lot of teenagers in Sunnydale, and they always needed a place to go to be alone with their boyfriends or girlfriends, or to hang out and drink with their buddies, or just to stay out too late and be with their friends. They should have been, but by and large, Buffy's peers weren't afraid of the dark, weren't afraid to gather in cemeteries or on the beach or up at the Point.

They should have been.

She still had a picture in her mind of Shauna Colburn, the girl they'd found in the park the night before. It wasn't enough that they had killed her. There had been twin puncture wounds on her throat, of course, but also on her arms and wrists and legs, as though she had been taken as supper for an entire litter of newborn puppies.

Newborns. And they might be, at that. But these were vampires, not puppies, and Buffy didn't want to see anything like Shauna Colburn again.

"He's right you know," Willow said softly, just to her right.

Buffy glanced at her, then looked away guiltily. She turned to peer over her shoulder at a sullen Xander. She slowed her pace and dropped back so that she was between them again.

"Sorry, Xand," she said quietly.

"Hey," was all he said, and he smiled. "You're scared for her."

"But Alan seems really nice," Willow offered.

Buffy grumbled.

"Well, not, y'know, that we could tell just from those few seconds, but basically nice, right? And basically nice is a start on the journey to really nice. And he's not bad looking for an older and-I-am-not-venturing-into-Xander-territory man," Willow said, eyebrows arched.

"It's just . . . I feel like I can protect her from the big honkin' evil, y'know?" Buffy asked, despairing. "Okay, she's been through some pretty rough stuff thanks to the whole Chosen One business, but I've always found a way to keep her safe. When it comes to the forces of darkness, I'm Power Girl."

She paused and looked at her friends. "But I can't protect her from this. I can't stop her from getting hurt. And I'm not going to lie, there's a whole selfish thing here, too. What happens if her life becomes some Meg Ryan movie, and she falls in love? I'm the Slayer. I can't change what I am. But that could mean I'm back in the closet, right? And then what? So she gets married again, and suddenly I've got a stepfather, and then I have to worry about what he thinks, and then . . ."

Buffy let her words trail off. Xander and Willow were staring at her.

"You do realize you're losing your mind?" Xander asked.

"Did you notice that you're afraid of your mother getting hurt but you're even more terrified of her finding happiness in a relationship?" Willow asked, her voice soft as though she were speaking to a mental patient with violent tendencies.

With a shake of her head, Buffy sighed. "Of course I know that," she said. "So what do I do?"

Xander nodded thoughtfully and scratched his chin.

He laid a comforting hand on her shoulder, glanced at Willow, and then looked back at Buffy.

"You were right," he said gravely. "You need to kill something. After which, something of the snack genus, perhaps of the chocolate species, would do us all a world of good."

"I don't think I'm in the mood for snacks," she replied.

Willow laughed. "Buffy, what are you thinking? The snacks aren't for you, they're for Xander."

Xander smiled innocently.

Deep in the park, where the sculpted gardens cast long shadows, someone screamed.

Buffy was running, stake gripped in her right hand, before Willow and Xander had even begun to react. Then they were behind her, their feet slapping the paved path as well. Ahead, there came another scream. Buffy listened closely, eyes focusing on the garden up ahead. There was an arch of green and flowers just off to the left, and she broke off from the path and headed for the arch on the most direct route.

Even as she passed beneath the arch and into the garden, Xander and Willow close behind, she heard the scuffle ahead. Buffy dropped into a crouch, hidden by the plant life and multicolored flowers all around her. She hustled, bent over like that, along one aisle of the garden. She could hear the sound of a fist slamming into flesh, and the whimper of a human being close by.

At the end of the aisle, she peered around the corner, and they were there. Vampires. At least five, maybe six of them. She couldn't be certain in the shadowy recesses of the garden. There was a corpse sprawled across the path behind them, a guy maybe twenty. But the vampires weren't done. They surrounded a park bench, and on the bench, a redheaded woman—the dead guy's girlfriend, most likely—was stretched between them.

As one, they descended upon her, fangs bared, faces contorted by the demons that lived within them.

Buffy launched herself along the path, rising to her full height. She grabbed the nearest vampire from behind, her fingers digging into the flesh of his throat, and drove her stake through his back with enough force to reach the heart. It wasn't easy, staking them from the back.

Easy didn't matter. The girl's life did.

The vampire exploded to dust in front of Buffy without making a sound. Before the others could even respond, she spun into a high kick and knocked a vampire backward. He stumbled and fell over the corpse on the path. Then they were on her. Buffy turned and met her first attacker with the stake, and he almost seemed to pop, a piñata bursting, filled with ash. But when the ash cleared, there was nothing left of him.

Then there were four.

"You interrupt the feasting," snarled a blond female vampire in high boots, jeans, and a black baby tee. "I'll have your eyes for that."

"Or not," Xander announced as he and Willow appeared behind Buffy, spreading across the path, stakes in hand, ready to back her up.

The blond girl hesitated a moment. Then she snarled. "Kill them."

The vampires attacked. In a release of all her pent up frustrations and anxieties, Buffy let out a yell that had no words, just anger. She grabbed the nearest vamp, a longhaired male with ritual scars on his face, and they traded blows. This one was good, a trained fighter.

Most of them weren't. She'd lost track of Willow and Xander, but had to assume they were holding their own. There wasn't anything else she could do for them at the moment.

She launched a straight-leg kick at the scarred vampire's gut, but he caught her foot before she could strike, and flipped her back, onto the ground. Even as she landed, she began to roll, to leap back up and face him again.

But it wasn't to be.

Scarface dropped on top of her, forcing Buffy down onto the path. She tried to bring up her stake, but then the blond girl was there, savagely stomping on Buffy's wrist, and she dropped the stake.

"Buffy!" Willow cried behind her.

She didn't dare even turn to see what danger her friends were in. The scarred vampire slammed her skull against the path, and pain shot through her head.

"Thanks," Buffy grunted. "I already had a headache."

But then her voice was muffled, her sarcasm stifled, as he clamped his fingers in a vicious grip around her throat. Choking her. Killing her.

"I want your blood," Scarface told her. "But it'll wait. You're too dangerous to live another second."

Buffy gathered her strength to hurl him off her, to thrust up and buck him away, turning the tables. But he'd cut off her oxygen, and her lungs screamed for air. She had to do it, had to throw him off.

Scarface started to laugh.

Then a long, thin wooden stake erupted from his chest, and he roared in pain.

He was dusted.

There was a figure above Buffy in the dark. As she

climbed to her knees, getting her bearings, she couldn't make out who it was, but she assumed it was Angel. He ran past her, and Buffy turned to see that he was aiding Willow and Xander with the vampire they were fighting. Past them, Buffy saw the blond woman who had apparently been their leader running off across the park.

The final vamp burst into a cloud of ash, and the wind carried it away.

"Oh," Willow said, glancing up at the new arrival. "Thanks."

"Yeah, man, timely save," Xander added.

Buffy rose to her feet staring at the stranger's back. He was tall and thin, with bleached blond hair. His clothes were baggy and faded. *Definitely not Angel.*

He threw his long stake onto the path in disgust, and suddenly Buffy didn't think he was a stranger anymore.

"I hate this!" he shouted. "Hate it!"

He spun to look at her. "See," he said, "this is why things never would have worked out with us. Don't you *ever* do anything else?"

Buffy's eyes widened, her mouth hung open. She whispered his name.

"Pike?"

Chapter 1

"Pike?" Xander asked. "Like in 'L.A.' Pike?"

Willow turned to Xander with a mischievous grin on her face. "Like in hot-with-the-smoochies Pike."

Buffy shot them both a dark look, meant to quiet them, and it worked. The two of them glanced around innocently. Buffy turned her attention back to Pike.

With a dark tan and his hair shaggy on top, short on the sides, and dyed a patchwork blond, he looked better than ever. That was the first thing she noticed. Mainly because she was trying not to pay attention to the whirlwind of conflicting emotions that rose up at seeing him. *Focus, Summers,* she thought.

Her eyes lingered on the bright pink scar that split his left eyebrow, and her mind drifted back to the night he'd received it. The last night they'd spent together.

"Hey," she said. *Eloquent as ever.*

Pike smiled, shook his head, and strode across the few feet that separated them. He wrapped his arms around Buffy, and she let him. In fact, she more than let

13

him. After a moment's hesitation, she returned the embrace, hugging him tightly to her.

"Buffy," he said, his voice barely above a whisper. "It is so good to see you."

Suddenly, Buffy stiffened. For a moment, she'd nearly forgotten that Xander and Willow were standing there. Now she pushed back, a bit awkwardly, from Pike's embrace, and glanced nervously at her friends before looking back to Pike.

"These are my friends," she told him, feeling more weight on the word than she usually did. It meant more to her than almost anything: friendship. "Willow and Xander. Guys," she continued, looking at them, "this is Pike."

Xander stepped forward, held out his hand, and Pike shook it. Buffy smiled at the oddly formal sight, mainly because it was something she'd never imagined she'd see. Though she'd received a letter from him now and again in the past couple of years, after that last night in Vegas she hadn't expected to ever see Pike again.

Strange wasn't the word for it.

"Nice to meet you," Xander said.

"You too, dude," Pike replied, then glanced up at Willow. "Both of you."

"Buffy's told us a lot about you," Willow said. "Okay, not a lot really, but . . . so what brings you to Sunnydale?"

At that question, Buffy watched Pike closely. It would have been the next thing out of her mouth if Willow hadn't beaten her to it. And it was abundantly clear, watching Pike's reaction, that the question made him uncomfortable.

With a guilty sigh, his eyes stopped wandering and

focused on Buffy's face, as if she, rather than Willow, had asked the question.

"Could we talk about this over coffee?" he asked.

They walked the half mile to the Espresso Pump. Buffy and Willow had pretty much declared it their spot to just sit and talk, something that wasn't easy to do at the Bronze. But the Bronze was about something else: dancing, flirting, meeting people, and more dancing. The Espresso Pump was coffee and conversation.

Xander and Willow walked ahead, and Buffy brought up the rear with Pike. With the purpose of his arrival in Sunnydale off-limits for the moment, she wasn't quite sure what to say to him. Thankfully, the others didn't have that problem.

"So, Pike," Xander said, with feigned nonchalance, "you're pretty good with a stake, and down with the ol' night beasties. Buffy said you traveled around a lot. I figure you for a fearless vampire hunter, or a homeless drifter."

Willow gave him an elbow to the side.

"No offense," Xander added quickly, gently touching his ribs.

Pike glanced at Buffy before replying. When he did, he was talking to her as much as answering the question.

"Not quite," he said. "Either way. Although I did the homeless drifter thing for a few weeks a couple of years back."

Buffy frowned, concerned and sad. Pike had never told her that, and the thought of him . . . *no, he can take care of himself. That's what he's best at.*

"And what've you been avoiding doing with your time since then?" Buffy asked.

Willow's eyebrows went up. Buffy knew she was surprised at her tone of voice, and didn't care. She had a lot of mixed-up feelings when it came to Pike, and it was up to her to work them out.

For his part, Pike didn't seem to notice. He shrugged.

"Last time I saw Buffy was the fall of sophomore year," he recalled. "Course, she'd totally been expelled by then, and I dropped out. After what I'd . . . well you guys obviously know what it's like. Once I found out what was out there in the dark, I couldn't really focus on school anymore. We went on a few road trips, checking out vamp activity and then . . . I sort of retired I guess."

"We both did," Buffy reminded him. "Only I didn't get the choice."

"Just when I thought I was out, they pull me back in!" Xander grunted dramatically.

They all stared.

"Pacino," Xander said, rolling his eyes. *"Godfather III."*

Willow patted him on the shoulder. "It's important you keep believing you can do these impressions."

"But it's also important you stop doing them around your friends," Buffy added before looking at Pike again.

Pike glanced away. "I couldn't look at the world the same way after I knew what I knew. It's hard to concentrate on the future when you know any day it might just get taken away."

He paused, looking up as both Xander and Willow dropped back slightly to watch him curiously.

"Sorry," he said. "Guess you guys live with that every day, huh? Anyway, I was kind of hiding out from the world, which is how I ended up on the street. But I had friends, some family, people I could get a couple of bucks from. I got back on my feet, moved down to Pacific Beach, got a new surfboard and a job driving a rehabbed VW Bug as a taxi, met some new people. Got my GED."

"The idyllic southern California life," Willow said. "Surfing and meeting girls. Or, in my case, boys."

"Y'know, as I think of it, that doesn't sound half bad," Xander pointed out. "If I could remember the words to any song by the Beach Boys, I'd sing."

"God help us all," Buffy muttered.

"It's not for everyone," Pike told Xander. "And it isn't as perfect as Willow makes it out to be. At least not for me. See, knowing what I know, I can't even read the paper the same way everyone else does. Where one person sees a horrible crime and shrugs their shoulders, I always have to wonder whether there's something behind the story that makes the news."

"So you're like Batman," Xander said. "You're out there tracking down the truth."

Buffy laughed at that, and Willow looked at her with astonishment, obviously thinking her unconscionably rude. But she knew Pike, and they didn't.

For his part, Pike only looked at Xander as if he were out of his mind. "Dude," he said, giving it all the meaning in the world. "Please."

"Not Batman," Xander corrected.

"Not even Robin," Pike explained. "I see something nasty, and maybe I wonder if there's more to it. And then I grab my board and go surfing and try to find a wave sweet enough to make me forget all about it."

There, Buffy thought. *That's the Pike I know.*

It wasn't always like that, though. She wasn't about

to forget what Pike was like when they'd first gotten to know one another. But that was a different story, a different time. He had a personal stake in what had happened at Hemery High two and a half years before. Not anymore.

Then Willow said something that surprised Buffy.

"Sometimes it doesn't work, though," she said, slowing almost to a stop as she studied Pike. "Sometimes you can't forget, and then you have to do something."

Pike shrugged. "There've been a couple of times," he admitted. "Maybe two years ago a little gang of bloodsuckers killed a bud of mine in the Gaslamp District in San Diego. That got personal. About four months ago, dude named Gorch and his girlfriend came through town, made a mess of a place I like to hang called Coasters."

"Lyle Gorch?" Willow asked, glancing at Buffy in surprise.

"We ran into him not that long ago," Xander added. "It wasn't the first time either. He's a member of Buffy's fan club, I think. Not to mention the first guy shot in every Clint Eastwood movie."

"Maybe he was on his way here. I don't know," Pike said. "Anyway, it doesn't matter, 'cause the cowboy was long gone after that. Never ran into him again. And I don't really want to. I hate all of this. It isn't my world, it isn't what I want."

They were walking along the street, past storefront windows, and the Espresso Pump was just a few doors up. But Buffy couldn't ignore Pike's words. They infuriated her. With all he'd seen, all he could have done to help if he'd set his mind to it—he was easily as capable as any of her friends, and even more so when it came to fighting vampires—she couldn't help feeling a little bitter toward him.

"So what *do* you want, then?" she asked, barely able to disguise her anger.

Willow and Xander had reached the door to the Pump, and Xander held the door for them. Pike paused, however, and turned to look at Buffy.

"I'm in trouble," he told her. "I need your help."

When they'd all paid for their ridiculously expensive exotic coffees, they slid into a booth together, Buffy and Willow on one side, and Pike and Xander on the other. She'd held back her questions, her conflicted emotions, and her opinions, up until now. But Buffy was through holding back.

"You've got a lot of nerve coming here," she told Pike.

"Y'know," Xander piped up suddenly. "It's a nice night. Maybe Willow and I should take our coffees for a walk."

"You don't need to do that," Pike said, looking at Buffy sadly. "If anybody leaves, it'll be me. And that's up to Buffy."

With a deep breath, Buffy regarded Pike. Then she looked at Willow and Xander, who immediately turned away and struck up a gibberish conversation with one another, sipping their coffees.

"I guess I hoped you'd be glad to see me," Pike said, with a half shrug.

Buffy sighed. "I am glad," she said. "Maybe it wouldn't be so weird if you'd called or something—"

"I couldn't call."

"—but you skipped out on me at maybe the most confusing and difficult time of my life. The threat was over, and you were just gone."

"The only reason I stayed in the first place was to

help you. I'd been wanting to get out of L.A. for a long time. You know that. And besides, you were done anyway. After what happened with Merrick and all, you didn't want to be the Slayer anymore."

Buffy glanced down at the table. Saw her coffee there, and had so nearly forgotten about it that she was almost surprised to see it. It was a mocha actually, a cappuccino with chocolate stirred in, and a bit of frothy whipped cream on top. A special treat. The kind of thing she only ordered when she was depressed or confused.

"You could've stayed. You could've said good-bye at least."

"Your mom had already decided to move anyway," Pike argued. "Look, Buffy, I'm sorry things worked out the way they did. And I'm sorry that you can't just walk away and live on the beach and surf and watch the fireworks over Sea World from the shore. But you're the Chosen One, not me."

"Yeah," she said bitterly. "The demons would love that. You'd be too busy waxing your board to sharpen a stake."

There was a long pause. Buffy could feel how tense Willow was at her side, and she glanced over to see that Xander was just as uptight. She didn't blame them. This was awkward for all of them. She should've taken Pike off and talked to him alone, but she honestly hadn't expected to react this way. In the few letters they'd exchanged, she'd felt only the barest hint of the hostility that rose up in her now.

Buffy shook her head, waved her hand in the air as if she could erase the previous few minutes. "Look, I'm sorry," she said. "You came here for help, and I owe you that much, at least. You were there when I needed you most, and that counts for something. No matter what came after."

Pike nodded gratefully. Then he looked directly in Buffy's eyes as if searching for something. He seemed quite melancholy in that moment. When it passed, he smiled tentatively.

"Would it help if I said I missed you?" he asked.

"Maybe a little," she admitted. She glanced down at the table, took a breath, and then looked up at him again. "How have you been? Really, I mean. Do you still have the dreams about Benny?"

Pike had lost his best friend to the vampires back at Hemery High, and nightmares had plagued him for months afterward.

"Once in a while," he told her. "But not like they used to be."

"I'm glad," Buffy said.

Simple as that, the past was behind them. For the moment.

Buffy glanced at her friends. "Now that we've ruined Willow and Xander's night—"

"Are you kidding?" Xander asked gravely. "You can't pay for this kind of entertainment."

Willow and Buffy both shot him a withering glare.

"And now that we've moved on," Xander said urgently, "I'd still like to know what Pike is doing here. Not that you're not welcome, Pike, but . . . okay, guy from Buffy's past shows up suddenly, there's a bad precedent here."

"And, strangely for Xander, he's not just thinking about the competition for Buffy's affection that a new/old guy in her life represents," Willow added helpfully. Then, when Xander glared at her, she quickly added, " 'Cause he's totally over that phase of his life and moving into a new and more mature Xander-hood."

"True," he agreed. "But I get a bit shy talking about my Xanderhood, so let's move on, shall we?"

Pike looked at Buffy. "Are they always like this?"

"Him, yes. Her, only sometimes," Buffy told him.

"Must get exhausting."

"Never really noticed," Buffy confessed. "But your usual crowd is a bit more laid-back."

"Wait till you meet Oz," Xander said. "You two are a match made in . . . whatever place laid-back guys come from."

"Great. I'll look forward to it."

Buffy sipped her mocha. "So," she said, her tone automatically moving the conversation forward from its stalled position. "You need my help. Now that I've vented my frustrations and might be willing to actually give it to you, what is it that you need me to kill?"

Pike blinked in surprise.

"Come on," Buffy prodded. "Why else would you come to me?"

He nodded, and gave a small shrug. "It was this friend of mine, Bone—"

"Bone," Buffy repeated. "Your friend's name is Bone?"

"Yeah?"

"Nothing. Just never knew anybody named Bone before," she said.

"You won't," Pike told her. "He's dead."

They were all quiet a moment after that. It was Willow who urged Pike to continue.

"He'd started to get into all this witchcraft stuff, or warlock, or whatever you call it when it's a guy," he explained. "He was an older guy, maybe thirty, and he'd been on the beach a while. Few years back he lost it in a curl, and his board hit him in the back of the head. Guys who knew him before then would tell me he was never the same after that. But I hadn't known him before, so to me he was always just Bone.

"The end of last month, I dropped by his place. We were supposed to go over to Coasters. When I got there, I rang the bell and knocked for a couple of minutes. I was like, dude's not home, I'm outta here. I'm about to leave, and the door opens. Bone looks like he's been on a three-day bender and I've just woken him up.

"But I'd never seen him drink. Not even on New Year's Eve. So I started asking him what was going on, was he sick or something, and he tells me yeah, that's it. He's sick. He'll call, y'know? It was a total brush-off. I was getting a little pissed, and then I notice his T-shirt."

Pike paused then, as if the memory was difficult for him.

"There was blood on it," he said.

Buffy wanted to interrupt, wanted to rush him, but she could see that it was painful for him, and so she let Pike reveal the details of the story at his own pace.

"It wasn't splashed on, y'know? More like it was soaking through from underneath. I tried to ask him what happened, was he cut, all that. He started getting all jittery, like a junkie needing a fix, telling me we'd hook up later, that he had to get some rest. 'Cause he was sick and all."

Once again, Pike paused. He looked down at the Formica tabletop. Buffy, Willow, and Xander all looked at him, waiting for him to go on. Nearly half a minute passed before Buffy spoke up.

"What did you do?" she asked.

When Pike looked up, his face was contorted with pain and guilt.

"I left," he said. "Damn it, I left. I should have put him in the Bug, taken him to a hospital. Or forced my way into the house. Maybe I would've been able to do something about it then.

"But I didn't. That isn't the way we do things, y'know? Bone's business was his business, not mine. Live and let live, right? Only he didn't. Live, I mean. Two days later he was dead.

"It was driving me nuts the day after, wondering what was going on with him. He didn't show up on the beach at all that day. I tried calling him, he didn't answer. When he didn't show up a second day, I figured I had to go over there. Even if he was just sick, nobody'd heard from him, he wasn't answering the phone.

"So I head over there again and I'm banging on the door. 'Let me in!' I'm yelling out there, and the neighbor's dog is yipping like crazy and I wanted to find a *real* dog to feed that little furry bastard to, and Bone is definitely *not* coming to the door.

"So I broke in.

"The place is a mess. It stinks like crazy—sour milk and rotten food and I don't even want to think what else. The shades are all drawn and stapled to the windowsill, and that's when I know for sure Bone's gone over the edge. I could barely move through the living room without tripping over all kinds of garbage. There were candles all over the place, black and white ones, and there were weird symbols written on the floors and walls. There was a bucket with a big sponge, and the wall was smeared like he'd been trying to wash it off.

"I'm almost to the kitchen when I hear Bone start shouting and crying like a lunatic. Part of me wanted to run. I'm not gonna pretend differently. But after what I went through back in L.A. with Buffy, well, I know there's evil. Real evil. And it was in that house. In my friend's house.

"And I've gotta tell you, evil pisses me off.

"Bone's shouting was coming from upstairs. I ran up, trying not to touch the walls 'cause they were so disgusting I couldn't even tell what was on them and I didn't want to know. At the top, I ran for his room. The door was closed, but I just hauled off and kicked it open, more afraid than I've been since the night Buffy burned down Hemery's gym.

"See, Bone had stopped shouting all of a sudden.

"When I kicked that door open, I saw why. There were black candles everywhere, and there were more symbols painted on the walls in blood. Bone's own blood, I figure. But he didn't have to worry about losing any more of it."

"He was dead," Willow said, speaking the words they were all thinking. After all, Pike had told them as much.

"He was stone," Pike told them. "Literally. Bone had been turned to stone, and the thing that had done it was right next to him. It was made of stone too, but this thing was moving. Not like Bone. The thing just looked at me, snapped off one of Bone's fingers, put it into its mouth and started chomping. I guess it figured it had me. I'd be too scared to do anything but die right there.

"It was so goddamn confident, it looked away over at the middle of the room. There was a pentagram there, drawn on the floor in chalk and something else, like sugar or salt, had been poured around the edges, and then there were candles. Inside the circle, the floor was glowing, kind of moving like water. All the candles were burning black smoke, and another one of those damn things started to climb out of the circle like it was a well or something instead of the wooden floor in a house by the beach.

"The thing that had turned Bone into a statue looked at the other one, the one coming through, and talked to it, but I couldn't understand any of it. It was like the sound of walking on gravel.

"I took one more look at Bone, and then I turned and ran down the stairs."

Buffy looked at Pike in dismay. She didn't blame him, couldn't blame him, but somehow, she had expected more. The idea that he had just run away without even trying to do something distressed her, though he'd already displayed more courage and calm than anybody could have expected. More than she would have given him credit for before tonight, when she wanted so badly to think poorly of him.

"You just left?" Willow asked, gently.

Pike narrowed his eyes. "Of course not."

Immediately, Buffy felt guilty for having judged him. And, ironically, furious at him for not having run after all. Bone was already dead, and he could have been killed.

"Is this one of those to-be-continued cliff-hangers?" Xander asked. " 'Cause I hate that."

Pike smiled weakly. "I ran downstairs, grabbed the bucket of water I'd seen when I first went in, and I went back up. When I got to the bedroom door, there were more fingers missing from Bone's hand. A little snack while it waited for its mate or whatever to come through. When I ran in, it was reaching down to help the other one out. It was maybe halfway through into . . . into our world by then.

"I took the bucket and heaved the water across the floor, and the candles went out and the chalk was washed away, and the passageway, whatever it was, closed right then, and it cut the stone demon that was coming through in half. The thing didn't even scream. The top half just fell over and shattered.

"The other one turned to look at me, started screeching in that gravel voice, and its eyes started glowing red like it had Superman heat vision or something. I turned and just bolted down the stairs. I could hear it coming after me, but I figured, a life for a life. And I needed to learn more about this thing if I was gonna fight it. I didn't want to end up a statue, y'know? So I'm down the stairs and on my Harley and burning out of there as the thing comes crashing out Bone's front door.

"Well, the thing's been after me ever since. Almost caught me a couple of times. I read up on it, too—"

"You were right," Willow interrupted. "It is a stone demon. I read about them in the Codex. Good move with the water, by the way, washing away the portal. How did you know to do that?"

"I didn't," Pike said. "How do you?"

"She's a witch," Xander said calmly.

Willow seemed embarrassed. "Well," she hedged. "Not a witch, exactly. Just a minor spellcaster."

"But she'll be called up to the majors any time now," Xander added.

Pike studied Willow for a long moment, then shrugged. "Sorry if I'm staring. It's just . . . I have an image of what witches ought to look like in my head, and you're not it."

"Gotta get you some of them witchy warts," Xander told her.

"So you just got lucky?" Buffy asked Pike.

"I guess," he admitted. "I figured with the chalk and the candles making up the door, or whatever, if I could get rid of them, maybe it'd close the door. And it worked."

"And now you've made a friend for life," Xander said happily. "And, lucky us, you've come to share."

Pike looked a bit guilty. "That's about it," he admitted. "After I read about the thing, I knew how lucky I was to have even walked away from it. If it touched me . . . *sayonara* man. I knew I needed help, and you were the only person I could think of."

He addressed this last directly to Buffy. It took her a moment to respond. In her mind, she was still with him in his friend's house, with the stone demons, and Buffy was afraid for Pike. No matter how angry she might have been at him, she still cared for him, and didn't want any harm to come to him.

Buffy reached across the table and covered Pike's hand with her own, held it briefly, and smiled. "You did the right thing," she said. "I'm glad you came." She pulled her hand away. "Not glad you've got the big honkin' evil after you, but you came to the right place."

She glanced over at Willow.

"Giles?" Willow asked.

"Giles," Buffy replied.

When the four of them walked into the library, Buffy was more than a little surprised to see Angel sitting at the study desk reading a dusty leather book that had obviously come from Giles's private collection. He glanced up at her, and was clearly as surprised as she was.

"Buffy," he said. "I didn't expect you back this early."

Behind her, Pike whispered to Xander. "Giles?"

"Angel," Xander replied. "Vampire. Good vampire. Usually. Don't ask."

"You didn't . . . ," Buffy began, and then blinked. "Not that I'm not happy to see you, but, what are you doing here?"

Angel shrugged. "Giles called. He had to go out on short notice. Said it was important. He asked if I could wolf-sit for a while."

As if on cue, the library cage rattled, and they all looked over to see the werewolf slamming against the metal mesh. It was the third night of the full moon, and Oz was hungry.

"What could be that important?" Willow asked aloud. "I asked Giles if it would be all right if I went out with you on patrol tonight, Buffy. The whole point of the question was to make sure he could sit up with Oz."

Willow went over to the library cage and began to whisper softly to the werewolf, which only stared at her, growling softly.

"Wait," Pike said, more confused than ever. "That's Oz? The laid-back guy that I'm supposed to get along with so well?"

Buffy smiled. "Give him time. He's a whole different person after he's had his morning coffee."

Angel stood up, placed the book on the table, and walked over toward Buffy, waiting expectantly. It took Buffy a second to realize what he was waiting for.

"Oh, I'm sorry," she said. "Pike, this is Angel. Angel, Pike."

"Pike," Angel said, raising his eyebrows. "From L.A.?"

"Used to be," Pike replied. "Not anymore."

Angel looked from Pike to Buffy. His face was expressionless, but Buffy could tell that he was jealous. Despite the fact that they could never truly be together as lovers, the idea that she might have something with someone else upset him. There'd been a time, however brief, when Buffy had fallen for Pike. It was a while ago, but Angel knew about it. Now he was looking for some sign from her, obviously hoping that those feelings were gone.

Buffy looked away.

"Well," Angel said to Pike. "Welcome to the Hellmouth."

Chapter 2

THE OLD, BATTERED MERCEDES MOVED SLOWLY ALONG Colby Street, riding low, thanks to the weight of the driver, and the solid corpse of the car's owner, which lay in the trunk. The Mercedes turned left at the corner and rolled along at that same pace until it drew adjacent to Hammersmith Park. Then, as though it had simply lost the motivation to continue, the car rolled to a stop. Several seconds slipped by before the car was shifted into park and the engine died, ticking as it cooled.

On the driver's side, the door opened slowly, was pushed slightly beyond its normal capacity, and snapped off, thunking to the pavement. From inside the Mercedes came the hushed, gravelly whisper of a curse.

Grayhewn, the demon, stepped out.

Formed from living stone, he wore a long coat to hide his body and an old-fashioned fedora to conceal the small horns that jutted from his forehead. And to shade the granite features of his face.

"Yes," he said, the sound of his voice not terribly different from that of his feet upon the road. "Yes."

Grayhewn walked across the street toward the entrance to the park. As he crossed, he was illuminated, suddenly, by the headlights of a car as it turned off of Colby, the same way he'd driven in the stolen Mercedes. It sped past . . . at the gates, he paused, seemed to listen to the air a moment. Then he crouched and reached out to touch the stone archway that was the entrance to the park.

To caress it.

His fingers melted into the stone. "Ah, yes, dear one," he rasped. "You've seen him. Share it with me, what you've seen."

And he knew then. The one called Pike had been here, and he had met others. Friends. Grayhewn smiled at the thought. If he had friends, they would die first. And Pike would watch.

As the demon stood, blue lights flashed behind him and a siren split the night just for a moment. If the burst of sound was meant to startle Grayhewn, it did not. He simply stood, and turned, curious to find the origin of the light and disturbance.

A police car. And coming toward him, two uniformed officers. Armed peacekeepers, he knew. The law. But Grayhewn believed in no law save his own, and he was already in search of justice.

"Hold it right there, mister," said one of the officers, who approached now on the left.

Grayhewn dipped his head, hiding his features beneath the brim of his hat.

"Step into the light," said the other officer, approaching from the right. "We've had a lot of trouble around the park recently, sir. What are you doing here tonight?"

"Looking for someone," Grayhewn replied.

They paused. Perhaps, the demon thought, a reaction to his voice.

"Step into the light," the second policeman asked again, his right hand moving down to the weapon holstered at his side.

"By all means."

He stepped forward, tilted his head back, allowed the blue light to flicker across his features. In the moment that the policemen hesitated, eyes wide, he reached out and touched them.

Just under a minute later, he drove the battered Mercedes away from Hammersmith Park, leaving the police car behind him, its lights still flashing, its engine running, its doors open. And in front of the park, some very unusual new statuary.

"Is he going to stay long?"

The question hung in the air for a moment. Angel watched Buffy's eyes, searching for an answer. She didn't look away, didn't want to hurt him that way. Instead, she shrugged.

"I don't know," she said. "I don't know what his plans are. But he never stays anywhere very long. Not since . . . not since Vegas."

"You never really told me what happened with that," Angel pointed out.

Buffy took a long breath, and this time, she did look away. They stood on the front lawn of Sunnydale High, not far from the bench where she often met Willow and Xander in the morning. Right now it was extremely peaceful. A light breeze blew across the school grounds. There was some low cloud cover, but from time to time the beautiful full moon broke through and shone down. It was the perfect temperature, warm enough to go without a jacket, chilly enough to make her shiver now and again, to make her long for arms around her.

Then again, maybe now wasn't the time.

"We have a weird history, Pike and I," Buffy said. "It's hard to explain."

Which was mostly her way of stalling. Back at Hemery High before she'd become the Slayer, she would barely have given a guy like Pike the time of day. She'd been in with the popular crowd, more concerned with her clothes and her image than her studies. One of the reasons why she'd always been willing to give Cordelia some slack was that she'd once been Cordelia. Or damn near.

But then Merrick, her first Watcher, had arrived to train Buffy to become the Slayer. She hadn't made it easy for him. Not that she even believed him to begin with. At least, not until Lothos came to town. And Merrick shot himself to avoid becoming a vampire, and to protect Buffy. And some of her classmates, kids she'd been through freshman year and the beginning of sophomore year with, had become vampires.

Her so-called friends were less than useless. The guy she was seeing went off with a girl she hung with, and the rest of them turned their backs on her. The only one who stood with Buffy against the vampires, despite his fear, was Pike.

She'd loved him a little for that. It didn't hurt that he was handsome, and funny, and oh-so-laid-back cool, and that he had what Buffy's no-longer friend Jennifer would have called Grrr. And things had begun to happen between them.

"What's hard to explain?" Angel asked. "He was

there when you needed him. You had a thing. You burned down the gym to save the rest of the school, and were expelled for it."

"And he dropped out . . ."

"To be with you?"

"I always wondered," Buffy confessed. "But by then, everything that had happened had already become the proverbial straw breaking the camel's back, and my mom and dad were getting a divorce, and Mom wanted to move, and it all happened so fast.

"Then I saw something on the news about these killings in Vegas that sounded so much like vampires. I didn't want to do it anymore. Being the Slayer had just completely torpedoed my world. School, home, image, all destroyed, and to top it off, y'know, vampires."

Buffy glanced at Angel apologetically. He nodded in understanding.

"I was done. Later for that. But people were dying in Vegas and I could do something about it, and when I told Pike, well, he said he'd come with me if I wanted him to.

"And we went."

Angel reached out to stroke her cheek. "Buffy," he said softly, "you've told me all this. What happened?"

"It isn't as big a deal as I'm making it," she admitted. "I mean, it was then, but not after all that's happened since. We went to Vegas. There were vampires. There was also a demon. Magick. Pike fell under the demon's control. I had to . . . hurt him . . ."

Buffy's voice trailed off. Angel reached out to embrace her, and she let herself be folded into his arms, but took little comfort in it. She barely responded, except to lay her head on his chest.

"The scar? Above his eye?" she went on. "I did that."

"But you saved him," Angel reassured her. "He's still alive, right?"

Buffy thought about that for a moment, then pulled back, out of Angel's embrace. She looked up at him.

"Vegas just reinforced what I'd already decided. I was gone for almost two days, told my mother I was staying at a friend's while she and Dad battled it out. When I got back, they'd already filed their papers, and she'd seen an ad in the paper about an art gallery for sale in Sunnydale. She'd always wanted a gallery of her own.

"I didn't want to go. But I didn't want to stay in L.A. either. I needed someone to talk to about it, and I couldn't talk to my mother and I didn't want to talk to my father. The only one who could understand what I was going through was Pike."

She stopped there, looked down at the ground.

"He was already gone?" Angel asked.

Buffy nodded.

"And now he's here," Angel said. "Do you still love him, Buffy?"

She cringed. It was the question she knew was coming, but least wanted to hear. Least wanted to answer. But she owed Angel that much, and more. Buffy looked at him and didn't turn away again.

"I don't know if I ever did," she told him. "Not the way that you mean. But we had something between us, that's for sure. Angel, you know how I feel about you. . . ."

Angel held up a hand to silence her. He shook his head when she began to speak again, and Buffy fell silent.

"Maybe this is right," he said, and she could see the pain in his eyes as he spoke. "Maybe this is what's meant to be. You know that, no matter how we feel, you and I can never really be together, be there for each other the way a couple ought to be. We can't allow ourselves the passion—"

"Angel," Buffy protested.

"No, just listen," he said. "I'm going to stay out of your way for a bit, if I can. You still feel something for Pike, you can't hide that. I think you need to find out exactly what it is."

He bent down and kissed her forehead, then his lips lightly brushed hers. Then he turned away and started off into the darkness. Buffy wanted to call after him, to tell him that he was wrong, that she knew things could never really be between them, and her unresolved feelings about Pike could stay that way forever for all she cared.

But she kept silent.

Buffy didn't like to lie to the people she loved.

As Buffy walked down the deserted high school corridor toward the library, she could hear low growls coming from the library, and voices as well.

"How did you find us at the park?" Xander was asking.

"I checked the papers as soon as I got to town. There'd been a bunch of attacks and disappearances and stuff around Hammersmith Park. I figured that's where Buffy would be. Right in the middle of the action."

She pushed through the library doors. Willow was still sitting by Oz, reading to him in a low voice from Jack London's *White Fang*. Pike and Xander both looked up at her.

"That's me," Buffy said, trying and failing to smile. "Action's my middle name."

"What happened to Angel?" Xander asked. "They having an all-night gore sale at the butcher shop?"

Buffy ignored him, but Pike frowned and turned to look at him.

"That's cold. I'm getting the impression you don't love Angel," Pike said.

"What's not to love?" Xander said, shrugging. "Dead guys are just so charming."

Pike raised his eyebrows and chuckled, but more in disbelief, Buffy thought, than amusement.

It was Willow who sensed her discomfort first. As usual, her best friend was the most perceptive of them.

"Buffy, you have that look," Willow said. "That something-bad look that always makes me nervous, only without the resolve face that usually gives me hope that we can deal."

"You have an eloquent face," Xander translated.

"Giles," Buffy said.

"Who isn't here but should be?" Pike confirmed.

Buffy nodded. "Do you guys think he's been acting a little too Hugh Grant lately?"

"Though he's always been pretty British, I never really thought of him as bumbling," Xander replied thoughtfully. "But now that you mention it, there's been a definite shift from Holmes to Watson the last week or so."

"Thanks Xand. A plain old 'yes' would've been fine. Willow?"

"I guess," Willow replied. "I mean, he's still Giles. But he's been kind of preoccupied—like you are now—and having Angel sub for him tonight with Oz after telling me he'd be here, well, it really isn't like him."

"No," Buffy agreed. "It's not."

Xander cleared his throat. They all looked at him. He glanced around, making a show of hesitating.

"You know," he said, "far be it for me to bring *sex* into the conversation, because, as you know, it really isn't like me to talk about sex, or think about it—"

"Or have it," Buffy said, one eyebrow raised.

Xander glared at her. "But in this case," he went on, "sex does sort of come into the picture. I mean, if I was dating Miss Blaisdell, I'm thinking I'd be a little of the preoccupied myself."

Pike looked mystified. But, Buffy reasoned, Xander had that effect on a lot of people.

"Xand," Buffy said, "Giles isn't dating Miss Blaisdell. They're colleagues. They went out for coffee. Maybe twice. And anyway, Giles probably had tea. And you both know he's still torn up over what happened to Miss Calendar. The idea of a date, the whiff of a date, would make him Mister Freeze."

"Yeah," Willow agreed. "And, okay, the roses he sent her could be just for, um, professional appreciation. And when she came by today to thank him, I'm sure the kiss was platonic."

Buffy stared at her. "Kiss?"

"Maybe not platonic," Willow confessed, defeated.

Buffy hung her head. "First Mom, now Giles." She threw her hands up. "Still, though, even if he is dating someone again, that doesn't explain the way he's been acting. It's like he's only half in his brain, and he walks around like his every move's slo-mo instant replay."

"Buffy," Xander said, slowly and earnestly, "men have been known to act like gibbering fools, and do utterly moronic things, simply due to the proximity of a female."

Pike nodded sadly. "Sad, but true."

Buffy rolled her eyes. "Yes, hence Cordelia."

"That's low," Xander chided her.

"I'm still worried about Giles," Buffy said. "I'm going to go by his place and see if I can find out why he bailed tonight. It might be he's onto something with all this vamp activity at the park."

"He would have waited for you to check in," Willow said, frowning.

"Not if he's suffering from the female proximity effect," Buffy said.

Xander raised his hands triumphantly, nodding. Buffy ignored him.

"Who's coming with me?" she asked.

Pike rose from the table. "I've got nowhere else to go."

"I'm wolf-sitting," Willow said with an apologetic smile.

Xander stood as if to accompany Buffy and Pike, but Willow reached over and pulled him back down into his chair. She stared at him meaningfully.

"You're wolf-sitting too," she told him.

"I am?" he asked, and Willow narrowed her eyes. "I *am*! Love wolf-sitting. As long as I don't have to change the papers."

Buffy smiled at Willow. "See you guys in the morning," she said, and started out of the library.

Pike said his good nights as well, and then followed. "I figured your life here would be interesting," he told Buffy, "but this is wild."

"What do you mean?" Buffy asked, honestly confused.

"Buffy, your best friends are a witch, a vampire, a werewolf, and whatever Xander is."

"Xander's just a guy."

"And he might be the scariest one," Pike told her.
Buffy smiled. "You haven't met Cordelia."

Before coming to the park, Pike had gone to Buffy's house. When he'd found no one at home, he'd left his Harley in the driveway, and walked to Hammersmith. Now, as she walked with him back to her house, Buffy remembered what it felt like to ride on the back of a motorcycle with Pike. It was a nice memory.

It was almost ten-thirty by the time they reached her house, and her mom hadn't gotten home yet. Buffy had a minor panic moment, and then she pushed it away. Willow and Xander had been right. Her mother had to have a life of her own. If that meant she was going to get hurt romantically, Buffy couldn't do anything about it. That was the chance they all took.

She should know.

With a start, she realized that she had just placed herself on the same level as her mother, and with an additional surprise, she found that it was an appropriate thought. She was eighteen, nearly out of high school. By any measure, graduation, at the least, would make her officially an adult. A grown-up.

Which was both exciting and depressing.

But a few minutes later, Buffy had her arms wrapped around Pike's abdomen and her hair was whipping across her face as he steered the Harley toward Giles's house. Maybe she wasn't a kid anymore, maybe the matters of her heart were a bit more grave, a bit more profound, than they had been when she'd first met Pike, but at that moment, she put all such serious thoughts out of her mind.

When they pulled up in front of Giles's apartment, Buffy dismounted the bike, her face flushed. She had a huge grin on her face, and when Pike looked at her, he smiled broadly.

"What?" he asked, stymied by her expression.

"I'm going to have to get myself one of those," she said.

Pike smiled, and followed her up the path to the apartment building. Buffy knocked on Giles's door, and they stood together, waiting. There was no response. After a few moments, Buffy knocked again, a bit harder this time.

"You're worried," Pike said.

She nodded. "Very. He's been acting so weird lately, kind of disconnected. Giles Unplugged. He wouldn't normally go off on a tangent without me even if the evil was something really funky. But it also wouldn't be the first time."

Buffy stared at the front door. "I really thought he'd be home," she said. "Before I was worried. Now I'm getting kind of scared. For him."

She hammered at the door, and shouted his name. Then she looked around to see if she'd drawn any unwanted attention. It wouldn't do for Giles's neighbors to question why a high school girl was pounding on his door late at night. But there didn't seem to be any activity in the surrounding buildings or the windows of the other apartments in Giles's building.

"So what now?" Pike asked.

Buffy thought a moment, then shrugged. "Now, I guess we have another ride on the Harley."

But just as they were turning to go, there came the sound of the deadbolt being drawn back, and the knob turned, and the door was pulled inward. Standing in the now open doorway, Giles stared at Buffy, jaw set stiffly, as it was when he was angry.

"Please tell me the world is coming to an end," he said, glaring at her.

He wasn't wearing his glasses. His eyes were bloodshot, his hair a scraggly mess. The collar of his shirt was open to the third button, and he seemed a bit rumpled all over. Buffy made the obvious connection, and felt badly immediately.

"Oh, Giles, I'm sorry," she said. "I didn't mean to wake you up. It's just, you bailed on Oz-watch earlier, and I figured something had come up. Angel didn't say anything about you not feeling well, and—"

"I feel fine," Giles interrupted, a bit abruptly. His voice sounded a bit slurred, and Buffy wondered if he'd been drinking before he crashed for the night. "Who is this?"

He was staring at Pike with narrowed eyes.

"That's what I came to talk to you about," she said quickly. "This is Pike. From L.A.? I've told you about him. Anyway, he's got a problem, a big nasty on his trail, and I just thought—"

"No. You didn't think," Giles told her. "We'll speak about this intrusion in the morning, Buffy."

Buffy flinched, her head moving back as though he'd jumped out and shouted "Boo!" She stared at him, frowning.

"Intrusion?"

"Do go home, please," he said wearily, and his fingers moved through his hair, smoothing and straightening it a bit.

"I'm . . . I'm sorry, I guess. Shoot me for worrying," she said, and grabbed Pike's elbow. "Let's go."

Then, from inside the door, a woman's voice called out, "Rupert?"

Giles blinked and glanced tiredly back into his apartment. Buffy stared past him and saw Karen Blaisdell standing in the living room, a glass of wine in her hand. The substitute chemistry teacher, whom Giles had known for only a few weeks, had long red hair and a perfect smile. She wore blue jeans and a copper-colored silk shirt. And no shoes.

She was very comfortable.

"Just a moment, Karen," Giles said calmly.

"Your wine is getting warm," she said impatiently.

Giles looked at Buffy. "Good night," he said dismissively, and shut the door.

Buffy blinked, turned, and stormed down the path toward Pike's Harley. At the motorcycle, she waited for him to straddle it, and climbed on behind him.

"Well, at least now you know why he's been acting like such a jerk," Pike said. "He's got other things on his mind."

"Yeah, maybe," Buffy replied.

But she didn't believe it. There was more to this than Karen Blaisdell, she was certain of it. Willow was very particular about wolf-sitting. If she couldn't sit with Oz herself, she wanted to make certain whoever was there was someone she trusted. Not that she didn't trust Angel, but he'd never sat up with Oz before, and that wasn't half the point. Giles knew how Willow felt. He had reassured her that he would watch Oz while she went on patrol with Buffy. Under normal circumstances, he never would have ignored her feelings and ditched his responsibility. Not even for a woman as beautiful as Karen Blaisdell.

It just wasn't Giles. And it wasn't the only example of his odd behavior of late.

Whatever was going on with him, Buffy was determined to get to the bottom of it. But it looked like it would have to wait until tomorrow. Already, as Pike guided the motorcycle away from the curb and down the street, other, more immediate concerns had begun to take precedence.

Like where Pike was going to sleep that night.

She'd just started to turn that problem over in her head, when something struck her as odd. Not a memory. Nor even a thought, really. Just a feeling. Buffy turned around as best she could while still holding tightly to Pike. As he turned a corner, she got a good look back at Giles's apartment building and the surrounding area.

In the dark shadows in front of the building across from Giles's, something moved.

Pike turned the corner, and Buffy couldn't see any more.

"Pull over," she told him.

"What?"

"Fast!"

Pike pulled the bike to the curb. Buffy got off instantly and crossed the street, keeping close to the shrubs around the house in front of her. At the corner, she paused long enough for Pike to catch up to her.

"What's going on?" Pike asked incredulously. "Are we gonna spy on your Watcher while he tries to score with his date?"

Buffy almost shot back a sharp remark, but then she remembered that Pike didn't know Giles. Not that it mattered. There wasn't going to be much more of his date as far as she could tell.

Staring around the corner, narrowing her eyes and wishing she had night vision or something, Buffy whispered back to Pike. "Vampires."

"Huh? Where? You think that Karen chick is a vampire?"

"No," Buffy said. "But there are vampires back there. They were watching us when we were at the door talking to Giles. And they're still there, watching his place."

"You saw them?"

"Sensed them," Buffy replied. "Then I saw something, one of them, I think, when I looked back."

"You sensed them?" Pike asked. "Maybe you're the one going schizo. You could never *sense* vampires before."

"I still can't. Not really. Or, I mean, not really ever before, except a couple of times I kind of thought I did. But when I first met him, Giles told me I should be able to sense them, or learn to sense them, or whatever." Buffy paused, and looked back at Pike. "Point is, I sensed *something*. The radar kicked in for some reason. It's possible it wasn't even me. I mean, maybe something's broadcasting on demon satellite network, and I'm the only one with a dish."

She turned back and stared into the darkness around Giles's apartment. The shadows coalesced, and the longer she stared, the better she could make out figures around that and nearby buildings.

"But they're here," she said. "One on the roof, at least. A bunch around the apartment. Like some kind of vampire task force. I'm the Slayer, Pike, and they let me walk away. Why would they do that?"

"You're the Slayer," he replied. "You'd only get in the way, probably end up killing most or all of them. Local talent's gotta know that, Buffy."

"So they're after Giles," she said, speaking the words for the first time, solidifying her concern for him.

"Or his date," Pike suggested.

Which was when the front door of Giles's apartment opened and Karen Blaisdell stepped out. She had her shoes on now, and Buffy found a kind of weird satisfaction in that. Miss Blaisdell was still just a visitor there. Giles kissed her at the door, and then watched as she walked down the path toward the curb where her car was parked.

Buffy tensed, waiting for an attack. But Miss Blaisdell unlocked her car, got in, started it up, and drove away without a single hostile motion from the things lurking in the darkness.

"Curiouser and curiouser," Pike said.

"What are they waiting for?" Buffy asked.

"The perfect wave," Pike told her. "They're choosing their moment, Buffy."

Then, as the taillights of Miss Blaisdell's car disappeared down the street, dark figures unfolded themselves from shadowy corners, stepped from behind shrubs, and scurried carefully down from rooftops as the vampires, at least a dozen of them, began to converge on Giles's apartment.

Buffy started around the corner, ready to attack, but Pike grabbed her shoulder.

"Wait," he said. "There's too many of them. Besides, if Giles doesn't invite them, they can't get in. Let's see what happens, then we can follow them when they leave. Figure out where they're holed up and hit 'em at sunrise."

With a deep breath, Buffy nodded. "Good plan. You're right. I mean, Giles looked like he was crashing for the night, and without an invitation—"

From down the street came the sound of glass shattering. Buffy turned and stared in horror as the vampires crashed through the windows and the door into Giles's apartment.

"That's not possible," Pike was saying.

And he was right.

But that didn't make it any less real.

Buffy was already running down the street, glancing around in search of a weapon.

Chapter 3

THE LAST OF THE VAMPIRES TO ENTER GILES'S APART-
ment was a slender blond girl in all black. Buffy recognized her from Hammersmith Park earlier in the night.

"The one that got away," Pike huffed, as he ran
alongside her.

"Yeah. But not again," Buffy replied, eyes narrowed.

They ran toward Giles's apartment, and Buffy
glanced around purposefully for a weapon. Any
weapon. Then she saw it. While most of the buildings
on this block were apartments, townhouses, whatever,
the one directly across from Giles's place was an old,
stuccoed, single home. With a mailbox. The mailbox
had a wooden post.

"What are you doing?" Pike asked as she veered
right.

Buffy didn't answer. She thrust a low kick at the
post, powerful and precise, and it splintered. The mailbox tumbled to the ground. The lower portion of the
post was still in cement, and too thick besides. But the

top half, which she now broke off from the mailbox, was split up the middle. Buffy tore it apart and ended up with four stakes.

Two for Pike. Two for her. But she didn't think she'd need the second one. Not the way she was feeling right now. Giles might have been acting freaky-deaky lately, but he was her Watcher, and her friend besides. No way was she going to let him down.

"Move," she snapped, and sprinted across the street for the door.

Pike was right behind her, silent and strong. That was the thing about Pike. He was very good at this for a normal, unenhanced human, and he did it without a joke, without any distraction. Sure, he was laid-back, but when it came to facing evil, he was as grim as they came. In so many ways, he was all the good things about Angel, Oz, and Xander rolled into one. Buffy was glad to have him watching her back, and glad to have him in Sunnydale and in her life, period.

Which made him dangerous.

As they moved up the front path, the door just a ways down from Giles's opened a crack and a man poked his face through.

"Get back inside," Buffy hissed.

The door slammed, and there were no other interruptions. She couldn't believe none of the other neighbors had responded to the noise yet, but it was possible they were just too afraid to poke their heads out to see what was going on. It was Sunnydale, after all. People were used to having to look the other way.

Without slowing a bit, Buffy launched herself through the shattered front door of Giles's apartment. Two vampires stood just inside the door, and they lunged for her as she passed by. Too slow.

She was in.

Both vampires reached for her, and Buffy batted away the hands of the one nearest her, then staked him in the chest. Dusted. Pike came up behind the second one, fast and efficient. He yanked the bloodsucker's hair, pulling back its head, and brought the stake around from behind to plunge it into the vampire's heart.

"Giles!" Buffy screamed, even as the other vamp was dusted.

Two down, ten to go.

There were six or seven in the living room, including the blond. Up in the loft, Buffy spotted three more. They were trashing the place. Smashing glass, tearing clothes, snapping antiques. With all the noise they were making, they hadn't really noticed her and Pike come in.

But Buffy couldn't focus on that. Her only focus was the barely conscious form of Giles. He lay on the floor at the center of the living room, vampires all around him. There was a long cut on his forehead, and he held his arms crossed in front of his face in a gesture of surrender and helplessness, a futile effort to protect himself.

"Stop it!" cried the blond vamp girl. "We're supposed to bring him in one piece."

"Come on, Rachel! We're just having . . . fun!" On the last word, the vampire aimed a hard kick at Giles's kidneys.

But Buffy was already in motion. When he cocked his leg back to kick, she dropped to the ground, landed on her hands, and swung her feet around swiftly to sweep his legs out from under him. Even as he fell, the others were turning, ready to pounce on Buffy.

She rolled out of the way and one of them landed next to her. Another dove for her, but Pike was there, stake in hand, and a cloud of dust exploded above her head. Dead-vampire ash sprayed her hair and eyes, and Buffy blinked. The vamp on the ground reached for her, but she reached over and pinned him, staked him fast.

"You idiots, kill them!" screamed the blond girl, the one they called Rachel.

Pike was fighting in close with a pair of vamps who had the better of him, one in front, moving in for the kill, and another holding him from behind. They had him. And why shouldn't they? He was just a guy. Not a vampire. Not the Slayer. Buffy had started to let herself think of Pike as her equal, and she couldn't let that happen. He could take care of himself better than most, but he was still just along for the show.

Her show.

"Pike, turn!" Buffy shouted.

He glanced up, his eyes gleaming with fear and rage, the pink scar over his left eye shining, and when he saw Buffy's face, he smiled. Then he gave a loud grunt and leaned forward, lifting the vamp that held him off his feet and spinning around.

Buffy ran at the bloodsucker in front of her, an ugly bastard with wispy white hair, and drop-kicked him to the floor. Then she used him as a step, springing up and bringing her stake down hard in the back of the vampire holding Pike. Wood against bone, but bone gave way.

He was dusted.

The jump had left Buffy off balance, and the vampire she'd drop-kicked was up again moving on her. But Pike had him. A very angry Pike. All the charm and humor of that face was turned back to fury now. The vampire tried to block Pike's stake, so Pike shoved it through his right cheek instead, tearing half the fang boy's face away.

The vampire screamed, lunged for Pike, who ducked and thrust the stake home. The vampire spun away even as he dusted, and Pike's stake clattered to the floor. But he had his backup still, and whipped it out, ready for more.

"Nice work," Buffy told him as the two of them turned to face the other vampires now.

"Yeah, well, I like to surf. And I'd like to live to do it again," he replied as the few upstairs in the loft ran down the stairs to attack.

Buffy looked around for the blond again. What was her name? Rachel. The vamp girl was at the front door, gesturing to the others, and Buffy didn't like what she thought that gesture meant.

Sure enough, she was right. As the vamps from the loft attacked her and Pike, the other surviving vampires, the ones who'd been beating Giles, lifted the Watcher off the ground. One of them, a huge bald ox of a man with a hooked nose and dark olive skin, threw Giles over his shoulder and headed toward the door, intending to follow Rachel out.

"Hey!" Buffy snarled.

Three vamps rushed her and Pike. Buffy didn't even bother with them. She gave the first one a backhand so hard it sent him crashing through Giles's coffee table. The second one got Pike's stake in his chest, and was dusted. Even as she set off after Giles, Buffy struck the third bloodsucker in the face, shattering his nose. Then she hit him again. And then a third time, all in quick succession.

He wasn't dead, but he went down.

Buffy left him there, running after Giles.

The other vampires—there were three left, not including Rachel—were moving quickly. They were already on the front lawn when Buffy caught up with Ox. She kicked him in the back of the leg and he crumbled to the grass, dropping Giles. The other vampires turned and prepared to attack as Pike caught up.

"Leave him, then, you idiots!" Rachel shouted at them. "There'll be another time."

They were running up the street then, with Buffy in close pursuit. Suddenly, headlights blinded her, and an engine roared. The lights jumped toward her, and Buffy had to dive clear and roll on the pavement as a long, black limousine skidded to a halt in front of Giles's house. Doors opened, and the four surviving vampires, Ox and Rachel included, climbed in the back.

A rear window rolled down.

Buffy glanced over at Pike, who was helping Giles to stand. Buffy didn't have a clear view inside that window, but from their standpoint, the guys obviously did. Giles was staring at whoever or whatever was in the back of that limousine, his eyes wide with horror.

The limo pulled away quickly. Painfully stretching, feeling to see if she'd broken anything, Buffy walked back to where Pike stood catching his breath, dabbing at some scratches on his neck where a vampire's fangs had grazed him. At their feet, the Watcher lay on the ground again, too tired, too sick, or too injured to remain standing. After a moment, Giles climbed to his knees and threw up on the grass.

"So," Buffy said, once she and Pike had gotten Giles inside, "what do you suppose that was all about?"

"And how did they get in here?" Pike added. "I mean, I have a feeling you didn't send out party invitations."

On the couch, Giles blinked and stared at him again. Buffy thought he looked shell-shocked, like he had in the days after Jenny Calendar's brutal murder. His eyelids fluttered as though he might fall asleep, and then he shook his head.

"I'm sorry, I didn't quite catch your name?" Giles asked.

"Pike, Giles," Buffy answered for him. "He's Pike, remember? I explained. L.A. Hemery. He's on the white hats team."

"Ah, very good," Giles said distractedly, as though nothing of note had happened. As though it were any other day.

Buffy used a damp towel to wipe the blood from his forehead. He'd need stitches probably. And he'd be lucky not to have a scar. They all had a few scars by now. Except for Buffy. As the Slayer, she healed differently. Faster. Better. Her only scars were inside, in her heart and mind, and couldn't be seen unless she revealed them. Something she rarely chose to do.

Now, for instance. She felt pain, a wound, a cold blade in her gut. Because something was so very wrong with Giles, and he either didn't know it or wasn't sharing.

"What did they want with you?" Buffy asked.

"I don't know."

"Well, how did they get in? How could they come in without being invited?"

"I don't know."

Buffy paused. Then, "Who was that guy in the limo?"

Giles only stared at her.

"Pike, want to get some water?" Buffy asked.

He nodded, realizing she wanted a moment with Giles. It wasn't like he could go very far. The kitchen was just a kind of cubbyhole open to the living room, but at least it gave Buffy and Giles some space.

"Hey," she said in a low voice.

Giles's eyes seemed to roam, unfocused.

Buffy prodded him. "Giles," she said. "Earth to Giles."

The Watcher looked up at her, seemed almost annoyed that she had brought him back to reality.

"What is it?" he asked a bit petulantly.

"We're not waiting for the cops. I'm driving you to the hospital," she told him. "You need to have your head looked at. That cut is nasty, and you look like you're flying blind, y'know? Lost contact with air traffic control."

"I'm fine," Giles rasped, pushing away the towel in Buffy's hand.

Buffy sat back and glared at him. "What?" she snapped.

He glared back. "I said I'm fine, Buffy. Why don't you take your little friend and run along, and we'll discuss all of tonight's events in the morning."

Pike had stepped back into the living room, a glass of water in his hands. Buffy stood up, glanced from Giles to Pike, her eyes narrowed, jaw set with anger.

"Let's go," she told Pike.

He set down the glass and followed her to the shattered door, leaving Giles to wait for the police to come. Even now she could hear the sirens. She wasn't really as angry as she knew she seemed. Actually, she was more hurt than anything.

At the door, she turned to look at him. "We will definitely talk about this in the morning," she said.

Then she went out, following Pike in silence as they walked back to his Harley where it was parked down the street. The entire ride back to her house, she couldn't get the picture of Giles out of her mind. She'd seen him be rude and sulky before, but never like this. Never to her.

Her mind flashed on the image of Karen Blaisdell standing in Giles's apartment with her glass of wine. Buffy didn't really think he had a concussion or anything. He just seemed cranky and extremely preoccupied. And secretive. *Just like a guy,* Buffy thought. *A woman pays him a little attention, and now his brain just isn't functioning right.*

She didn't miss the fact that, even as she thought this her arms were wrapped tightly around Pike's waist, her face against his back, hair blowing in the breeze. Angel was probably home at the mansion, but it felt good to be there, on the back of the Harley with Pike. Pike, who was human, a regular guy, who knew everything about her, and didn't care.

So maybe men weren't the only ones whose brains malfunctioned around the opposite sex.

Still, a new girlfriend was no excuse for Giles's behavior. In the morning, they were going to have a serious talk. Right after they figured out who Sunnydale's latest vampiric visitors were. They had wanted Giles, that seemed clear enough. And alive, which made Buffy shiver with memories of other times Giles had been captured. And one time in particular, when he'd been tortured by . . . but her mind refused to go there.

Instead, as the Harley dipped low around a corner, her mind focused again on the vampires. Rachel. The one Buffy had dubbed Ox. Whoever had been sitting in the rear of that limo. If they wanted Giles, Buffy had to figure they wanted to use him as bait. It made sense they'd go after the people closest to her.

The instant that thought hit her, Buffy gave a tiny gasp.

"Mom," she whispered.

"What?" Pike asked, raising his voice as they sliced the air around them, the Harley's engine roaring.

"Just hurry," Buffy told him.

And held on more tightly.

As the police officers milled about his apartment, Giles simply sat on the couch nodding and grunting in response to their questions. When he had to, he offered a more cogent response. He sipped from a small tumbler of whiskey he'd poured himself the moment Buffy had left. Part of him had been glad she was gone.

But somewhere inside him was a voice that wanted to shout, to stop her, to call her back.

After that, he started to get a headache that had nothing to do with the beating he'd taken, or the deep cut on his forehead. His mind felt quite fuzzy, as though he'd taken a few too many decongestants.

He told the police about the horrible street gang that had broken into his apartment, beaten him and trashed the place. He invented a gold watch that he said had been his father's, and a little over four hundred dollars in cash that he claimed the gang had stolen, only because he knew it would make the police feel better if they didn't have to do all the work when it came to pretending Sunnydale didn't sit on top of a Hellmouth.

Beyond that, he just waited. Waited for the carpenters to arrive, called by the police. Waited for the EMT to tell him she thought the cut wasn't as bad as it looked. Waited for her to put three quick dissolvable stitches in right there in the living room. Why waste the money on a trip in the ambulance? All of which was fine by Giles.

He sipped his whiskey. And then, at some point, in the small hours of the night, he looked around and realized he was alone. They'd all gone.

And, finally, he allowed his mind to confront a horror unlike any he'd known before. The horror of a face. The countenance he had seen—or thought he had seen—peering out at him from the backseat of that limousine.

He knew that face. It was as familiar to him as his own.

Of course, it was patently impossible that he'd seen the man he'd thought he'd seen. It couldn't be him.

It couldn't be.

A little after midnight, Alan and Joyce pulled up in front of the Summers's house in his Audi. She felt a little light-headed, and not just because of the three glasses of Chardonnay she'd had to drink. Nope. In fact, she was pretty sure the main reason for her light-headedness was driving the car.

Alan wasn't just handsome and funny, but sweet and intelligent as well. Of course, his ex-wife probably didn't think that way, she reminded herself. But still, how many men her age who were available hadn't been married at least once?

They'd been to dinner at Altobelli's, a wonderful restaurant specializing in the sweet northern Italian cuisine that Joyce favored. There'd been candlelight. Soft music. And later, they'd gone down to the beach and walked along the sand hand in hand.

There had been a kiss, too. Soft and tender.

A lot of talking.

Her heart felt lighter than it had in such a very long time. The full moon shone across the water. She opened up her heart as much as she dared. She had been out with Alan only five times, but at her age, she knew if she was going to like someone or not after date number one.

She liked Alan.

Enough for another kiss. One she was going to instigate. One she leaned in toward him to give, smiling, perhaps even giggling a little. Until Joyce had stiffened, growing uncomfortable as a strange thought entered her mind.

That it wasn't right. It wasn't fair. That this kind of sweet, idle romantic moment was precisely the kind of thing that being the Chosen One had stolen from her daughter, and somehow, it was a kind of betrayal for Joyce to be enjoying herself so.

She knew it was nuts. That was the thing. She was a relatively young woman with an entire life ahead of her. If Hank Summers couldn't stick around when things got a little difficult, well Joyce wasn't going to grow old waiting for life to repair itself. As the mother of the Slayer, she'd learned nothing if she hadn't figured out that wasn't how life worked.

You had to grasp the future, to take it and make it yours.

Alan had looked at her oddly, there on the beach, and been about to ask her if anything was wrong. It was almost as though she could hear the words, though he'd yet to speak them. Then she gave him the kiss that her mind had interrupted, and his questions disappeared.

Now she got out of the car, and Alan stepped out to walk her to the door. They moved up the walk in silence. He reached out for her hand and she let him take it. At the door, he gave her a light kiss on the lips, and she let him. But that was all. For now.

"I'll call you tomorrow," he told her.

"Good," she said, smiling coquettishly.

She watched him for a moment as he went down the walk toward his car. Then Joyce bit her lip, crossed the fingers of both hands, and just *hoped* that he was all he seemed. 'Cause she liked him.

A lot.

With a jangle of keys, she let herself in. Behind her, she heard the roar of the Audi's engine as Alan pulled away. She shut and locked the door, then let her purse fall to the floor. The lights were off, and she reached for the switch.

"Ssshhh," Buffy whispered from the darkness.

"Buffy?" Joyce frowned.

"In the kitchen."

As her eyes adjusted, Joyce saw the body curled up on the sofa, and realized why Buffy was whispering. They had a guest.

"Who is that?" Joyce whispered as she followed Buffy to the kitchen.

"Pike."

"You're kidding," Joyce replied.

Buffy didn't answer.

In the kitchen, Joyce pulled out one of the chairs and sat down.

"So," she said happily. "You're up awfully late. Waiting up for me, now? That's a switch."

But then Buffy slumped down in the chair opposite her, and Joyce saw the circles under her daughter's eyes, the haggard look, the anger there, and she lost her sense of humor.

"Honey, what is it?" Joyce asked.

"Where've you been?"

It took Joyce a moment to separate out the different inflections in her voice. Anger, sure. But there was much more to it than that. Fear. That was the number one thing. Real, profound fear.

"We only got back half an hour ago," Buffy told her. "We've been riding around looking for you."

Joyce shook her head, not understanding. "I was on a date, Buffy. Why were you looking for me?"

So Buffy told her. About the night, and the attack on Giles, and her concern that the vampires might be after her loved ones. It had happened before. As long as she still had people she loved, she figured it would happen again. It was the thing she feared most.

Joyce let out a deep breath when Buffy finished.

"Well, I'm sorry to worry you, honey," Joyce said. "But I couldn't have known what was happening. I didn't see anything odd tonight. Nothing strange happened, unless you count Alan and I having a wonderful time as bizarre, which might not be far from true."

Joyce expected her daughter to smile. Buffy didn't.

"I don't like him," Buffy said bluntly.

With great effort, Joyce controlled her reaction. She wanted to get mad, to tell Buffy that she was just being paranoid and overprotective, that she hadn't even given Alan a chance. But Buffy was eighteen years old. An adult. She knew all of that.

"You just met him," Joyce said, but without any effort to convince Buffy. "But you'll have other chances, Buffy. And if you don't like him, well, we'll have to live with that."

Buffy opened her mouth to respond, but instead, she dropped her gaze and sighed.

"I'm sorry, Mom," she said. "It's been a long night."

Joyce nodded. "That's okay, honey. Maybe in the morning you can tell me what Pike's doing on our couch."

Buffy smiled.

"In the meantime," Joyce went on, "about this thing with Mister Giles? Maybe it isn't about *you* this time."

The granite edge of the sidewalk whispered to Grayhewn where he stood in front of the house on Revello Drive. He stared at the windows as the lights went out one by one.

He waited.

Pike was inside. He knew it for certain. But he wasn't alone now. There were others within, and at least one of them was a being of great power. The Slayer. The stone had told him as much.

Grayhewn had never met a Slayer, but he had heard so many stories of them. He feared her. And stone demons did not, as a rule, fear anything or anyone. The mountain in Hell that had calved him would be appalled. Still, Grayhewn knew he could master his fear. His mate had been destroyed, and for that, he would turn Pike to limestone and eat him bit by bit. If he did it right, and slowly, the boy might actually be able to feel it as he was consumed.

That would be nice.

His right foot had been buried, enmeshed, in the granite curb. Now Grayhewn removed it, and began to move slowly up the walk. A breeze blew across the lawn, sudden and cool, and Grayhewn paused. There was something odd about that breeze, the way it caressed his rocky flesh, the way it energized him.

It was an ill wind.

"Hello, demon" said a voice, just behind him.

Grayhewn turned hurriedly, astonished that he had been taken by surprise. For the voice had whispered almost over his shoulder, a voice pleasant and yet so filled with savage cruelty it brought the first smile to the stone demon's face since his mate had been destroyed.

The being behind him was a stranger. A vampire. Its yellow, feral eyes glowed in the darkness, and its grin was punctuated with the longest fangs he'd yet seen on such a creature. The vampire wore a dark suit, suitable for human mourning. He was tall and slender, his thinning hair brown and gray, but there wasn't the barest hint of weakness about him.

"Good evening, vampire," Grayhewn replied.

He'd always believed that courtesy should be repaid in kind.

"She'll destroy you, you know," said the vampire. "The Slayer, I mean. You're a fierce chap, and powerful, that's certain. But I've seen this girl at work, and it's strong work she does. You'll need friends, old man."

Grayhewn frowned, looking at the stranger with deep suspicion.

"Friends such as you?" the demon asked.

"Indeed," said the vampire. "Your quarry is in her protection. Alone, you cannot defeat her. But together . . . well, perhaps we can be of assistance to one another."

"You want the Slayer dead, then?" Grayhewn asked. "And you need my aid."

"Oh no," the vampire replied. "I care nothing for the Slayer. And it isn't death I'm after. It's pain. Suffering."

Grayhewn held out his hand. The stranger took it, and shook.

"An alliance, then," Grayhewn said. "Favor for favor."

"There's a good lad."

Chapter 4

BUFFY SAT AT THE KITCHEN TABLE DRINKING A TALL glass of pulpy OJ, only a scant few Cheerios left in her cereal bowl, when her mother walked in. Joyce was in her usual morning mode—scattered as hell—and Buffy smiled as her mom moved through the kitchen in a whirl.

"You look nice," she told her mother.

Joyce looked down to double check what outfit she had on. Then she smiled and looked back at her daughter. "Thanks, honey. I really like this, and haven't worn it in months. I don't even remember why I stopped wearing it."

Buffy grimaced. "That'd be the stain on the skirt. Right hip."

With a gasp, Joyce looked down at the skirt, cursed heartily, and then marched out of the kitchen. "Back to the drawing board," she said.

Buffy only shook her head, loving her mom. Weekdays, Joyce was nearly always of the frenzied. Today was no exception. She had offered to drive Buffy to school, and then she had a full day at the gallery, including lunch with an antiquities dealer from Paris. But somehow, she managed it all. She always had. Through the divorce, and single parenthood, and, okay, discovering that her daughter was champion of the still-breathing, Joyce had lost it a few times. But it was pretty amazing that it had been only a few. It took a very strong woman to go through all she had and not break.

Buffy had issues with her father. She knew that. And there was no question in her mind that some of her general disregard for authority came from the divorce. Or, not from the divorce so much as from the invisible man act Hank Summers had been pulling ever since.

In Giles's case, it was a little different. He was the Watcher, which meant she was supposed to do what he said. That part of it never did sit right with her. But she could work with him, and respect the fact that he was usually right, and she wouldn't deny that, after all this time together, she cared a great deal for him . . . and she could not ever forget that her first Watcher, Merrick, had taken his own life in large part to protect Buffy herself.

So Buffy figured she had Watcher issues too.

Then there was Mom. Everything came full circle back to Joyce Summers. Where her father had abandoned his responsibilities in classic Peter Pan fashion, Buffy's mother had only tried to love her. And sure, she'd been distracted by work, and—God forbid—by her own life, sometimes. But Buffy knew that everything her mom had done had been for her, that she'd experienced things no mother should ever have to suffer, and still wanted to make sure Buffy had a decent breakfast in the morning.

I wonder what she would say if she knew, Buffy thought, *that I might have totally blown off the whole Slayer duty issue if I didn't have her as an example.*

Better not to tell her. She might start bleeding from her ears or something.

Anyway, now she was eighteen. Nearly out of high school. And Buffy knew she'd changed. She figured that, as the Slayer, she might be a little more self-aware than other kids her age. Or maybe that was all crap, and she was just deluding herself like everyone else in the world. Didn't matter. What was important was that she believed she'd come into her own, that she'd finally reached a point in her life where she wasn't looking for everyone else's approval, or even opinion, anymore. And she probably had her mom and Giles, and even her father, to thank for it.

Maybe there's something to this whole adulthood thing, she thought.

Which was when Joyce walked back in, in brown slacks and a very stylishly cut brown jacket. She caught Buffy's eye, turned around, glancing at her daughter over her shoulder.

"Do these pants make my butt look big?" Joyce asked.

Then again, Buffy thought, *maybe not.*

"You look great, mom," she said. "Very sexy. I thought you were having lunch with an antiquities dealer, not Alan."

Joyce rolled her eyes slightly. "Remy is from Paris, Buffy. Everyone looks good there. Sure, he's an antiquities dealer, but that doesn't mean his fashion sense is antique." She ran her hands over the outfit, smoothing imaginary creases, and when she seemed essentially satisfied with her appearance, Joyce glanced over at Buffy again. "You ready?"

"Born that way, remember? You were there."

"As I recall," Joyce said wistfully, "you were born red-faced and screaming, with a conehead and the face of an alien, like most other children."

Buffy stood up and grabbed her bag. "Aw, Mom, you just make childbirth sound so transcendently rewarding."

"It was the best day of my life," Joyce reminded her quite earnestly. She kissed Buffy on the head. "And you were the most beautiful thing I had ever seen. Still are."

With a grin, Buffy linked arms with her mother. "Now that's the way to start the day," she said happily.

In the living room they passed Pike, who was still asleep on the sofa. The blanket Buffy had given him barely covered his torso, but barely was the key since most of his clothes were in a pile on the floor.

"Not exactly inhibited is he?" Joyce asked.

"Not a word I'd ever use to describe him, no."

"Think he'll sleep all day?"

Buffy looked at Pike. "It's possible. He's been living only to surf for the past year or so, at least. Without his board, he might be in hibernation or something."

Joyce laughed, and by then, Buffy was pulling the door closed behind her.

On the way to school, Buffy grew quiet. The closer she got to graduation, the more she found herself thinking about it, about growing up, about her parents. Most of her peers, she knew, were equal parts psyched and freaked about graduating and going to college, or whatever. Buffy was just sort of surprised. Surprised, mainly, to find herself alive. Average Slayer life span usually didn't allow the Chosen One to become an adult.

She liked the idea. She couldn't wait to pick up her

diploma and look down and see her mother in the crowd. Her mom deserved that moment as much as she did. They both needed it.

Then, as they neared the high school, her quiet reflection grew more somber. Almost grave. For thoughts of her mother brought her back to the night before, and the attack on Giles, and the thought that her mother might also be a target. Sure, Joyce had dismissed the notion last night, but that didn't mean Buffy was going to stop worrying.

"Hey, Mom, do me a favor, all right?"

Joyce looked over at her, concerned. "You've been quiet. What's wrong?"

"Nothing," Buffy lied. "Just thinking about last night again. I know you think it's nothing, but just for my peace of mind, will you try to stay alert? There could be danger—"

"Isn't there usually?" Joyce asked earnestly.

"More than usually."

Her mother smiled. "I'll keep my eyes open," she said.

Then she looked back at the road and cursed, applying the brakes and swerving to avoid an older woman crossing the street with bags of groceries in her arms. Joyce's knuckles were white on the steering wheel, her arms locked in position as she brought them back into a straight line.

"Yeah," Buffy said, eyes wide. "You do that."

Giles wasn't in the library before class. Considering his behavior the night before, Buffy was tempted to panic. But she controlled the urge during her first few periods. It was, after all, legitimately possible that he'd had some other business to attend to. Or he might have simply slept late. Not something she'd normally suspect of Giles, but with the way he'd looked the previous night, and having to deal with his broken door, and the cops, and all of that . . . well, okay, sleeping late.

She had a free period just before lunch, and went to the library to check in. When she pushed through the double doors, there was no immediate sign of Giles. Then Buffy noticed that the door to his office was open slightly, and she was certain it had been closed when she'd dropped by that morning. With concern and caution, she moved to his office door and peeked in.

Giles sat at his desk, back straight, eyes slightly downcast, as though he were staring at something on his desk. But there was nothing there for him to be looking at. No papers, no books. It was unusually neat, actually. She watched him for a few seconds, and was disturbed by his motionlessness.

"Giles?"

After a moment, in a kind of delayed reaction, Giles looked around, raising his eyebrows. "Ah, Buffy," he said, "good. I was wondering when you'd arrive. I'm sorry I missed you this morning. A great deal to attend to at the apartment. Now, why don't you tell me about your patrol last night."

Buffy blinked. It was a new Giles. A reenergized Giles. He still seemed unfocused, as if his mind was on something else, but at least he wasn't quite as much of a zombie as he'd seemed the night before.

"Patrol was . . . fine," Buffy replied.

She was about to go into an explanation, complete with her frustration that they hadn't been able to get any leads on the rise of vampire activity in the Hammersmith Park area, and then hopefully segue into its connection to the attack on Giles the night before. She was *about* to.

Then Giles raised his eyebrows, smiled, and nodded. "Excellent," he said. "Well then, carry on."

He stood and crossed the office, pulled a book from a shelf seemingly at random, and began to leaf through it. Buffy stared at him, waiting to be let in on the joke. Finally, after an exasperating thirty seconds or so, she called his name.

Giles looked up. "Hmm?"

"Don't you think we have a little more to discuss? Isn't there anything else you want to know?"

He looked at her fondly. "Buffy," he said, in an attempt to comfort her, "I trust you implicitly." Then he shut the book and moved toward his office door, about to leave her there, staring after him.

Buffy moved to block his exit. Giles seemed legitimately surprised when he looked at her.

"We need to talk," she said. "Maybe you're done. I'm not."

"Now see here," he said grumpily, "I'm not sure what this is all about, but I have things to attend to, and—"

"Oh, I'm sure you do. Just like you had things to attend to last night when you blew off Oz, freaked Willow out, and basically slammed the door in my face."

Giles frowned and glared at Buffy. He looked pissed.

Good, Buffy thought. *At least he's focused on something.*

Giles crossed his arms. "What I do on my own time, with or without Miss Blaisdell, is none of your concern, Buffy. You'd do well to remember that."

"The hell with that," Buffy snapped. "I don't know what's up with you. Maybe you're acting bizarre because the last time you fell for someone she ended up dead in your bed, or maybe it's just typical male behavior. Doesn't matter. It is my concern. It is my business. You're my Watcher, you're part of the team, and all of this is affecting your behavior and your efficiency. So don't tell me what is and isn't my concern."

"How dare you!" Giles said, taken aback.

"Somebody has to," Buffy told him. "Now sit down and listen to what I have to say, and see if you can pay attention."

Though he looked more furious than she'd ever seen him, which was saying quite a bit, Giles did indeed go and sit back in the chair at his desk. Buffy thought, for just a moment, about parents being caretakers of their children, and children eventually being forced to become caretakers of their parents. That was the cycle of life, she'd read somewhere.

She could relate.

"There was a girl last night, a vamp chick named Rachel. She was in Hammersmith. The only one who got away. She was also there when you were attacked last night."

Giles looked thoughtful, even confused. There was an expression on his face Buffy found difficult to read, but it was as though he were trying to remember something.

"The blond?" he asked.

"That's the one. She and the huge guy, that ox? You saw him. They took off in a limo with someone else. I get the feeling there are a lot more vamps where last night's cannon fodder came from. There's something going on here, Giles. Somebody new in town, I think, and they're trying to get to me through you."

He thought about that a moment, then nodded. "That

may well be," he agreed. "Do we have any other clues?"

"How did they get in last night? Did you invite them?" Buffy asked.

"Don't be absurd," Giles replied.

"Well, the way you've been behaving—"

"I don't know how they got in, but I certainly didn't invite them," he insisted. "We'll just have to stay alert, and see if we can find out who's . . . behind all this."

Giles put a hand to his forehead and pressed his palm against it. He winced, then took a breath.

"Are you okay?" Buffy asked, concerned.

"A bit of a headache actually, which ought to come as no surprise after last night. I'll be all right, though," he reassured her.

Buffy didn't feel reassured.

"What about Pike?" she asked.

"Who?"

"Pike," Buffy frowned. "Cute bleach-blond surfer guy at your door with me last night. Helped save your life. Not to mention coming to the swashbuckling rescue last night at the park."

"Ah, yes, sorry," Giles said. "What about him?"

"He pissed off something called a stone demon. It's hunting him. I'd like to get to it before it gets to him," she said.

Giles nodded thoughtfully in the best imitation of concentration he'd managed since Buffy had walked in.

"Yes, well, first off, don't let it touch you," he instructed her.

"Pike's buddy was turned to stone," Buffy said. "Which has got to make dancing difficult."

For a moment he looked at her, and she had the eerie

feeling that Giles was trying to make sense of her comment. Something he'd never bothered with in the past. Usually he just let the banter go right past him, and wisely so. But this time, it was as though he wasn't sure if he was supposed to understand or not.

"Giles?"

"Aside from not letting it lay hands on you, legends claim it can communicate with stone. Certainly, it would feel more comfortable somewhere it might find a lot of stone. Older buildings. Cemeteries."

"Okay, so we patrol and we find it, and then we . . . how do we destroy it?"

"To the best of my recollection there's no real trick to it. Save for getting close enough to do it enough damage to destroy it. Oh, and I believe there was something about separating the parts afterwards, but I could be confusing that with something else. I could look it up?" he suggested as though it were a novel idea.

"Would you mind?" Buffy asked.

"Come back after the final bell, and I should have something for you," Giles told her. "In the meantime, while you're searching for this stone demon, don't forget that you're also trying to get to the bottom of this new vampire infestation."

"Not to worry," Buffy replied. "I can kill two birds with one blunt object."

Again, Giles got that confused look on his face.

"Hey," Buffy said, more gently now as she moved closer to him. "Are you all right, Giles? Seriously. It takes a lot to bring out my motherly instincts, but you don't seem well."

The Watcher returned her smile with a very strained, exhausted one of his own.

"I'll be fine," he told her. "But thank you for asking, Buffy."

"I don't know what's going on with Giles, but he's either hiding something uber-nasty from us, or he's under some kind of spell," Buffy said firmly.

She looked around the lunch table at Willow, Xander, and Oz. As Buffy had shared her observations about Giles's behavior and the events of the previous night, they'd all grown more and more concerned. But now they shared that determined look that she loved them for.

"All right, so what do we do about it?" Xander asked.

From behind them came a familiar voice. "For starters," Cordelia said, "you can keep your voices down."

Buffy turned to see Cordelia holding a few textbooks in her arms. She looked killer, as usual, a reflection of both her fashion sense and her general attitude.

"Hey, Cordelia," Willow said. "We're trying to find out why Giles has been acting so weird. Wanna help?"

"Help?" Cordelia asked, and looked at Buffy as though she were insane. "Don't get me wrong, I'm all with the help thing, but usually only when my life or the world is in dire jeopardy. Giles blinded by the scent of a woman isn't exactly the danger zone. You guys should just butt out, stop spying on him, and let love run its course."

"We're not spying on anyone!" Xander snapped defensively.

"Giles needs our help," Willow said.

"As clueless as he may be when it comes to gender

relations, I really doubt he needs help from anyone at this table," Cordelia explained dubiously. "Maybe you should all be more concerned about your own love lives."

With that, she turned on her heel and marched from the cafeteria. They watched her go, and Buffy turned back to look at her friends.

"All right, so there are four of us. That'll have to do. Willow, see if you have any spells that can detect if someone's been enchanted or whatever. Now, we don't have any reason to think Miss Blaisdell's really the cause of any of this, but it did start when she and Giles got together."

Willow looked sad. "I really like Miss Blaisdell. I hope she's not something evil."

"She's a woman," Xander interjected.

He was rewarded with withering glares from both Buffy and Willow. Oz looked bemused.

"Your timing and lack of mental editing never cease to amaze me," Oz told him.

"Thanks!" Xander said happily, smiling with self-satisfaction.

"Don't mention it," Oz replied.

"Xander," Buffy said, "I want you to keep an eye on her. Let's see what we know about her, try to figure out if there's anything strange about her."

"Check," Xander said, with great enthusiasm. "Spy on Miss Blaisdell. Does this include in her bedroom . . . I mean, her house?"

Buffy ignored him, turning to Oz.

"I'd like your help keeping an eye on Giles," she said. "You're not in class much, and neither am I. Between the two of us we ought to be able to get an idea if there's anything weird going on."

"So we *are* spying," Oz observed.

"Don't think of it as spying," Willow said, concerned. "Think of it like a stakeout, or . . . or, like espionage. James Bond. Or a life study. Observation."

They all looked at her. Willow glanced away.

"All right, spying," she said. "It just seems wrong to spy on Giles."

"I think he's in danger," Buffy told her.

Willow nodded.

"See, isn't it nice to have a reason to do something that might get you branded a stalker or a sociopath on any other day?" Xander asked. When they all looked at him, he stood and moved back toward the cafeteria line. "Anybody else want more pudding?"

Pike woke up just before noon. Or, more accurately, he woke up again. The first time, just after nine, he'd realized that the Summers women had left him alone in their house, and quickly abandoned any ambition for the day. Buffy would be at school, and her mom at work. That meant he had nothing at all to concern him.

Except rest. Much-needed and hard-earned.

But when he awoke the second time, he actually began to feel a bit uncomfortable. They'd let him into their home—though Buffy's mom hadn't had much of a choice, what with coming in late and finding him on the couch—and here he was snoring and drooling on the cushions.

Pike dragged himself, scratching his head and the stubble on his cheeks, from the couch and into the kitchen. It felt sort of strange to be in the house alone. Women lived here, and there was something sort of intimate about wandering around by himself. He felt a kind of weird temptation to snoop, but ignored it. That might have been cool when he and Benny were twelve and searching for Benny's dad's *Playboys*, but not now.

He downed two glasses of OJ, cooked himself some scrambled eggs with cheese and ham, then wolfed that down and did the dishes. Even the ones already in the sink. *Gotta do something to earn my keep,* he figured. *Besides the occasional monster killing.*

After a shower, he pulled some clean clothes out of his duffel, and washed the dirty ones. Making himself right at home, and it concerned him. Buffy's mom might not approve, but he knew that if Buffy couldn't kill this demon thing, he might be on the run for a long time. No way to tell when he'd have a hot shower and a chance to wash his stuff.

Man, what are you thinking? he wondered. *Buffy's the Slayer. Rock guy's got no chance.*

Still. Better to be prepared.

Later, he picked up as best he could, put his clothes in the dryer, and went out to take a ride around on the Harley. Check out Sunnydale. He left an upstairs window open in case he had to sneak in, but he figured he'd hook up with Buffy or she'd end up home before he needed back inside.

With the familiar and welcome rumble of the Harley under him, Pike cruised the streets. He went downtown past the Bronze, the club Xander and Willow had told him about. He was tempted to take a swing by Hammersmith Park, but didn't. With the demon on his trail, he'd kind of formulated an unwritten rule: don't go anywhere you've already been.

Of course, hanging around Buffy was going to force him to break that rule. Not half an hour after he'd decided to forgo the park, he found himself driving by Giles's apartment. The scene last night had given him a major chill, and he still didn't get how the vampires had gotten in.

The door had been replaced by something as temporary as it looked. Pike figured it would do as well as anything. Certainly, it wasn't going to keep the vampires out if they came back. He wondered what Buffy was doing about all that, and figured it was time to go by the school. Classes would be over soon, and maybe they could hook up.

Riding through Sunnydale was eerie. Buffy had told him the town was literally sitting on the mouth of Hell. What creeped him out the most, though, was how normal it all looked during the day. How everyone went along doing their business like they had no clue there was anything evil going down.

Talk about denial.

On his way, he stopped at a convenience store to get a Coke. Caffeine withdrawal had struck, and he was in need of a fix. The girl behind the counter looked like she should still be in school, and when Pike smiled at her, she gave him a very broad, too friendly grin in return.

It made him think of Buffy. And Angel. *And what the hell am I doing here, anyway?* he thought.

The answer came back from his subconscious instantly: *Saving your ass.*

True, but then there was Buffy. He'd never met a girl like her, before or since their time together. And he knew he never would. As long as he'd put it off, he knew that somehow, this trip to Sunnydale to seek her out had been inevitable.

As he left the store, Pike glanced down at the headline of the *Sunnydale Press*. "COPS MISSING," it said. "2 OFFICERS DISAPPEAR, BIZARRE STATUES FOUND."

Pike was already outside on the Harley when he made the connection. The way the headline had been written, it was vague. But he got it, then. Knew what it must mean. The statues that were found would have been *in place of* the missing cops. Because they *were* the missing cops.

The demon had arrived.

All afternoon, with very infrequent interruptions by students in search of books, Giles sat in his office alone, doing little. Doing, he had to confess to himself, nothing.

His mind was dull. His memory blurry at best. Something was not right, he knew that. He'd seen that face last night, the face in the back of the limousine. It had disturbed him deeply, hurt him, sickened him. It was impossible, of course, a hallucination perhaps. Or some hurtful psychological warfare.

And oh, it had hurt.

It couldn't be. He was certain of that. There was simply no way that the person in the back of the limousine could have been who it appeared to be. He was dead, after all.

Giles had delivered his eulogy.

Still, the sighting was haunting him. That and the beating and the vampires—*how* had *they gotten in?*— and Buffy's questions. He wondered why her questions confused him so, left him feeling so hostile and defensive.

It was as though his whole mind was wrapped in a thick mist. In many ways, it reminded him of some of his more social experiments from the dark age of his life when he was running with Ethan Rayne and dabbling in things better left alone. But he hadn't been dabbling in dark magicks of late, or anything else for that matter.

Still, in spite of the fog that enshrouded him, Giles could feel the dawn coming. He could sense that the fog was about to lift, that all would become clear to him. His mind was struggling to be free of this disorientation, and he knew it was only a matter of time.

This train of thought was interrupted by a knock at his office door. He turned and saw Karen Blaisdell standing on the threshold. She had a beautiful smile, and her eyes sparkled in a way that was deeply enchanting. Giles returned her smile.

"You seem troubled, Rupert," she said lovingly.

"I'm all right," he replied. "Just a bit preoccupied."

Karen moved slowly across the office, then reached out to remove his glasses. Giles responded instantly. He pulled her to him and she slipped onto his lap, her lips meeting his, her mouth opening to the kiss. She ran her fingers through his hair and Giles felt a passion rise in him like nothing he'd ever known. This was a woman whose femininity was almost primal, a woman to war over, a face, like Helen of Troy's, to launch a thousand ships.

And that kiss . . .

In Karen's kiss, all of Giles's concerns and troubles disappeared so completely, that when she'd left his office, he could only dimly recall what he'd been so worried about.

Alone again, he touched his fingers to his lips and found them warm from her kiss. From the clock, he knew that nearly forty minutes had passed, and he barely remembered them. There was the tiniest flash of panic in his mind, the sense that something was horribly wrong, and then it was gone.

All he could think about was Karen and her kiss.

That woman is something else, he thought.

Chapter 5

OKAY, BUFFY ASKED ME TO DO THIS, AND IT'S FOR A *good cause, so it isn't like stalking, right?* Xander thought.

He stood at a T-junction in the corridor, peering around the corner and watching Miss Blaisdell walk down the hall. Her long, red hair fell perfectly across her back and shoulders, and Xander couldn't help being slightly hypnotized by the rhythmic sway of her hips.

Not a pervert, he told himself. *Just normal, red-blooded American male. And for a good cause . . . how can it be wrong when it feels so right?*

With a grin, he watched the teacher knock lightly on Principal Snyder's door. As she stood in the hallway, she glanced around and Xander pulled his head back. He was pretty sure it wouldn't be the first time a student paid a little bit too close attention to Miss Blaisdell, but he didn't want to get caught. If she was up to something, it would tip her off. Plus . . . then he couldn't watch anymore.

She knocked again on Snyder's office door. After a moment, the muffled sound of the principal's voice came from within.

"Whoever the hell is out there, go away!" came Snyder's response, friendly as ever.

"It's Karen Blaisdell, Principal Snyder," she said aloud. "I was hoping you could spare me a few minutes."

Miss Blaisdell dipped her head and swayed, tossing her long hair back away from her face. Xander watched, fascinated by the little movement and wishing she would do it again.

Snyder opened the door, smiled his little ratboy smile, and let Miss Blaisdell in, mumbling something as close to pleasant as his generally curmudgeonly demeanor would allow. Then he closed the door behind them.

"Damn," Xander mumbled.

Keeping an eye on Miss Blaisdell meant standing there in the hall, waiting for her to come back out. He didn't mind spying when there was something or someone to spy, and still had never gotten an answer from Buffy as to whether spying included peeking into Miss Blaisdell's bedroom windows, but he figured he'd have to use his own prerogative on that one.

Prerogative said yes.

But until then, he stood in the hallway watching Snyder's door, and wondering how long Miss Blaisdell would be able to stand the man's company.

Xander was also wondering what kind of pajamas Miss Blaisdell wore to bed. If any.

"It's *not* stalking," he whispered to himself.

* * *

Buffy and Oz sat together at the study table in the library, searching through dusty volumes for information on stone demons. They weren't having very much luck, and Giles hadn't been any help at all. He'd mumbled the titles of a few volumes, but when pressed to fish them out, he couldn't recall where he'd had them last.

The absentminded thing was wearing on Buffy in a big way.

Still, she did her best to research, even though she and Oz were really there keeping an eye on him more than anything else. She wanted to leave, wanted to be out trying to track the thing down. But she'd called home and gotten no answer, so she figured Pike was either riding around, or on his way here. So she waited.

In his office, Giles puttered, doing very little. For a short time, while they flipped through books, he actually came out and used the trusty old inkpad to stamp books that had been returned to the library. It was an archaic system, but though he'd come to accept computers, he certainly didn't trust them yet.

He went back into his office and actually shut the door. Buffy couldn't remember the last time he'd done that.

"What do you make of that?" Buffy asked.

Oz glanced up from his reading, glanced at the office door a moment, then closed his book. "Let's see," he said, and rose from the table. He went over to the office door and walked past, peering through the glass window set into the wood as he did. Then he sauntered back to the table as though he'd wandered away by mistake.

"Well?" Buffy asked.

"I could be wrong, but I think he's sleeping," Oz told her.

Buffy stared at him. "Huh?"

Oz nodded. "Looks that way. Which, y'know, fine, since I have to do some research for my English paper anyway."

The library doors swung open, and Pike poked his head in. He still had a lot of stubble on his chin, and Buffy decided she liked the look.

"Thought I'd find you here," he said, and then came all the way into the room.

"I thought you would too," Buffy replied, then glanced at Oz. "Oz, Pike. Pike, Oz."

"Hey," Oz said.

"Hey," Pike replied.

Both of them nodded in greeting, and that was that.

"You want to sit for a few minutes?" Buffy asked Pike. "I just want to do a bit more of this until Willow comes back, and then it's home. I told my mother we'd have dinner with her and Alan tonight."

"Really?" Pike asked. "I thought you hated Alan."

"Hate's a strong word," Buffy said. "Let's just say I don't really trust him. I have issues trusting men, period. Especially when they're dating my mother."

There was a long moment of silence between them, and Buffy did nothing to alleviate it. No question, there was a romantic tension between herself and Pike, and she knew she was doing nothing to diminish it. She couldn't help it.

"Hey, why don't you guys go," Oz suggested. "Willow should be back soon, and I'm cool here."

"Really?" Buffy asked hopefully. "Thanks, Oz. I want to be on patrol tonight, to try to get to the bottom of the weirdness from last night. This way, maybe I can sneak out of dinner early."

"Consider him covered," Oz told her, then looked at Pike. "See you."

"Cool," Pike replied, nodding.

Willow had locked the door to the bio lab. It wouldn't do for someone to walk in on her while she was handling some of the ingredients in the spell she was casting. It was one thing to put herbs into a small beaker of water as it boiled over a Bunsen burner. She could be making soup for all anyone knew.

But once you added insects to the mix, not to mention the powdered shark cartilage, well, people weren't always charitable, and Willow didn't want rumors to start spreading that she tortured puppies for fun, or whatever.

Patiently, she read through the spell again, making certain she was following the instructions to the letter. The shark cartilage was in place of "the bones of a sea monster," but she was starting to get a handle on the whole magick thing, and figured that it would be a decent substitute.

It had taken her nearly an hour alone in the bio lab to get everything just right. When the moment was perfect, she checked the clock. Going on four in the afternoon. That was fine. She struck a wooden match, and waited for the second hand to come around to the twelve again, and then dropped the match into the mixture.

A potent combination. Flames roared up from the water, searing the inside of the beaker, turning it black, and evaporating into a puff of black smoke. Willow glanced up at the clock. The second hand had stopped. She waited, counting silently to herself, as the smoke from her spell coiled away like a tiny air serpent, sliding under the lab door and out into the school.

Willow had counted to thirty before the clock on the wall started ticking again. She wondered where the smoke had gone.

Oz was skimming through a biography of Nikos Kazantzakis when he smelled smoke. It was just the barest whiff, something anybody else might have missed. Maybe. He looked up to see a tiny cloud of black smoke drift across the library and under the door of Giles's office.

Eyebrows raised, he watched the door with interest to see if anything else strange would follow the entrance of the sentient smoke. But nothing did. In fact, though the bio on Kazantzakis was interesting, he found his eyes drooping not long after the incident with the smoke. It was four-thirty, and the shadows outside would be growing long.

It was a relief, however, after three nights of the wolf, to know that he could enjoy the coming of the dark without the dread that accompanied him everywhere during the full moon. As usual, he had excuses to make to the Dingoes, and homework to catch up on. But Buffy thought Giles was in trouble, and needed help getting to the bottom of things.

Duty called, and that came first. But at least Willow would be with him. When Willow was with him, nothing else mattered.

Then, as if on cue, she walked in, looking around the room tentatively as if searching for something.

"Smoke?" Oz asked.

Willow nodded.

Oz hooked a thumb in the general direction of Giles's office, and Willow nodded, eyes lighting up with an excitement that she tried her best to hide. The circumstances weren't the happiest, but Oz knew she was always pleased when a new spell succeeded.

Willow sat down next to him at the table, and they exchanged a soft kiss. Oz liked the soft kisses best. They were the most Willow. She took a look at what he was reading, then at the stack of books on stone demons that Buffy had been searching through earlier, and slid the top volume in front of her.

"Might as well make myself useful."

"Your middle name," Oz told her.

Willow smiled bashfully. Pretty much the only kind of Willow smile. Well, that and what Xander called "geeker joy," but that was reserved for things related to magick and computers. Or magick with computers, as the case may be.

It was nearly five when Giles stirred inside his office. He came to the door, opened it, and looked out at them with a vaguely confused expression on his face. His hair was a bit mussed, and Oz thought that pretty much confirmed his suspicion that Giles had been sleeping on his desk.

"Ah," the Watcher said tiredly. "I didn't realize anyone was still about. I must have dozed off for a bit. Too much excitement last night, I suppose. What are you two up to?"

Oz watched Giles, expecting Willow to take the burden of responding. After a moment, though, he realized that Willow was too busy staring at the small black smattering of dust on the sleeve of Giles's shirt to say anything.

"Kazantzakis paper," Oz told him. "And Willow's Research Girl."

"Research Girl," Willow repeated, her tone almost as devoid of emotion as Giles's own.

Oz found the similarity a little eerie. But where Giles would normally have asked Willow with great concern if she were feeling all right, the Watcher didn't even notice her behavior.

"Ah, right, indeed. Well, go about your business, then. There are several leads I've been meaning to follow up on concerning our latest vampire infestation. When that's done, I'll try to lend a hand as regards our stone demon."

"Great," Willow said weakly. "Thanks."

Giles nodded and moved up the stairs and into the stacks. When Giles was deep among the books, Willow glanced over at Oz, and he lifted an eyebrow in response.

"Smoke?" he asked again.

Willow gave a little shrug. "I guess. It was supposed to mark anyone currently under any kind of magickal influence, and the one who was exerting that influence," she whispered. "So Buffy's right about part of it, at least. Weird Giles is not just distracted-by-a-woman Giles. There's magick. Now we just have to see what Xander comes up with."

Xander had to go. It was getting pretty unbearable. There wasn't anything he wouldn't do for Buffy, and Giles was, well, Giles, so helping him was high on the priority list.

But he wasn't going to wet his pants for anyone.

Miss Blaisdell had been in Snyder's office for a very long time. More than an hour and a half by now. Xander had seen the little puff of black smoke float down the hall and under the door. Bizarre, sure, but hanging with Buffy, and living in Sunnydale, he knew from bizarre.

Besides, Willow had told him to expect something strange if her marking spell succeeded.

But since the smoke, nada. Only the custodian and a couple of basketball players had come by while he was standing there. None of them had said a word or even looked at him oddly, but Xander still felt very silly standing in the middle of the hall doing nothing.

Now there was the whole bladder thing to contend with. The bathroom was just down the hall a short way. In his mind, he kept trying to figure how fast he could go and get back here. Maybe Miss Blaisdell would still be in there with Snyder, he thought.

What are they doing in there? Xander wondered for the millionth time. Of course, there was one answer that kept coming to mind, but he pushed it away again and again. In his mind, it just wasn't possible. Not the foxy redheaded substitute teacher and ratboy himself.

Of course, she was dating Giles, so . . . but no, on a scale of one to ten, Snyder was still Snyder. Giles, in spite of the thrilling life he didn't lead as a librarian, was at least still on the scale.

Finally, Xander couldn't take another second of clenching his entire body to try to hold off the impending trip to the bathroom. And just as he turned to go, a door at the far end of the hallway opened, and the cheerleading squad streamed through.

"This is hell," he whispered, and stood back as the cheerleaders ran by him, pom-poms swishing.

Several of the girls looked at him and rolled their eyes. Which was, in some ways, better than the rest of them, who didn't bother noticing him at all. Once again, none of them seemed to question the fact that he was loitering in the hallway of the school after five o'clock.

"Y'know, I *could be* a stalker," he muttered bitterly.

Then he saw Cordelia, and he had an idea. She was one of a trio of girls bringing up the rear, and he looked at her with what he hoped was an imploring glance as she came up next to him.

"Um, Cordy, could I talk to you a second?" he asked hopefully.

Cordelia sneered, half amused, half disgusted. It was a look she did well. She'd had a lot of practice with it.

"Please," she said.

Then she moved on with the other cheerleaders, down the hall, and through the far doors. Xander bit his lip, glancing nervously at the door to Snyder's office. Nothing to be done about it, though. He had to go, and that was that.

Which was when Cordelia pushed back through the door she'd gone out, and came padding quietly up the corridor toward him, looking furious and beautiful.

"What's wrong with you?" she hissed at him. "Here I've taken pains to attempt to repair my reputation, even the littlest bit, and you go trying to ruin it all over again. I told them I had to use the bathroom. What do you want?"

"Um, to use the bathroom?"

If she'd had heat vision, Cordelia would have torched him on the spot.

"No, see, I'm helping Buffy. Watching Miss Blaisdell. Spying, if you want to call it that."

"Oh, that again," Cordelia sniffed.

"Yeah, well, she's been in with Snyder for almost two hours, and I have to go. If you could just stand here for two minutes. Really, that's all. I'll be right back."

Cordelia looked at him dubiously.

"Please, Cor," Xander said, too desperate to insult

her. "Something's wrong with Giles, and I know you don't have anything against *him* at least, right?"

She rolled her eyes. "Hurry," she said.

"Bless your soul," Xander prayed, and then hurried down the hall toward the bathroom as fast as he could waddle.

"So, Pike, how long are you in town?"

At her mother's question, Buffy looked up from the pan in which she was cobbling together a lasagna she and her mother were making. It was a question she had wanted to know the answer to for a while, but would never have just come out and asked. When it came to emotions, she was bad at guessing, worse at second-guessing, but somehow, she was worst at coming out and asking what she wanted to know. She had always supposed that was because she was never sure if she really *wanted* to know.

Like now.

"Not sure, really," Pike replied, without glancing at Buffy. "Right now I'm . . ." He paused, looked at Buffy's mom, and gave a soft laugh. "I'm sorry, Mrs. Summers. It's just so weird talking to you about this stuff. Guess I never thought Buffy would tell you about the whole Slayer thing. It's crazy."

"It is that, for certain," Joyce agreed.

"Anyway," Pike continued, "what I was going to say is that for now I'm just trying to stay alive. After that . . . I guess I'll probably head back to San Diego."

Buffy was watching Pike closely, and when he looked her way, she met his gaze a second before looking down. She didn't know what she had hoped to hear. It wasn't that she wanted him to stay, not with how complicated that might make things with Angel—as if they weren't complicated enough already. But she didn't want Pike to leave either. Angel wasn't her boyfriend. Not really. Never would be.

But neither would Pike. It wasn't meant to be for them. She knew that. Knowing didn't make it easier. All along, she'd thought the big problem with being the Chosen One was that it interfered with her being a normal teenager. Now she was beginning to realize that there was more to it than that. She wasn't going to be a teenager much longer. She was an adult now. And being the Chosen One interfered with that, too. With everything.

"Buffy?" her mother asked, gesturing at the pan in front of her. "Do you think that's enough ricotta?"

With a downward glance, Buffy realized she'd dumped far too much cheese into the pan. She rolled her eyes and started scooping it back into the plastic container.

"Sorry," she said. "Just distracted, I guess."

This time when she looked over at him, it was Pike who looked away.

"I hope Alan likes lasagna," Joyce said idly.

Buffy smiled. "Don't worry, Mom. Who doesn't love lasagna? Pasta, sauce, meat, and cheese. Maybe a little spinach for flavor, right? What's not to like?

"Besides, if Alan doesn't like it, we kick him out and trade him in for a new model," Buffy added, giving her mother a mischievous glance.

Joyce looked at her, pretending to be scandalized, and then laughed along with her daughter.

"It isn't that easy when you're a fortyish single mom," Joyce replied.

"Oh, 'fortyish,' " Buffy teased. "Isn't that a nice way to dodge around numerical specificity. And I've got news for you, Mom. Maybe you've forgotten, but it was never that easy."

Joyce only smiled and began placing a second layer of cooked lasagna noodles over the cheese and meat sauce that Buffy had spread across the pasta in the bottom of the pan.

"He really is a nice guy, you know," Joyce said quietly.

Buffy paused, looked up reluctantly, and then nodded. "He seems it. I'm just looking out for you. I'm your daughter. It's my job."

"And thank goodness I have my Slayer around," her mother replied, teasing. "What would I do if, heaven forbid, Alan didn't fall madly in love with me—as if that's a possibility? I can take care of myself, Buffy, but I like that you're worried for me."

The Summers women fell silent then, working well together, happy for each other's company. It was a rare moment. Alan wasn't due for half an hour, and Pike seemed content to set the table.

But then Pike was done. And speaking. "Anything else I can do?" he asked.

Buffy shot him a hard look. "Can't you see we're bonding?" She and her mother both laughed, and after an indecisive moment so did Pike.

"You could make a salad, if you don't mind," Joyce suggested.

"I'm king of salad," Pike told her.

"Everyone has to have some ambition in life," Buffy said. "Well, except Xander, of course."

Cordelia lasted about thirty seconds standing guard in the hallway, watching Principal Snyder's door. Not only did she think the whole concept of spying was offensive—unless it held some personal benefit—but she didn't for one moment believe that Miss Blaisdell was the evil creature everyone else suspected her of being. In fact, even though, if Xander could be believed, the woman had been in Snyder's office half the afternoon, Cordelia was actually pretty fond of Miss Blaisdell.

The teacher had an excellent eye for fashion.

So, after that first half minute or thereabouts, Cordelia wasn't exactly inclined to put up with the sneaking around stuff. Instead, she walked down the hall to Principal Snyder's office and rapped hard on the door. She waited a few seconds, and when there was no answer, she knocked again.

Still nothing. Which was weird. Xander had said they were in there, and if he'd been standing out in the hallway all that time, he ought to know. Curious, and also a bit concerned—she didn't want anything bad to happen to a teacher who set such a good sartorial example for her peers—she tried the knob, and it turned.

Cordelia pushed the door open slowly, peeking in. She didn't want Principal Snyder to bite her head off if he simply hadn't heard her, but then, with the way things went around the Hellmouth, she also had to be concerned that he might bite her head off in a more literal sense.

"Hello? Principal Snyder?"

She didn't see him at his desk. In fact, the office looked pretty deserted. She was about to turn and leave, just shut the door behind her and leave Xander and his friends to their bizarro games.

Then she heard the moaning.

Cordelia blushed, and her opinion of Miss Blaisdell sank to lows Cordy had never imagined. *I mean, God . . . Snyder? That's depraved,* she thought. And cheating *on Giles* with Snyder? Giles was no stud-muffin, but compared to Snyder, he was Ben Affleck *and* Matt Damon.

She started to back up, wanting desperately to be out of there. Then there was another moan, and something about it stopped Cordelia where she stood. She cocked her head, listening, hoping that didn't make her a pervert. But there was something wrong about that moaning. She'd heard plenty of moaning in her time.

This sounded painful.

Cordelia took a tentative step forward. Then another. After a long moment, she took a third. Then she could see down behind Snyder's desk, where the principal's legs shuddered, his heels tapping the linoleum lightly in time with his moaning. His eyes were rolled up in his head as though he were having some kind of seizure. His shirt was open to his navel.

Miss Blaisdell was above him, straddling his body, her face pressed against his. Almost covering his. Her mouth was distended, lips stretched impossibly, inhumanly wide. Cordelia let out a little shriek, and the thing that was Miss Blaisdell turned to look at her.

It changed in an instant. The black, soulless marble eyes and the wide, red, dripping mouth seemed almost to melt away as her features returned to their usual appearance.

Miss Blaisdell smiled. "Cordelia," she whispered.

Cordelia tried to scream again, but she couldn't seem to open her mouth, couldn't tear her eyes away from Miss Blaisdell's gaze. Her heart hammered in her chest, and she worried that it had finally come, the moment when Xander and Buffy and the others had managed to get her so deeply into trouble that there would be no time for a rescue.

She was paralyzed as Miss Blaisdell, or whatever she was, reached out a hand and brushed soft fingers across her cheek. Touched her hair. Leaned forward and gave her the tiniest kiss on the forehead.

"You're such a sweet girl," she whispered. "Now close your eyes."

Cordelia couldn't help but obey.

When Xander came out of the bathroom, he noticed Cordelia's absence immediately. He strode angrily to the corner, ready to cuss Cordy out with all the bad words he'd ever learned—most of which he'd already used on her, but not necessarily to her face—only to find her standing in front of Principal Snyder's office talking to ratboy himself.

Snyder looked up and saw him, and frowned.

"Harris, you're here too? To what do I owe this nausea?"

"Ah, Principal Snyder," Xander said reluctantly. "I see you're as chipper as ever. Just doing a little extra-credit research. And going home now."

"See that you do," Snyder snapped, but it seemed to lack some of its usual cruelty.

He went into his office and shut the door. Xander turned to Cordelia, staring at her wide-eyed.

"What was that all about?" he demanded. "You were supposed to watch, not have a coffee klatch."

Cordelia blinked. For a moment, Xander thought she was going to lose her balance. Then she smiled, and the expression was completely devoid of the revulsion she usually exhibited around him.

"Miss Blaisdell was leaving. I walked down the hall like I was coming from practice. We talked. She walked. Snyder asked if I was doing my part for the basketball team's morale. I think he meant something vaguely disgusting by that, but I let it go."

"Wait, she's gone?" Xander asked. "But I'm supposed to be tailing her."

"Don't let me stop you," Cordelia said dismissively, then turned and walked off.

Xander stood and watched her go, uncertain how to proceed. Willow had told him about the whole marking spell, but if he didn't see Miss Blaisdell before she showered or changed clothes, he might not ever know if she'd been marked or not. He didn't want to blow it here. It was important that they figure out what was happening to Giles.

After a moment, Xander realized what he had to do. Taking a deep breath, summoning his courage, he knocked on Snyder's office door.

"Go away, it's after hours!" the principal shouted.

Xander knocked again.

Snyder whipped the door open. "What?" he barked.

On the principal's neck was a splotch of black, like soot. Xander stared at it.

"Do you . . . have the time?" he mumbled.

"Time to go home," Snyder said angrily. "Good-bye."

He slammed the door.

It could all be a coincidence. Xander knew that. But if it wasn't, well, suddenly, he wasn't all that excited about the possibility of peeking through Miss Blaisdell's bedroom window.

Chapter 6

GILES'S FACE LAY NESTLED AGAINST HIS ARMS—FRAMED by them—where they were crossed on top of his desk. His right cheek pressed against the cold wood, and his glasses dangled from his left hand. His breathing was slow and deep. His mind whirled with images, mostly disturbing, and he moaned softly, his eyes tightly closed.

But he wasn't asleep. Not really. Whether it be at night in his bed, or during a nap—which in itself was very unlike him—Giles's condition couldn't be called sleep, exactly. There was no rest involved. He did not wake feeling in any way rejuvenated, or relieved of his exhaustion. The ghosts which flitted through his brain were not exactly dreams, or nightmares, though they were the work of his subconscious.

In his heart, and in the recesses of his mind, Giles knew that he was being toyed with. Something had him in its vile control, something that fed off of his emotions and his memories and his vitality. It sapped him of precious life. In time . . . it would kill him.

In those times when he closed his eyes and his body desperately attempted to find some respite from its deteriorating state, he knew all of this. And he could focus, once more, on the face in the backseat of the limousine that had appeared in front of his home the night before.

As he tried to rest, Giles shuddered slightly, an aching sadness stealing over him, taking away even what little will to fight that his subconscious mind could muster. He saw pictures in his mind, of Karen Blaisdell, and the way her kisses seemed to overwhelm him, to weaken him . . . he saw her true face, and understood . . .

But only for a moment.

The instant his subconscious began to focus, began to reach out for his conscious mind in an attempt to shake free, to escape from the numbing mental prison he had been in, Giles felt a sharp spike of pain travel along his spine and thrust into his head.

Then he settled down, his half-sleeping mind relaxing, relieved of the burden of independent thought. He had combated magick before. Spells and charms and wards. But this was something he had not seen coming.

And now it was simply too late for him.

"It's weird knowing he was here last night. That he's here in town," Pike said, hitching up his baggy pants.

"You need a belt," Buffy told him. "Maybe even some clothes better suited for fighting."

He looked at her as though she were out of her mind.

"What?" Buffy demanded.

Pike shook his head. "First of all," he said, "I thought being the Slayer had cured you of the fashion-snob infection you had back at Hemery when you were shallow and popular. Second, I'm sharing my creepy feelings here, and you're blowing me off. And third, I don't need clothes better suited for fighting, 'cause I don't plan to do a lot of fighting. My clothes are my clothes, and they ought to be suited for hanging out or driving my beat up VW taxi, 'cause that's all I need them for."

Buffy looked away, properly admonished. There was a long, awkward moment, then she turned and started walking deeper into the park toward the gardens where they'd been reunited last night. Pike followed, also silent. When Buffy paused again, listening to the wind, scanning the darkness with her eyes, Pike came up next to her.

Very close.

"Buffy—"

"I don't want you to die," she said abruptly, cutting him off. "I don't care what you wear, otherwise. And excuse me for not wanting to think about your stone demon, and how close he might be."

Her heart beat rapidly in her chest. She didn't remember ever being this confused about what she felt. There were so many things right about Pike, so many things that could make it perfect, but then there was Angel . . . and even if there wasn't, it seemed pretty clear to her that Pike didn't have the same feelings. He was just looking for her help, letting her risk her life for him because that's what she did. After that, he'd be back to San Diego in a heartbeat.

"Let's go," she said, and started off again. As she walked, she scanned the gardens ahead, and the park around them. "Maybe we scared them off last night. They've been using this place as their stalking ground for a while, but now that they know we know, it looks like they've moved on. This place is just empty."

After a moment, Buffy realized that Pike was not following. She swallowed hard, and turned. He stood half a dozen feet away, looking at her with sad eyes, his expression reflecting the confusion and turmoil that was in her own heart.

"Buffy, I . . . this isn't easy for me," he said. "Coming here. To you, I mean. After L.A. and Vegas, and, y'know, us . . . it's all complicated inside. I want it to be simple, right? I always did. Boy meets girl, boy throws popcorn at girl in movie theater, boy falls in love, the end. But boy helps girl in her fight against forces of darkness, isn't in there, y'know?"

Buffy looked away, her eyes beginning to brim with unspent tears she couldn't attribute to sadness or happiness or anything else. Just to Pike. But she wouldn't cry in front of him.

"I'm not saying I even know what's in my own heart," she said. "I have romantic issues bigger than Everest. But I hear you say that, and all I can think is, 'coward.' "

Pike looked as though she'd hit him. Except without the blood.

"That is so not fair," he said angrily. "I never felt for anybody else what I felt . . . what I feel, for you. But this . . ." He spread out his arms, indicating the park, the fact that they were patrolling, maybe Sunnydale and Buffy's life in general, she figured.

"This isn't reality."

"Yes," Buffy said darkly, moving across the few feet that separated them, getting up in his face, "it is, Pike. Maybe it's a reality you don't want to face, but this is it. Demons are real. Hell is real. Those things moving in the shadows? They're gonna rip your throat out. Maybe you can't handle that, but I don't have a choice.

I can't just grab my board and hit the waves, I have to turn and face it."

Their eyes locked for a long moment. Pike was the first to look away.

"I don't," he said.

"Tell that to your demon friend," Buffy said. "Tell that to *them,*" she added, pointing past him.

Pike's eyes went wide, and he spun quickly, but there was nothing there. Nothing but trees and benches and all the shadows in between.

"That wasn't funny," Pike told her.

"It wasn't meant to be," Buffy replied. "Just proving a point. Maybe you can't see them. Maybe they're not right over your shoulder, but they're out there. So you're afraid to die," she went on, bitterly. "We're all afraid to die. But it's still gonna happen, one way or another."

Buffy wasn't looking at him. She wrapped her arms around herself, though she wasn't cold at all. Pike moved closer to her. She could feel his nearness, but she didn't want to continue. This—bringing him on patrol—had been a terrible idea. He didn't want to be here. She ought to have just tracked and killed the demon by herself and then told him to go home.

But Pike had a part of her, a little shard of her past that she cherished. She cared for him, no matter how much his attitude hurt her. And now she had begun to realize there wasn't anything she could do about that.

Pike reached out with two fingers and touched her chin. He tried to turn her face toward him, and for a moment, Buffy resisted. Then she turned to look up at him. Standing so close like that—he was much taller than she—she felt, well, like a girl. It was different with Angel, somehow. There was passion of course, a love like she'd never known and never would again. An impossible love. But as powerful as Angel was, his strength and immortality were a constant reminder of what Buffy herself was. Of her own power. It was an incendiary combination.

But Pike was just a guy. He made her feel like just a girl. And that was very, very nice.

"You don't understand," he told her, without a trace of anger, or bitterness, but with more than a little melancholy. "Sure, nobody wants to die, but that isn't what keeps me from staying. I just . . . I can't stay in one place too long, Buffy, because then I start thinking about you again. Thinking about what you're going through. And I can't stay with you because I don't want to see you die."

Thunderstruck, her throat going dry, Buffy stared at him.

It was so sweet, Buffy felt a surge of simple happiness rise up within her unlike any feeling she'd known for a very long time. In her life, a normal relationship was impossible. But with Pike . . . it would be as close as she might ever come.

Then she turned away, head still awhirl with conflicting emotions, but knowing that at that moment, it was the only thing she could do. The only thing her heart could stand.

She knew it was only a fantasy, that Pike would never stay, no matter what he felt. And that she could never leave. Would never leave. Her love for Angel was impossible, but she knew that trying to make things work with Pike was also beyond her reach.

Pretending things were different wasn't fair to either of them, Buffy knew. But when she looked up at Pike again, and he reached out for her, she let him take her in his arms, let him hold her.

Well, maybe I can pretend just for a little while, she thought. *Even if it's only a day or an hour, it couldn't really hurt. At least, not any worse than it already does.*

Willow's posture was the picture of anxiety. She sat on her hands, alternately rocking gently back and forth or bouncing her legs up and down on the balls of her feet. It was a lot of nervous energy to manage in one hard wooden chair, but she'd given up all pretense of research a while ago.

At the door to Giles's office, Oz looked in through the window and sighed. He turned toward Willow and raised his eyebrows.

"Sleeping again?" Willow asked.

"And not too comfortably," Oz replied.

Willow frowned, eyes darting around aimlessly. Then she brightened.

"Idea?" Oz asked.

"Well, what if it isn't Miss Blaisdell?" she asked. "Okay, I know Buffy thinks it has to be her, but I don't feel like we're married to that idea, right?"

Oz nodded. "Conjectural matrimony is always a mistake."

"Exactly," Willow said firmly. "Giles has been sleeping a lot. Bad dreams. I'm not suggesting Freddy Krueger, but there are plenty of sleep- and dream-related demons that could be preying on his mind, eating his subconscious, trying to drive him insane . . . I'm getting carried away, aren't I?"

Oz walked over to the study table and bent slightly to kiss Willow on the head. "I like you carried away," he said. "It makes you bold, which is kind of sexy."

"That's me," Willow confirmed happily. "Bold . . . what was I talking about again?"

With a grin, Oz looked away and pointed at Giles's door.

"Right. Giles. Dream demons. Which means time for more research," she said emphatically. "You with me?"

Oz looked at her oddly. "Where else would I be?"

"Sorry," Willow rolled her eyes, smiling sheepishly. "Just, y'know, bold. Gung ho, John Wayne, morale-building leadership."

"Very working," Oz reassured her. "So, where do we start?"

"At the beginning," Willow told him. "With the symptoms Giles is showing, the obvious exhaustion and the disturbed sleep, it could really be anything."

The library doors swung open and Xander rushed in, face pale and eyes wide. He paused and took a deep breath.

"It's her."

Willow blinked, looked at Oz, then back at Xander. "Are you sure?"

"She spent about two hours in Snyder's office—with Snyder, which don't get me thinking about again please—and while they were in there, your little 'black magick marker' drifted in. Afterward, Snyder had a mark on his neck."

"Mark?" Oz asked, suggestively.

"Not that kind of mark," Xander replied, shuddering visibly. "The thought of that, well, if I don't throw up I might have my stomach pumped just for a cleansing. But yeah, he had a black mark on him."

"I did that," Willow said proudly. "And Miss Blaisdell? She had the mark too?"

Xander shuffled. "Well, it would help if I knew the answer to that, but I don't."

"Which brings us to the why-aren't-you-still-watching-her question," Oz noted.

"Right," Xander said. "I can explain that. See, I had to go, and Cordy came by, and I asked her to spell me, and she did, but then when I got back, Miss Blaisdell had already left."

"You had to go?" Willow asked. "Go where?"

"Go," Oz said, as if sharing a secret.

"Oh," Willow said, crinkling up her nose. "And eew. But I guess we can't blame you for that."

"Why thank you, Your Highness," Xander snapped.

Willow smiled. "I'm being bold today."

"A cause for celebration," Xander noted. "But back to the point we've strayed so far from? I didn't get to see whether Miss Blaisdell was marked, but c'mon, guys, she'd have to be, right? I mean, she's dating Giles, he's acting all funky-dunky, and now she's in with Snyder and he gets marked too."

"That could mean a lot of things, Xander," Willow said, frowning as she thought of it. "It could mean Snyder has put a spell on Giles, or that someone is doing something to both of them. But it doesn't have to be Miss Blaisdell."

"Come on, Will," Xander argued, "the babe's workin' the mojo. You know it, I know it, Buffy knows it, Oz has unexpressed knowledge of it, even Giles probably knows it, but is too blinded by booty to worry about the fact that his brains are practically leaking out his ears."

Off to one side, there came the sound of someone

clearing their throat. As one, Willow, Xander, and Oz turned to see Giles standing in the now open door to his office.

"Oh, Giles, there you are," Xander said nervously. "Right there. Hearing me. Practicing. For the debating team."

Giles glared at him, face pale, dark circles under his eyes. "Really, Xander," the Watcher chided. "Booty?"

Xander opened his mouth as if he were going to reply, then obviously, and much to Willow's surprise, thought better of it.

"You know what?" Xander said. "I think I hear my mother calling me. Or . . . something similarly urgent. If anyone needs me I'll be off doing what Buffy told me to do. Not the keeping my foot out of my mouth part, of course. The other part."

As he babbled on that way, Xander backed out of the library. When he was through the doors, Willow thought she saw a look of intense relief cross his face, and then they swung shut and Xander was gone.

After a moment, Willow realized that Giles was staring at her. She glanced guiltily over at him and smiled.

"And the two of you are here researching some school project or other, I presume?" Giles asked, quite dubiously.

Willow nodded innocently, though she knew she was a horrible liar. When Giles merely raised an eyebrow, she shook her head slowly and looked at the tile.

"Actually," Oz spoke up, "there's still research. But since stone demon research equaled fruitless, we've moved on to trying to figure out what's got you so wacky lately."

Giles glared at him. "Define wacky."

Oz frowned. "Not sure I could, but I can provide

synonyms. Wigged, funky, weird, odd, bizarre, creepy, kooky, ooky, nuts, bananas. I'm not sure crazy as an outhouse rat would qualify here, though. A bit too extreme, I'd say. But the jury's still out."

With a nod, Giles said, "I see." He looked at Willow. "And what have you deduced thus far?"

Willow was about to answer when Giles held up a hand.

"Realize, of course, that if you use the word booty, I shall thrash you both within an inch of your lives."

He smiled as he said it, but it was a very strained smile. Then he squinted, and reached up to massage his left temple.

"Headache?" Willow asked sympathetically.

"Oh yes," he replied. "In fact, I retract my question. I'm fine. Perhaps a bit preoccupied, but that's not an uncommon state for one with my responsibilities. Now, I'll leave you to your research."

"You're leaving?" Willow asked, somewhat panicked.

They were supposed to follow Giles, to keep an eye on him, but now that he knew that they were supposed to keep an eye on him they couldn't exactly follow him home. The Watcher must have seen the look on her face, however.

"I'll be home," he said, with a small sigh. "Should you have any further need to express your concern. Which, by the way, I'm certain I'll appreciate much more when I've had a chance to get some rest."

Willow blinked, glanced at Oz, and saw that his expression was troubled as well.

"You've been sleeping off and on all afternoon," Willow said. "Now you need to rest. Don't you think we have reason to be worried about you?"

Giles seemed stumped by that one. Then he winced in pain and massaged the back of his neck.

"I've got to get home," he said, dismissively.

Then he turned and walked out the library doors. They swung shut behind him, and for a moment, Willow felt paralyzed. They knew he'd had some kind of spell on him, or her own marking spell wouldn't have worked. But they had no idea what was wrong with him, and every time she thought he might actually respond to her questions sensibly, his headache had seemed to grow. That had to be part of the spell.

She looked down at the books she'd been flipping through. Oz came to stand next to her, and she looked up at him slowly, mind racing.

"Next?" Oz asked.

Willow snapped one of the books closed and slid out of her chair. She stood up, determined to make sure Giles was safe.

"We follow him," she said, and started for the door, Oz right beside her.

Which was when the lights went out.

Frustrated and confused, head feeling like it was filled with ground glass, Giles walked down the locker-lined corridor toward the main doors of the school. He fished in his pockets to be certain the keys to his Citroen were there. He'd been so absentminded lately, it was best to be sure. Somewhere off to his right there was a sudden crash, like a heavy desk being overturned.

Then the lights went out.

A moment later, the emergency generator kicked in and the orange backup lights clicked on, bathing the hall in an eerie, unnatural light. Someone was there, inside the building. Someone who didn't belong. And it would do him no good to be trapped here in the hall if he had to defend himself. Better to be outside, with room to maneuver, and a chance to run for help if he should need it.

In spite of the pain in his head, Giles was about to sprint for the exit when he remembered that Willow and Oz were still in the library.

"Damn," he whispered harshly.

He turned to go back the way he'd come, and saw her there, the beautiful blond vampire girl who'd been at his home the night before. Rachel, he thought her name was. She had two others with her, a thin, long-haired male and a tall, exotic-looking woman who was missing an eye.

"Hello there, Watcher," Rachel said amiably. "A pleasure to see you again."

"All yours, I'm afraid," Giles muttered. "The lights are your doing, I expect."

She shrugged. "Some of my friends have a flair for the dramatic."

"So you're here to kill me, then?"

"Oh, worse than that," she assured him. "But not us, really. Our master has sent someone else to do the honors."

Giles frowned. *Someone else. What in God's name does that mean?*

Even as he wondered, the hallway erupted with the sounds of running feet, and Willow and Oz began calling his name.

The pain in his head worse than ever, Giles winced and held both hands to the sides of his skull.

"Stay back!" he cried. "Vampires!"

Rachel glanced at the longhaired male.

"Gunther, kill the girl," she said before turning to the

Amazonian, one-eyed female. "Jocelyn, if you can capture the boy, fine. We'll wait for him to turn next month, and keep his pelt. Otherwise"—she turned to smile at Giles again—"gut him."

A horrible nausea welling up in his stomach, his head tight with pain, Giles began to stumble toward her, enraged in spite of his agony.

"You can't believe I'll just let you kill them," he said, his own words sounding strange to him.

Then he lunged for her. Rachel's face changed then, contorting into the ugly visage of the vampire. Her yellow eyes blazed as she gave him a savage backhand, knuckles cracking against his cheek. Giles flew backward and slammed into a row of lockers, then slid to the cold tile floor.

Down the corridor, he heard Willow begin to scream.

He whispered her name.

"Nothing you can do to help her now, Giles," said a horrible, deep, grinding voice.

Disoriented, he looked up into the chiseled face of a stone demon, red eyes blazing like cinders set back in granite orbits. Giles shook his head slightly, his vision fading in and out, his mind trying to make sense of it all. *The stone demon . . . after Pike . . . but the vampires are here as well.* He didn't understand anything, but the more he tried to focus, the worse his head felt, agonizing spikes shooting through him.

The stone demon grabbed Giles's face and began to lift him off the ground. Flailing, Giles grabbed the creature's arm, concerned, momentarily, that the thing would tear his head off. Instead, the demon lifted Giles and threw him over its shoulder. He batted at it with his hands, and only succeeded in scraping and bruising his fingers and knuckles on the solid rock surface.

For a fleeting moment, he realized that the thing had touched him and he was still flesh and blood. It was not there to kill him, then. No matter what he'd been told, he hadn't quite been able to believe that.

The stone demon strode with Giles toward the front entrance of the school. Its footfalls scraped the floor, grating, echoing off the metal faces of the lockers.

In a haze of pain, Giles spared another thought for Willow and Oz. He heard shouting, scuffling down the hall, and was heartened by the thought that they were still alive. He tried to force his body to move, to rise and go to their aid, but he could barely move a muscle, even if he hadn't been held by the demon.

He felt the blackness begin to envelop him, felt himself slipping out of consciousness. Then suddenly the demon stopped, perhaps ten feet from the large doors that would take them outside to the stone steps at the front of the school.

"The gravel whispers and Grayhewn listens. My gray brothers speak . . ." The demon's words trailed off. "Yes . . . ," he rumbled slowly.

Grayhewn slipped Giles from his shoulder and dropped him to the tile. A jolt of pain shot through him, and he opened his eyes wide for just a moment. A moment of clarity before oblivion claimed him again.

In that moment, he heard Grayhewn's gravel-growl just in a whisper. The demon spoke a single word: "Pike."

Then the front doors crashed open, kicked in from the outside, and Buffy stood there on the threshold, Pike at her back.

Giles closed his eyes, and slipped away into the dark.

Chapter 7

ANGEL WANDERED AROUND DOWNTOWN SUNNYDALE watching humans going about their lives. They lined up for the Sun Cinema, and waited just inside the doors of the latest trendy restaurants, hoping to be seated soon. They window-shopped and held hands and laughed out loud. They shivered at the unexpected chill. It was warm during the day, but at nightfall there might still be a cool breeze now and again. It would have been smart to bring a coat.

But they weren't thinking about that. They were thinking about spring. Humans loved spring. Nature returned to its full vigor. The warm rains came and washed the darkness of winter away. The days began to grow longer, the sun stealing the world back inch by inch, minute by minute, asserting its dominance once again.

That was the key, Angel knew. Somewhere, deep in their consciousness, in ancestral memory that likely stretched back to their days in caves, humankind knew that the gray, short winter days were cause for celebration to the creatures of darkness. Spring began to drive them back, to chain them once more to the brief nights of summer.

But that was summer. That's where the humans always got it wrong. Angel had seen them year after year after year. As soon as spring arrived, they grew more confident, more carefree, they stayed out later.

Spring was a cruel tease. Night still fell quite early. Even now, it was barely seven o'clock and the darkness had swept across Sunnydale nearly an hour before. The vampires were abroad in the night, hunting, and the humans behaved as though the arrival of spring was enough to protect them from the evil that lurked in the shadows.

It wasn't.

Nothing Buffy, or Angel himself, did, could change that. Buffy would simply have to do her best. For his part, Angel had decided during the bright spring day to wander the town tonight. He'd been unable to sleep, unable to keep his mind off of Buffy.

And Pike.

Much as it pained him, he knew that the best thing he could do for Buffy at the moment was stay away. Not that he believed there was a future for Buffy with Pike. Though he wondered if he'd ever allow himself to believe such a thing. No matter, though. What was important was that he keep his distance, give Buffy the opportunity to find out for herself.

It was a little like having his heart violently torn from his chest. But that was how much he loved her. Angel knew that he could never be what Buffy needed. She loved him, that much he knew also. But the dream of being what might be called a couple, of being lovers, of sharing every intimate secret and moment, sharing heart and soul . . .

That dream was dead.

So he had no choice. It wasn't for Angel to know if Buffy would ever be truly in love with another, or if she would ever be able to find a human partner or lover with whom she could truly be happy, nor was it for him to stand in the way.

It was one of the most difficult things he had ever done.

At sundown, he had wandered out into Sunnydale, and now walked its streets, thinking to do what he could to alleviate the Slayer's burden. Certainly he could not fulfill her duties. Only Buffy was capable of that. But Angel could help at times, and he could listen and try to discover what the recent rise in vampire activity, especially in Hammersmith Park, was all about.

To do that, he'd have to find a vampire, hunt the hunters. The best place to do that was to mingle among their prey. So Angel walked and watched as the humans let spring convince them it was safe. And he tried desperately not to think about Buffy and Pike, tried not to focus on the human couples walking by on the sidewalk. He let them just drift by him without more than a casual glance at their faces.

Until Cordelia walked past him.

Angel blinked, turned, and watched her move away in the opposite direction. She was with a guy, arm in arm. Which wasn't all that unusual. But she'd passed right by him, within inches, and when Angel had noticed her, Cordelia had been looking right at him, her expression sort of lost and disturbed.

But she hadn't stopped, hadn't said anything, not even to flirt with him, or disparage Buffy and her friends. And there was one more thing. Something he felt bad for even thinking. The guy that Cordelia was with—with his shaggy, unkempt hair and tall, bony frame, not to mention glasses—well, he wasn't exactly the kind of guy you'd normally see out on a date with Cordelia Chase.

Curious and a bit concerned, Angel started after her. Almost simultaneously, the lanky guy began to steer Cordelia toward a small alley that separated Sun Cinema from Villa Francesca Ristorante. Growing alarmed, Angel picked up his pace. He shoved through the throng of people on the sidewalk. Someone shouted at him, but Angel ignored it and kept on. When two couples walking side by side blocked the sidewalk, he dodged out onto the street.

A car horn honked at him, but Angel paid no attention. Cordelia and her companion had disappeared into the alley. Angel jumped back onto the sidewalk and sprinted for the alley. Dozens of people saw him, must have seen where he was running.

Most of them probably heard the high-pitched scream from the alley.

But this was Sunnydale. Nobody moved to stop him. Nobody moved to help him. They went about their lives, and didn't get involved with whatever dangerous business was going on in that alley.

It was spring, after all. Time for joyous renewal.

Angel rounded the corner of the theater and ran into the alley. Cordelia was against an alley wall with a vampire holding her by the throat, admiring her before he feasted. Her companion was on the ground, nose bleeding, probably broken, and scrabbling backward, ready to flee from the scene, to just leave her there.

Cordelia's eyes were dead, staring straight ahead.

She wasn't screaming, despite what he'd heard. She didn't even really seem to be afraid. Just there. About to die. With a snarl, Angel reached inside his jacket and withdrew a stake from the pocket sewn there, his face shifting, altering, becoming the face of the vampire.

He leaped over the bleeding kid on the ground. Just as the vampire leaned in to sink his needle fangs into Cordelia's nicely tanned throat, Angel grabbed the soulless creature by the hair and yanked his head back hard. The vampire stumbled, began to fall into Angel, and Angel caught him around the throat from behind, as if to choke him. Instead, he lifted the stake and brought it down into the creature's heart.

It exploded to dust in his arms, leaving Angel face-to-face with a completely expressionless Cordelia. She seemed almost entranced. He looked at her and frowned.

Then he heard the heavy breathing and the panicked movements of the guy on the ground, who'd steered Cordelia into the alley in the first place. Angel didn't know what the kid had to do with any of this but he wanted answers.

Out on the street, people passed by, studiously avoiding even glancing into the alley. The kid hauled himself to his feet, glancing fearfully behind him. Angel's face had returned to normal, but the kid had seen him. He was terrified. He was running.

"Stop," Angel commanded.

The kid faltered slightly, but didn't obey. He took off.

Angel caught him right at the mouth of the alley, and dragged him back into the shadows where Cordelia stood leaning against a wall, still completely out of it.

"What's your name?" Angel demanded.

"H-h-henry. Polk. Are you gonna kill me? Please don't kill me," the kid begged.

For the moment, Angel didn't answer that question. Instead, he hauled Henry up onto his tiptoes, despite the kid's height, and pointed at Cordelia.

"How'd she get that way?"

"She was like that when I ran into her," Henry sobbed. "I swear, man. I swear. It was totally innocent. I mean, she's Cordelia Chase, y'know? I've been watching her in school for years. She's untouchable. But then I see her wandering around like, I don't know, like she needed a friend."

Fury burned in Angel's heart, and he narrowed his eyes dangerously.

"So you saw she was like this, helpless, and you figured you'd bring her into this alley and be her friend, huh?" he growled.

"No, listen, it wasn't like that—"

"If she was like that already," Angel asked, suddenly confused, "how did she scream?"

Henry flushed, eyes darting around. "She didn't," he said softly. "That was me."

Disgusted, Angel gave him a hard shove toward the entrance to the alley. "I should've let that thing have you."

"What *was* that thing?" Henry asked. "It was horrible."

"Yeah," Angel said acidly. "Imagine attacking a defenseless girl in a dark alley. Just go. Don't ever let me find you within a hundred yards of her again."

Henry blanched. "But I'm in her history class."

Angel started toward Henry, letting his lip curl back in a furious snarl. "I guess that's your problem, isn't it?"

When Henry ran from the alley, he screamed again. It didn't get him any more attention than it had the first time. Finally, Angel was able to turn his attention to the strangely silent Cordelia. He moved to where she still leaned against the wall and bent slightly, looking directly in her eyes. Her eyes didn't really seem to focus on him at all, and Angel moved back and forth to see if they followed him.

They didn't.

"Cordelia?" he ventured.

No response.

"Can you hear me? Do you know who I am?"

She still didn't look at him, but this time, her eyelids fluttered a bit, and the edges of her mouth turned up in the hint of a smile.

"Angel," she said breathily.

He grabbed her face, somewhat roughly, and turned her to look at him. Again, he stared into her eyes, and this time, he thought he saw a bit of recognition there.

"Do you know where you are?" he asked.

Cordelia looked troubled, and didn't respond.

"What's the last thing you remember?" He knew her mind had been toyed with, but he didn't know how or why. It could be traditional hypnosis, but he'd never known it to be this effective. Which left magick. Some kind of spell or glamour.

"Cordelia," he snapped. "What's the *last thing* you remember?"

She frowned. At least that was some expression, Angel thought.

"Xander," Cordelia whispered. "He was in the hall . . . at school . . . he was spying for Buffy. Stupid. Spying. He asked me to stand watch, just for a second, and then . . ."

Her face went blank and Angel swore.

"You don't remember what happened?" he asked.

She shook her head.

"Do you remember who you were spying on? Who was it Xander asked you to watch? Come on, Cordelia, remember!" he said harshly. For if she didn't remember, he wasn't sure if he would ever be able to remove whatever magick was clouding her mind.

Cordelia blinked, winced as though the very act of thinking caused her pain.

"Cordelia?" Angel prodded.

"It was . . . Miss Blaisdell," she whispered. "I was spying on her, and then . . . I don't know. I talked to Xander, but I don't know what I said."

Her eyes began to lose their focus again. After a moment, she was staring off into the shadows of the alley, just as she'd been before. Angel knew he had to figure out a way to get Cordelia out of this fog she was living in. But first, he had to warn the others.

"Come on," he said. "We've got to get to the school."

It had all become clear to Angel now. Buffy had been concerned about Giles's behavior since he'd been seeing Karen Blaisdell. For good reason, it seemed. Moments earlier, he had thought Cordelia was simply under a spell of some kind.

The truth was more sinister.

"Oz, come on!" Willow shouted, and slammed through the library doors.

Behind her, Oz pulled over a large plastic trash can, hoping to buy them even a heartbeat longer. That's all. A heartbeat. Or maybe a lifetime's worth.

When the lights had gone out and they'd heard Giles cry out in the corridor, they'd run out after him and seen the vampires. Worse, the vampires had seen them and attacked. At first it seemed there were only three, the blond female, Rachel, and two others. Gunther and Jocelyn, she'd heard Rachel call them.

Rachel hadn't paid any attention to them, just told the others to kill them. Willow and Oz had scuffled with them—he had fang scrapes on his neck and she had what was going to be a nasty bump developing on her skull— but they'd managed to stay alive for a minute.

Then, from the shadows, the vampires had reinforcements, a pair of short, muscular vamp-boys with reddish Marine crew cuts. Twins.

"Double your pleasure," Oz had said drolly, before barely eluding the newcomers.

The odds were not good. Down the hall, they'd seen the stone demon taking Giles, but could do nothing to stop it. Then Buffy and Pike had arrived, and that changed everything. Willow knew she and Oz had only one chance. So she'd grabbed his arm and muttered, "Library," and with a meaningful look, they'd both run for their lives.

Oz plowed through the swinging doors behind her, but Willow wasn't waiting. They had scant seconds. The one-eyed, Amazonian Jocelyn slammed into the room behind him, and Gunther was right behind her. Willow ran for the library cage. The mesh door was open, the key still in the lock. She ripped the key out, and jumped in.

"Oz!" she screamed.

Then Oz barreled in behind her, and pulled the cage shut as he passed. The metal door clanged against its frame, and the pursuing vampires slammed against it. Jocelyn hissed and spat, and Gunther only grinned and reached out for the mesh. He tugged at it, hard.

It didn't look like much, Willow knew that. It wasn't supposed to. But what it was supposed to do was hold her boyfriend when he was in werewolf mode, and if Oz couldn't get out when the moon was full, she was banking that these guys couldn't get in.

Metal cried out a little under the strain, but the cage held.

"Forget it," Willow told them. "No way are you getting in."

With the twins standing behind them, Gunther and Jocelyn worked together to pull on the cage. Again metal shrieked, but did not let go. Together, Willow and Oz moved to the back of the cage, just in case.

"I thought about taunting them, but I figured now might not be the best time for 'nyah, nyah,'" Oz confessed. "I don't want us to come off as overconfident."

"That . . . wouldn't necessarily be my first concern," Willow said, reaching out to hold Oz's hand as the twins came up and put their hands on the cage as well.

Suddenly the library door was kicked open and Rachel stood there, looking furious. "Gunther, Jocelyn," she said angrily. "Grayhewn's dropping the ball. Get out here."

The one-eyed vampire woman looked at Willow and smiled, her carved and empty eye socket even more unsettling. "I'll come back for a taste, girl," she said.

"That's . . . thoughtful of you, but don't trouble yourself," Willow replied, tentatively.

"It's no trouble," Gunther snarled, flipped his long greasy hair back, and followed Jocelyn out of the library.

The crewcut twins didn't smile. They didn't threaten. They didn't grunt or groan or bluster. They just set to work, hauling on the cage like monkeys at the zoo, trying their best to tear the metal from its moorings.

"Hey," Willow said. "We're in the library cage."

Oz looked at her, one eyebrow raised, and then suddenly he got it. They turned to the shelving units where Giles still had a great many of his old books and journals and things stored. There was a cabinet in his small office where he kept most of Buffy's weapons. *Most* being the operative word. Oz reached up and grabbed the box on the top shelf, pulled it down. He and Willow looked inside, and smiled.

Willow whipped out a cross. The twins hissed and drew back from the metal for a moment. Then, turning their faces as if from bright light, they started to yank on the cage again.

Which was when Oz uncorked the bottle of holy water and splashed it in their faces, over their arms and hands. The vampires hissed and roared in pain and anger, withdrawing a short distance from the cage.

Oz had his back turned, so he didn't see the fury in their yellow eyes and the way their fangs jutted out when they hissed. They inspected their smoldering burns, only sparing the occasional angry glance at Oz and Willow every few seconds.

They didn't even see Oz as he turned with the now-loaded minicrossbow.

"Hey," Oz said.

The twins looked up.

"Should've been more polite," Willow admonished them gently.

Then Oz shot a wooden crossbow bolt into the heart of the twin on the left. He grunted, then exploded in a cloud of dust that blinded his brother. By the time the remaining vampire turned, enraged, to approach the cage again, Oz was loading another bolt into the weapon. The vampire saw him, stared at the weapon for a moment, then began to back away, glaring murderously at them.

"Somehow that look makes me more nervous than Jocelyn's threats," Willow whispered to Oz.

He only nodded, and let out a long breath. After a moment, Willow's eyes widened.

"Oh, no," she said. "Buffy!" Then she held up the key, shoved it through the cage mesh and began trying to work it around so they could free themselves.

"Not that I'm adverse to life-threatening situations," Oz said, "but is this wise?"

"We don't have a choice," Willow insisted.

"There's that," Oz agreed.

"Buffy, don't let it touch you!" Pike shouted.

"Funny," Buffy replied. "That's what my mother always says."

Grayhewn lunged at Pike, who dodged to the right, down the corridor, leading the demon away from Giles. Buffy dropped, and rolled out of its way and quite purposefully, landed near Giles. She glanced at him, made sure he was still breathing, and then she stood up, and turned to face the demon again.

It had no interest in her. None at all. Slayer though she might be, its vendetta was for Pike. The thing was one of the oddest looking creatures Buffy had ever seen: like a granite statue, sculpted and chiseled by human hands. But the way it moved, and the low rasping sound its movements made, amazed her. It was stone. Before she'd seen it, she imagined that it would be slow, its movements stunted. Which was not the case at all. Grayhewn was not the fastest of creatures she had seen, but its movements were fluid and deadly.

"Pike, just run!" she cried, as the demon pursued him down the hall.

If he'd just gone on, he might have been able to out-run it. But instead, he turned, reached out and opened a classroom door, just as the demon was lunging for him again. Its upper body crashed through the glass window in the door, and Pike ducked low to avoid being touched by its hands as he drove the door against the wall, pinning the demon between them. Then he started back in the opposite direction, and met Buffy as she ran toward him.

"Let's just get Giles and go," he said. "It's too dangerous to fight him. You can't get close enough to hurt him without being close enough for him to touch you."

Buffy was almost willing to agree—withdraw and come back to fight later, when they'd figured out how—when the demon roared its gravel-voiced roar and bounded at them again.

"Move!" Buffy snapped, and shoved Pike out of her way. The hall was lined with lockers. Buffy reached out and grabbed the handle of one, tensed, and yanked. The lock shattered, the door swung open, and then Buffy tore it off its hinges.

"Pike!" Grayhewn rasped. "You killed my mate, boy. Now I kill you and yours."

The demon reached for them. Buffy frowned, whipped the locker door up and blocked its attack, batting its hands away. Grayhewn roared again and turned to face her. Buffy held the metal door by the bottom and swung it around. There was a loud clang as it connected with the demon's head, and the creature seemed momentarily off guard.

In that split second, its hands still reaching for them though it was disoriented, Buffy lifted the door and brought it down like a guillotine, snapping off one of the stone demon's hands. The hand hit the floor and broke apart into pieces.

Red eyes blazing, the demon snorted with pain and rage and began to roar again, furious now with Buffy as well as Pike. Buffy brought the dented locker door down on its head again, and it stumbled backward.

"Buffy!" Pike shouted, his hand clamping on her shoulder.

"I'm a little busy here," she replied, moving in for another attack on Grayhewn.

"They're taking Giles!"

Buffy spun and saw that Pike was right. Giles wasn't on the floor anymore. Rachel was far down the hall, with Jocelyn and Gunther behind her carrying Giles between them. A red-haired vamp with a buzz cut came out of the library and started to follow them.

So much went through Buffy's mind then. They were taking Giles. But where were Oz and Willow?

"No!" she shouted.

Buffy set her legs firmly on the floor, held the locker door up, cocked her arm back and threw it with all her might. The rectangular metal door spun through the air, powered by the strength of the Slayer, and with a wet thunk, imbedded itself into the neck of the redheaded vampire, throwing him forward. The door hadn't cut all the way through, but it had severed the spinal column, leaving his head connected only by ragged muscle and tissue. When the vampire hit the floor, the door clanged against the ground. The flesh holding head to neck tore away.

The vampire was dusted.

"Giles!" Buffy cried.

Behind her, Grayhewn held the stump of his severed

hand against his chest and lurched toward Pike. Buffy spun, kicked the demon in the chest as hard as she could, and then turned and ran down the hall, pursuing the vampires.

As she passed the library, Oz and Willow rushed out, nearly colliding with her.

"Oh, Buffy, you're okay!" Willow said happily.

"They've got Giles," Buffy snapped, and kept running. "Oz, stay with Pike."

Willow fell in behind her. But by the time Buffy rounded the corner, Giles was nowhere to be seen. The vampires were gone. Buffy paused a moment, listening for them, and heard a loud crash and a shattering of glass not far away. She swore and ran as fast as she could. At the next turn, though, she knew it was too late.

There was a long floor-to-ceiling window in the hall outside the bio lab that looked out onto the campus lawn. The window had been shattered.

Too late.

"They've got him," she muttered as Willow raced up behind her. "We'd better get back."

Together, they ran back the way they'd come. Buffy was turning the whole situation over in her head. The vampires wanted Giles, but alive, which didn't make sense, unless they wanted her. But it didn't seem to be about her. And she'd thought Miss Blaisdell was in on the whole thing, but now she wasn't sure.

And Grayhewn . . .

They rounded the corner that led to the front door. At the end of the hall, past the library, two lone figures lay on the hard floor. Oz was slowly getting to his knees, shaking his head.

"Oh, God, Oz!" Willow cried, and ran for him.

Buffy ran as well, panic welling up inside of her. The other figure that lay there on the floor was Pike. And Pike wasn't moving.

"What happened?" Willow asked as she reached Oz.

"The demon, Grayhewn," he replied. "He's not very friendly. Also gone, by the way."

Buffy dropped to her knees by Pike. The first thing she noticed was that he was still breathing. A huge wave of relief swept over her.

"Pike," she whispered.

His eyes fluttered open. "Hey, Buff," he croaked. "Did you get Giles back?"

She shook her head. "But I will."

Pike nodded painfully.

"What happened to Grayhewn? Why did he leave? I didn't think he was on board with their kidnap-Giles program after he saw you," she said.

Pike smiled weakly. "Dude didn't have any reason to stay," he said simply. Then he raised his left hand, and Buffy saw what he meant, saw the long stretch of skin on Pike's right forearm that had turned to stone.

"He touched me," Pike said. "And it's spreading."

Chapter 8

IN THE SEVENTIES, CATALINA ROAD AND THE STREETS around it had been pretty much *the* cutting edge middle-class neighborhood in Sunnydale: small, contemporary single-family dwellings. But that was a quarter century earlier. At the turn of the millennium, it was just another cracked and faded street lined with run-down houses in desperate need of a paint job, a major renovation, or in some cases, a bulldozer. Buyers wanted older homes with sturdier construction, or something bright, shiny, and new.

They weren't going to find that on Catalina Road.

Xander and his family didn't live that far away, and didn't have any money to speak of. But his father cracked the whip every couple of years and they got the house painted. His parents had always taken care of the yard pretty well, even if they screamed at each other while doing it. Their house wasn't much, but at least it wasn't on Catalina Road.

Karen Blaisdell lived at number twenty-nine Catalina, which could have been Cordelia's house in comparison to the others around it. Freshly cut grass. New paint job. Recently rebuilt front steps. And a nice, shiny chain-link fence running the perimeter of the property. Looking at that fence, Xander was completely convinced that there must be a dog inside, some kind of vicious, slavering beast that would have given Oz a run for his Milk-Bones during a full moon.

But as he walked along the outside of the fence between Miss Blaisdell's house and number thirty-one next door, Xander was surprised to find no sign at all of the hellhound he'd been expecting. No doghouse. No chain or runner. No chewed Frisbees or paperboy limbs.

It didn't usually work that way for Xander Harris, but for once, luck was with him. He hopped the fence and ran to the corner of the house as silently as he was able. Miss Blaisdell's car was in the driveway, and there were lights on inside, so he knew she was home. Which was also lucky. He didn't want to let Buffy and the others down. They were trying to figure out why Giles was acting all personality-impaired, even for Giles, and he wanted to do his part.

And if doing my part involves peering in the windows of a beautiful sultry vixen who happens to be a substitute teacher, well, I'll just have to make that sacrifice.

At least, that was what he was telling himself. Unfortunately, Xander realized with some disappointment that the prospect of peering in Miss Blaisdell's windows—even if it was under "orders"—wasn't as much of a thrill as it might have been at thirteen. In truth, he found that he was nervous, even embarrassed. The titillation factor was there, no doubt—he was a teenage male, after all—but it felt wrong, too. Just . . . wrong.

Xander had a grim expression on his face as he moved from window to window, trying to get a glimpse of Miss Blaisdell inside. He couldn't go around front, but there were enough trees and shrubs along the side, and it had gotten cloudy enough, that if he stuck to the back and sides of the house, he probably wouldn't be seen by the neighbors or passing cars.

A perfect night for peeping, he thought uncomfortably.

Somewhere down the street, a dog barked loudly, and Xander started nervously, his heart racing. His mind had gone back for just a moment to the monstrous mutt he'd imagined would be in Miss Blaisdell's yard and he thought he might have sprouted a few gray hairs. Eighteen and gray hairs were a volatile combination, but he figured that was better than a heart attack, which was likely to happen if he was startled again.

When he turned back to look in the kitchen window, he saw that Miss Blaisdell had come into the room. Xander being Xander, he didn't fail to notice that her hair was wet from the shower and she wore a blue terry cloth robe belted around her waist. Belted loosely.

Xander swallowed self-consciously. His heart was racing again, but it had nothing to do with any dog. Well, unless he counted himself. The needle on his internal guilt-o-meter was pretty high.

Paying very little attention to the swish of her robe, Miss Blaisdell picked up some papers from the kitchen table and piled them into a small stack, which she then slid into a briefcase. Then she turned, the movement revealing enough leg to freeze Xander's brain cells for a moment. His face felt warm and he knew he was blushing. When she didn't come back, he moved to the next window.

The living room. Hair still damp, Miss Blaisdell reclined in a lazy sprawl, robe now barely tied, on a plush sofa. The room was dark, save for the light coming from the kitchen and the flickering of the television screen, which illuminated her.

Xander didn't know how long he stood there, staring, barely breathing, waiting for her to move. To do something suspicious, of course. 'Cause that's why he was here, after all. Spying on her to see if she was something evil.

But Xander didn't see anything at all evil about Miss Blaisdell. And he could see a lot of her right then, so he should know.

A few minutes later, Miss Blaisdell stood again, and Xander had to blink to get the image of what he saw then from blinding him for life. His mind wasn't really functioning properly when she left the room, but he moved back to the kitchen window as slowly and carefully and soundlessly as he could.

He stood next to the window, then, crouching low, moved in front of it to peer in.

Karen Blaisdell was right on the other side of the glass, staring out at him with a sly grin on her face.

"Yah!" Xander shouted, stumbled backward trying to hide his face and run at the same time, and ended up falling on his ass on the lawn.

Miss Blaisdell raised the window, still smiling with amusement.

"Hello, Xander," she said pleasantly. "I presume you've got some school-related question for me, and just wanted to make sure this was my house?"

Xander blinked. Then his eyes widened. "Absolutely," he said with relief. "That's it exactly."

"Well," she drawled, making no move to cinch her

robe up tighter as she leaned over at the window. "Why don't you come on in, then?"

It was Xander's turn to smile.

Buffy felt panic rising up within her, so many thoughts crashing through her mind, and she pushed it all away. She had to control herself, had to stay calm, if they were to have any chance at all of saving Pike's life.

"Oz," she snapped. "Get his legs."

Willow and Oz were there instantly. Buffy lifted Pike by the hands, ignoring the feel of stone under her fingers as Pike's left hand slowly changed to stone. Oz grabbed Pike's feet and they hefted him, Buffy handling most of the weight.

"Where to?" Oz asked.

"Library," Buffy said in clipped tones, forcing herself to remain in control. She looked at Willow. "Can you do anything about this? Anything?" Buffy demanded.

Willow looked uncomfortable, but then nodded grimly. "I don't know if I can stop it, or even save him, but I think I know a way to slow it down long enough to buy time to figure it out. I'll need some stuff from the bio lab, and from Giles's office, but—"

"Do it."

"But, Buffy," Willow said, following Buffy and Oz as they pushed through the library door with Pike between them. "I mean, what about Giles?"

Without pausing, Buffy and Oz slid Pike onto the long study table in the library. The glass and brass banker's lamp was shoved off the edge and shattered on the floor. Buffy looked at Pike's arm, saw the gray stone spreading up his arm, and went to Willow.

"This was the second time they came after Giles," she said. "If they wanted to just kill him, they'd have tried to do that already. Whatever nasty fun they've got planned for him, he'll be alive a little while. Pike won't."

Willow nodded. "Going," she said. Then she turned and ran from the library.

Buffy paused a moment, then looked after Willow with concern. She glanced at Oz. "Maybe you'd better—" she began.

But Oz was already moving. "Just in case they aren't all gone," he agreed, and went after Willow.

Leaving Buffy alone with Pike. He was unconscious. Whatever that demon, Grayhewn, had done to him, however the whole infection thing worked, it was already traumatic enough for Pike's body to have completely shut down. Pike had told them the story of how his friend had died. It had sounded like it was pretty quick, not like what was happening to Pike at all. The only thing Buffy could think of, the only explanation, was that Grayhewn had wanted Pike to suffer.

He'd come with those vampires to get Giles, but seeing Pike, he'd figured the hell with Giles. Pike had to suffer. Pike had killed Grayhewn's mate, and that had obviously been more important to the demon than whatever they wanted Giles for.

They *all* wanted Giles, which Buffy still couldn't figure out.

She bent over Pike and pushed his hair away from his eyes, traced her finger over the scar that ran through his left eyebrow and bit her lip as she remembered giving it to him. *And now this,* Buffy thought.

The demon was turning Pike to stone, but somehow he'd made it happen so slowly, so painfully. He wanted

Pike to suffer. And now, the very hatred that had made the demon so cruel toward Pike had given them the only opportunity to save his life.

Grayhewn. Buffy vowed to herself that she would take a sledgehammer to that demon the second she had the chance. She wanted to tell him to his face what a coward she thought he was. Sure, he'd already gotten what he'd been sent for—Giles—and managed to even the score with Pike, but then the demon had run away, instead of facing Buffy herself. She looked forward to calling him a coward, seeing how Grayhewn liked that.

"What the hell's going on?" she whispered to Pike, and kissed the scar on his brow.

From behind, a voice replied. "I think I have part of an answer."

Buffy pulled away from Pike and stood up straight. Angel stood holding open the double swinging doors of the library. She gazed at him a moment, feeling horribly awkward, wondering if he'd seen her kiss Pike, and wondering if, in the end, it really mattered. Of course it would pain him. Angel loved her and she loved him. But they just couldn't have any future together.

And you've been through this, Summers. Can you really have a future with anyone?

Which made her look back at Pike, reminding her that if Willow couldn't come up with something fast, he was a dead man. His shirt had ridden up when she and Oz had put him on the table, and Buffy could see that much of his left side had already started to turn to stone.

Buffy looked back at Angel. "I'm glad you're here," she told him, and despite her discomfort, she wasn't lying. Somehow, having Angel there gave her hope.

"What's wrong with him?" Angel asked, nodding toward Pike.

Buffy glanced down, swallowing. "Stone demon," she said. "It touched him."

"I'm sorry," Angel said.

She looked into his eyes from across the room, and she saw the pain there, and knew he meant it. Angel didn't know Pike at all, but he loved Buffy. Her pain was his. She knew that because the reverse was also true.

"So, what were you saying?" she asked.

Angel shook his head, raised his eyebrows a moment, then let one of the doors swing shut and reached back out into the hallway. A moment later, he pulled Cordelia into the library by her hand. Buffy was about to ask what was going on, then she noticed the expression on Cordelia's face. Or, rather, the lack of any discernible expression at all.

"Cordy?" Buffy ventured, moving toward her.

But Cordelia barely even reacted to her name. Angel propelled her gently toward the study table where Pike was sprawled, and pulled out a chair. He guided Cordelia to the chair, and she sat down.

"I found her like this downtown," Angel explained.

"Well," Buffy said reasonably, "I'm not sure this isn't an improvement. None of the people in Oz complained when they melted the witch."

Angel nodded. "Yeah. But the novelty of Cordelia keeping her mouth shut wears off after a few minutes, and then it's just eerie."

"Wait," Buffy said, turning to him. "When you came in, you said—"

"That I could explain it, or at least part of it," Angel confirmed.

The library doors flew open, and Willow and Oz rushed in, arms loaded with supplies from the bio lab—

including a beaker and Bunsen burner, and what Buffy tried to tell herself wasn't one of the fetal pigs they had to dissect first semester—as well as some jars of herbs and less wholesome things that had to have come from Willow's locker.

"Out of the way, guys, we've got work to do!" Willow declared, shoving past Angel. Then she paused. "Oh, hi, Angel." Another pause. Willow looked from Buffy to Pike's still form, and back to Angel. "Oh. Hi, Angel," she said again.

"You said that," Buffy told her, the awkward feeling rushing over her again.

"And Cordelia," Oz told Willow as he started laying some things out on the table around Pike. "It's a shindig."

Willow looked at Cordelia and frowned. "What's wrong with her?"

"Your next patient, Doctor Rosenberg," Buffy explained.

"Witch Doctor Rosenberg," Oz corrected.

Willow smiled adorably. "I like that," she said. Then she looked over at Buffy, opened her mouth to ask, and then shook her head. "No, we don't have time for explanations." Then Willow ripped Pike's shirt open.

Witch doctor Rosenberg didn't even react to the sight, but Oz uttered a slight "Whoa," and Buffy flinched and looked away. Pike's entire left side was stone now, and it was creeping across his abdomen and throat. Willow touched the side of his face and Pike's head lolled slightly to one side, revealing that the left side of his face was also stone, all save the eye, which was open and staring, though the other was closed.

"Oh, God," Buffy murmured, reminded of the villain

Two-Face from the Batman cartoons. "Willow, you've got to stop it."

Angel came up behind Buffy and put his hands on her shoulders. She turned, emotions still warring with one another but needing him so desperately, and fell into his embrace. He held her tightly a moment and then Buffy composed herself and turned back to Willow.

"So what are you doing?" she asked as Oz got some water cooking in the beaker over the Bunsen burner and Willow spread some nasty ingredients across the table.

"Helping," Willow replied hurriedly. "Angel, go into Giles's office and get me the *Athol Demon Concordance*. Oz, prepare the pig."

"There's something you don't get to say every day," the laconic guitarist replied, and unwrapped the plastic that covered the dead animal.

Finally, Willow looked at Buffy. "I think I can stop it. If I can, I can probably reverse it. But I need time, and space, to focus. Let me do what I do, and you should, y'know, probably do what you do. In this case, finding Giles."

Buffy nodded. She looked at Pike, trying to steel her emotions. Whatever happened to him now, it was out of her hands. But she could kick Grayhewn's ass to make herself feel a little better, even just for a few minutes. And if she could find Grayhewn, maybe she'd find Giles.

Angel came out of the library and handed Willow a book, even as Oz lifted a scalpel. Buffy was ready to grab Angel and drag him out hunting Giles, but then she looked over and saw Cordelia. She took a deep breath and looked at Angel.

"You were telling me?" she said. "About Cordy?"

He nodded slowly and walked over to look down at Cordelia again. Angel waved his hand in front of her face, and she blinked, but offered no other reaction.

"She's been mesmerized," Angel explained. "There are a number of ways this can be done, mostly magickal, some just psychological. But I don't think either is quite the case here. I talked to her, got her to come out of it, just a little. I think she saw something she wasn't supposed to, and the thing she saw didn't want her to remember, or talk about it."

"What thing?" Buffy asked sharply. "We don't have time for twenty questions."

Angel blinked, and Buffy started to apologize for being so harsh, but he held up a hand to stop her, to indicate that he understood.

"It's called a glamour," he told her. "They're a race of minor demons who control the minds and feed off the passions of their victims, not that much different from succubae, only the glamours look beautiful and human. Also, they don't kill so much as drain their victims. A glamour wouldn't want to kill, you understand. They'd rather keep the victim alive as a source of sustenance for as long as they could."

Buffy felt a wave of icy cold spreading through her body. She took a breath, looked at Cordelia, and then back at Angel. "But eventually they die?"

"If the glamour isn't stopped, yes," Angel admitted.

Willow looked up from her spellcasting, concern haunting her face. "Cordelia walked in on Miss Blaisdell with Snyder. It's probably Miss Blaisdell, right?"

Angel nodded.

Suddenly, Buffy wasn't cold anymore. Anger began

to rise up in her. Her brow creased, teeth gritted together. "Which explains why Giles has been acting so funky." Buffy paused, trying to make sense of it all. "But what I don't get . . . I mean, I was sure the way Giles was acting had to do with whoever's behind our little Watcher-napping. It just doesn't . . ." She raised an eyebrow.

"What?" Angel asked.

"Last night, Miss Blaisdell left right before the vampires attacked. They just let her walk away. Even if they were there on a mission, no red-and-cold-blooded vampire posse is gonna let a hottie like Miss Blaisdell just walk by. There's a connection."

"Okay," Angel said. "But what?"

"We're going to find out," she said, and turned to face Willow and Oz, who were finishing up a chant over whatever magickal concoction was now boiling over the Bunsen burner.

Buffy waited until the chant was through. Oz took a breath, seemingly tired out a little by the magick. Willow sort of nodded to herself, face etched with determination.

"Will?" Buffy asked.

After quickly examining Pike's throat and face, Willow turned to look at Buffy. "I don't think I stopped it, but I slowed it way down," she said. "Now I'm Research Girl again. I think I can figure out how to reverse the process."

Buffy nodded. "What about Cordelia?"

Willow glanced at the silent, unmoving girl. "I don't know," she said. "It's sort of nice and quiet in here." Then she smiled guiltily. "But I'll snap her out of it as soon as possible."

"First I need you to do that computer voodoo you do

so well," Buffy told her. "I need Karen Blaisdell's home address."

"That's easy," Willow said. "Twenty-nine Catalina Road. I looked it up for Xander before he starting spying on her."

"Oh, God," Buffy said, shaking her head in dismay. "Xander." She glanced at Pike, looked at Willow and Oz. "Don't let him die," she said before turning and grabbing Angel by the hand, and dragging him out the door.

In his dream . . .

Giles was kissing Karen. He could feel the ruby red softness of her lips on his own. She removed his glasses, let them dangle at her side, and just when he began to relax, before the kiss became more than a kiss, she twined her fingers in his hair and wrapped a leg around him, pulling him close. Closer. And her lips moved down his throat to his chest, and back up once again.

Only they didn't feel soft anymore.

There was pleasure, unlike anything he'd known.

But there was pain, as well. Horrible pain. Clutching, aching pain, as though his heart had seized, his breath stolen away, his stomach tightened, about to revolt.

He was jostled awake, his head bouncing slightly on the hard metal floor of the van. For a moment, Giles's mind was clear, the dream fresh in his memory, and he knew that he'd been used, been violated. Then his eyelids fluttered, and he descended into a haze of mental numbness that had become too familiar to him in recent days.

There were vampires all around him. That he knew. And against the rear doors, Grayhewn the demon sat facing them all, eyes glowing red in the darkness of the vehicle. The back of the van dipped toward the street; the van obviously riding too low.

"He's awake," said a beautiful, lilting voice.

Giles saw blond hair, and blinked, recognizing Rachel, the vampire girl who'd twice tried to engineer his abduction. Now here he was in her hands.

But alive. At least he was alive.

Twice more, the van jostled up and down, and Giles had the vague idea they were driving over speed bumps. Then the driver braked and the van pulled to a stop. Nobody moved until the two vampires up front had jumped out and come around the back to open the doors. Grayhewn stepped out—his stone flesh scraping paint off the floor of the van—and the vehicle rose several inches.

His mind grew even more muddled, though he sensed some of the vampires moving past him. Then he was staring into the ragged, empty eye socket of the one called Jocelyn.

"Out," she ordered.

Giles tried to command his limbs to move, but they weren't paying any attention. He felt helpless, almost frozen.

"Come on," Jocelyn growled, and grabbed him by the hair, almost dragging him from the van that way.

"Aaagh," Giles mumbled painfully. "Hurts." He tried to say more, but couldn't make his mouth obey. He felt lost, a prisoner inside his own body, his own foggy mind.

"That hurts?" Jocelyn asked harshly as she forced him out of the van, forced him to start walking across the pavement toward a large, featureless building. "How about this?"

She'd warned him. Her words told him what was coming. But as numb as he felt, Giles couldn't even react, couldn't get out of her way. Jocelyn kicked him in the side, and Giles went down hard on the pavement. He cringed, trying to catch his breath, his kidneys in pain, and he was grateful she hadn't kicked higher where she might have broken some ribs.

His eyes flickered open a moment, and he saw several of the vampires above him. The demon seemed to have gone inside already, or moved on his way. Jocelyn, Rachel, and the other, the thin, longhaired male called Gunther, they all looked down on him.

Rachel ripped open his shirt. Giles blinked, and didn't really see Jocelyn strike out at him, her claws raking across his chest, drawing deep furrows, drawing blood. Giles screamed, and opened his eyes wide, and that was how he knew it had been Jocelyn, for she was licking his blood off her long nails.

"Now *that* hurts," she told him. "And it's just the beginning."

He was barely able to open his eyes or focus on anything as they forced him to stumble his way into the large building. Somehow his ability to concentrate was diminishing by the moment. They marched him down a long hallway dotted with doors. At the end of the corridor were a pair of heavy double wooden doors.

Rachel opened them.

Gunther shoved Giles inside, into the darkness.

He slammed into a long wooden table, nearly falling on top of it, and then slid down to sit, swaying with disorientation, on the floor. The door slammed shut, and he could hear them locking it. Barely able to keep from throwing up, he lay down on the carpeted floor, his eyes closed.

Sighing, he tried to think, tried desperately to focus on anything. If he couldn't think, he'd never get out of here. He forced himself to open his eyes.

There in the darkness, just inches from his face, was the cooling corpse of a woman whose eyes were wide with death and whose throat had two ragged, bloody puncture wounds in the soft flesh.

There were others in the room as well.

Despite his dazed state, Giles began to wonder if they were truly dead. Or if they'd be coming back. And if so, how long he had.

Chapter 9

AFTER THEY'D DRIVEN PAST KAREN BLAISDELL'S house for the second time—without seeing any sign of Xander—Angel pulled Oz's van to the curb just down the street, shut off the lights, and killed the engine. For a moment, they sat there, engine ticking as it cooled.

"He's fine," Angel told her. "He may not even have been here."

Buffy glanced over at him. It wasn't like Angel to offer hollow reassurances, and she didn't like it coming from him. From other people, she sometimes liked to be comforted with empty hopes. Sometimes, that was all that got her by. But not from Angel. Especially not when they both knew Xander wouldn't have just blown off something Buffy had asked him to do, something that could help Giles.

"Let's go," she said.

Silently as they were able, Buffy and Angel climbed out of the van and gently shut the doors. Angel pocketed Oz's keys, and they started back down the street toward Miss Blaisdell's house.

"How do you want to do this?" Angel whispered. "If the glamour is someone else, you could get in—"

"It's not someone else," Buffy said confidently. "And we don't have time to be clever. If there's a back door, we go in that way. If not, the front will do."

Buffy ran swiftly and silently around to the back of the house with Angel following closely behind. There was a light on in a small window, and Buffy could see kitchen cabinets through it. There was a door that apparently let into the kitchen. The idea of a home invasion, of kicking down a teacher's door in the middle of the night, didn't sit well with her.

Until she thought about all the people this creature, this glamour, had already hurt. It had to be Miss Blaisdell. She was certain. And if she was wrong, well . . . she'd been in trouble before.

She started to move forward, but Angel put a strong hand on her shoulder and Buffy paused to shoot him an inquiring look.

"I know this isn't the time," he said, glancing down uncomfortably. "But I just wanted to say, about Pike—"

"You're right," she said quickly. "This isn't the time. I just . . . I can't right now."

Angel nodded. "I know. I just wanted to tell you I understand how hard it is for you. All of it."

With a deep sigh, Buffy turned back to the house. "Let's go," she said. And in her heart, she prayed that Angel really knew, really understood. It seemed like every month that went by, every day older, life became more complicated. The rule for growing up seemed to be that no choice, no decision worth making was without some cost.

She almost welcomed the danger and the horror sometimes. Like now. Buffy shook off all the thoughts and questions that had been haunting her, and focused on the issue at hand.

"Go," she whispered harshly.

Buffy and Angel sprinted across the lawn. She paused in front of the back door, but only for a second. Then she bounced on her left foot, raised her right, cocked the leg back, and kicked straight out. The metal door dented, the frame around it splintered, the door tore free and the chain ripped loose. It slammed open, wood shards from the frame flying to the shiny linoleum of the kitchen floor.

Then she was inside, and Angel entered behind her, ready to fight.

But there was no one to fight. The kitchen was bright and spotless as a showroom. It didn't look as though it had ever been used. Though she didn't hear any sounds from other rooms, or upstairs, Buffy proceeded quickly and quietly into the living room straight ahead, where the television flickered silently in the darkness. Angel went around the other direction, into the dining room. They met at the bottom of the stairs near the front door.

Buffy glanced around the downstairs again, still not certain they were alone, no matter how things looked. There was the basement, as well, but they were dealing with magick and demons, not vampires, so she figured upstairs first.

Angel raised his eyebrows, nodded silently toward the stairs. Buffy thought for a second, then nodded in return. Angel started up the steps and she followed. It was profoundly dark up there, they didn't dare turn on a light, and Angel could see much better in the dark than she could.

After half a dozen steps, Buffy had to wonder if the darkness that enveloped them, the deep shadows, was natural or some kind of camouflage mechanism. Angel was only a step or two above her, and granted he was wearing black clothes, but she couldn't see much more than his outline.

This can't be natural, she thought.

Then she reached out to grab Angel's jacket, to give him a tug, to slow him down, maybe rethink things. Maybe she should have just put the light on to begin with?

Which was when a figure sprang from the dark at the top of the stairs, stood firm, and swung something metal at Angel's face. There was a crack, and then Angel was falling back toward Buffy and the shadowy figure was moving down toward them.

Buffy flattened against the stairwell wall, holding the rail, and let Angel tumble right past her. The metal rod, what turned out to be a fireplace poker, whipped toward her head as well, but Buffy saw it coming, reached up, and stopped it. She ripped it from the hands of Angel's attacker, then charged up the last few stairs at him. With a hard kick, she slammed him against the wall of the upstairs hall, then she hauled back the poker, ready to bring it down on his head, to shatter the creature's skull if that was what it took.

At that moment a car turned onto Catalina Road somewhere down the street. Headlights cut the darkness, slipped into the house, and washed over the shadows in the hallway, and Buffy saw her attacker.

With a wide-eyed, vacant stare, Xander knocked the poker from her hand and then shoved her, and Buffy went tumbling painfully back down the stairs.

* * *

In the library, Willow sat on the steps that led up to the stacks, and sighed. She rocked a little bit and stared at Pike where he lay on the study table. Her eyes drifted over to the shattered banker's lamp on the floor, and she wondered idly who would end up paying to replace it. Then her eyes, and her mind, returned to Pike.

She had slowed down the painful process that was turning him to stone. But she hadn't stopped it. Even the hair on the left side of his head was stone now, and it was deeply disturbing to watch the rise and fall of his chest, knowing that when his heart or his lungs turned to stone, he would die. They had maybe an hour, given how slow the stone was creeping.

Oz came out of Giles's office with a cup of tea and handed it to her. He sat down beside her. Willow took a sip, found that she couldn't taste a thing, and set the cup down on the step next to her.

"I'm so afraid," she confessed.

"It's freaky," Oz confirmed. "But you can do it. You've got this stuff down."

Willow shrugged. "I can do it. Yeah. But even if I do it exactly right, there's still a chance it could kill him. That's just . . . just . . ."

"Not fair?" Oz suggested.

With a soft, painful smile, Willow leaned against Oz, her cheek against his chest, and just enjoyed that moment of escape. "If I do nothing, he'll die anyway, but I don't want to be the one, y'know, who kills him," she said. "I'm not up to making decisions like this. I'm just me. I'm Willow."

"Who better?" Oz asked. "And besides, is it really a decision?"

The question stopped her. How selfish she was being, even for the few seconds that she had wasted thinking about it. The guilt she would feel if she caused Pike's death would be nothing compared to the knowledge that she might have saved him but let him die.

"No," she replied. "No, it isn't."

Her tea forgotten, Willow stood and moved swiftly to the table where Pike lay, still unconscious. His one still-human eye moved under the lid. Whatever part of Pike was still alive, he was dreaming. Willow hoped it was a pleasant dream.

Taking a deep breath, she snapped off a piece of stone that had once been Pike's hair. It was risky. The spell would work better if she had something that had previously been flesh, like the tip of a finger or something, but she worried that if she tried to chip off the end of his pinky, for instance, she might end up shattering the whole finger, or even the entire hand. The hair would have to do.

"Oz."

He came up beside her and Willow gave him the bits of stone. While he took them to Giles's desk and used the heavy tape dispenser to pound the bits to dust on top of a white cloth, Willow opened a book called *Human Alchemy: The Mysteries of Transmutation.* She had only ever seen the book once before, in a dusty box Giles kept on a shelf in the cage, but she had remembered it. Mainly because it was among the books Giles had forbidden her to read.

"There are certain kinds of magick which are both simple and dangerous," he'd told her. "Transmutation spells are simple, as long as you have the right words and the right concoction. But they are also unreliable. Even the most experienced of spellcasters try to avoid them."

Well, Willow didn't have a choice. If Giles ever

came out of the weird stupor the glamour, or whatever it was, had put him under, Willow figured he'd understand.

"All set?" Oz asked as he emerged from Giles's office.

Willow looked at the words on the page again, whispered them to herself, making certain she understood the meaning of the spell. Sometimes it didn't matter, but for the most part she'd found that if you truly understood what you were asking, spells tended to show better results. Right now, it mattered.

"Okay," she said uncertainly. "I guess this is it. Put it in."

Oz shook the white cloth over the mixture still boiling on the Bunsen burner, and the stone dust and fragments slid into the liquid. Willow watched it swirl around in the steaming, bubbling brew. There were certain shapes inside, coagulated things, that she hadn't put into the beaker. They had formed in there as a result of the magick, and Willow didn't think she wanted to know what they were.

The book lay open in her hands, and Willow looked down at the spell again. Simple as anything, just as Giles had told her. But no matter how perfect she performed the spell, spoke the words, there was still a chance it would speed Pike's death instead of saving him.

As if he could read her mind, Oz moved up next to her and kissed her cheek. "Don't think about it," he told her. "You're his only shot."

She nodded. Then she read:

"Malleable flesh of man, now twisted from its natural form;

"To your flawed, original, human state revert.

"Neither spell nor charm nor curse may erase the first;
"Now face, now heart, now soul all reassert."

A blast of steam shot from the glass beaker, and Willow saw that nearly half the potion within had been evaporated in an instant. Gone. She didn't know if that was supposed to happen, but she didn't have time to wonder about it.

"He's not changing," Oz said.

"I know," Willow replied.

Then she moved down the table, picked up the white cloth, and used it to lift the beaker from the burner without searing her fingers on the hot glass. The mixture within immediately began to calm its boiling. She couldn't wait, couldn't even take the time to be careful. Instead, she reached across Pike with the beaker in her hand and poured the mixture over the stone half of his face and shoulder and chest.

It slipped from the cloth and shattered on the floor, but Willow had already done all she could.

She stood back to look at Pike, waiting for a change. Oz was with her, and that made it easier somehow. Then the worst happened.

The stone began to spread.

It grew across Pike's flesh with incredible speed. In moments, his entire body was the gray of granite, his features chiseled like a statue's. His throat, his ears, his fingers, the little scar over his eye.

Willow let out a little whimper, closed her eyes, and hung her head. Her only thought was what she would say to Buffy, and her eyes began to fill with tears of repentance.

"He's breathing," Oz told her.

Blinking, Willow looked up doubtfully at Pike's

chest. But Oz was right. He was breathing. More than that, his breathing seemed to be cracking the stone, now nothing more than a thin shell. Pike moved. Twisted his neck. Raised a hand up and stretched, as though waking from a particularly restful sleep.

With every motion, the thin stone shell cracked and fell away.

"You did it," Oz whispered to her, and Willow was elated.

Pike opened his eyes wearily, and sat up on the table, moving around painfully. He looked down at the debris falling away from his body, then up at Willow and Oz, and smiled in wonder. He slipped from the table and went over to them, stared for a moment, and then hugged Willow tightly to him.

"Dude, that was the worst nightmare I ever had. I could feel it all, y'know? It hurt so bad, I just tried crawling inside my brain, but . . . Willow, you saved me."

"That's my witch," Oz said proudly.

"It's a calling," Willow confessed, glancing down shyly.

Pike looked around, smiling, and then, slowly, the smile slipped from his face.

"Where's Buffy?" he asked.

Angel shouted to her to get out of the way, but Buffy was already moving, rolling, leaping to her feet. Xander came stomping down the stairs. Buffy had dropped the fireplace poker when he'd kicked her, and he had it in his hands again as he ran down at Angel, who was rushing up to meet him. Xander lifted the poker over his head in both hands and prepared to drive it down toward Angel.

"Don't hurt him!" Buffy shouted.

With a grunt, Angel deflected the poker with his left forearm, then hit Xander with a hard right to the gut. He collapsed, falling down on top of Angel, who caught the mesmerized Xander over his shoulder. Angel turned, came down the steps, and dropped Xander to the ground on his face, then kneeled on him holding his hands behind his back.

"All the times I've wanted to hurt him and didn't," Angel reminded Buffy, "you're worried about me hurting him now?"

"This is all just getting out of hand," Buffy said grimly, then looked up into the darkness at the top of the stairs. "I think it's time Doctor Laura had a brutal talk with our little demon nymphomaniac." She looked back at Angel. "Hold him."

Then she started up the stairs.

Below, Xander struggled, but Angel held him easily. Buffy went up fast, but on guard. She knew how important it was to be cautious. She also knew that Giles was missing and Pike was dying and Karen Blaisdell, or whatever her real name was, might well be the one to tell her how it all fit together, and how to tear it all apart.

At the top of the stairs, it didn't seem quite as dark as before. The lights from outside now penetrated the rooms and the corridor more fully, not muted as they had been moments ago. Buffy glanced in both directions, and then started off to her right.

To the left, the rasp of a match being struck, then blazing to life.

Buffy spun, ignoring the sounds of Xander struggling against Angel below, and walked toward what appeared to be the master bedroom. The door was only half-open, but she could see the flickering of candle-light within. Another match was struck, another candle lit.

When Buffy slowly pushed the door open, she saw that the room was beautiful. Silk and soft colors, candles burning, a wide bed with a canopy of fine lace. Then Buffy stopped and simply stared. For sitting on the bed was Karen Blaisdell, looking extraordinary with her lush red hair falling over her shoulders. She wore a lace and cotton shift that looked as though it belonged in another age, delicate and yet modest.

There was nothing modest, however, about the smile on Karen Blaisdell's face.

"Buffy," she said, rising from the bed and beginning to approach. "What a lovely surprise. I never imagined I'd have a visit from you, here in my home. I suppose I'm a terrible hostess for not meeting you downstairs, but I'm just so comfortable here. These surroundings make me feel so relaxed, so warm and content."

For a moment, her muscles seemed to go slack, her mind slowing, her head lolling slightly to one side.

Karen reached out, then, and caressed Buffy's cheek. "Such a lovely girl," she said, a playful smile on her face.

Buffy returned her smile. Then she hauled off and cracked the glamour hard across the cheek. The beautiful demon's head rocked back, she stumbled, and nearly fell.

"Pay attention, there, femme fatale," Buffy said darkly. "I'm the Slayer. That crap doesn't work on me."

But the glamour turned on Buffy, lips distending, stretching, her mouth becoming an obscene, toothless thing. Her eyes were wide, and red now, as if filled with blood. She glared at Buffy.

"Look at me, girl," the glamour croaked through its too huge mouth.

"Gosh, do I have to?" Buffy asked, then rolled her eyes. "Didn't we just have this discussion?"

Hissing, slobbering, the glamour leaped for her. Buffy thought, for half a second, about spinning into a high kick. But Karen Blaisdell, or whatever her name was, just wasn't worth the effort. Instead, Buffy shot out a stiff arm, palm open, and stopped her cold with a blow to the chest. The glamour staggered. Buffy grabbed her by the hair, spun her around, and slammed her head into one of the bed's wooden posts.

"And by the way," Buffy added. "A little overboard on the collagen. Just thought you should know."

She drove the glamour to the floor, sat on its chest, and held her hands around its throat. Rage pulsed through Buffy's veins, and she didn't know how to get rid of it. Didn't even know if she wanted to.

"Talk to me," Buffy snapped. "Giles. Snyder. Tell me what I need to know, and maybe you can relocate your ugly butt out of Sunnydale in one piece."

The glamour began to hiss again and Buffy slapped her in the face. "Could we please have a normal mouth? I don't think I can have a real conversation with the catfish from the Black Lagoon."

Suddenly, she was staring into the face of Karen Blaisdell again, and Buffy realized she had miscalculated. It was one thing to defend herself while under attack, or to smack around a hideous demon. But when the demon had a familiar face, it got a little bit more difficult. She relaxed her grip, and in that moment, the glamour tried to buck her off.

Buffy pinned her to the ground by her throat, and bent over angrily. "Let's start again," she said. "Giles.

Snyder. On the one hand, why? And on the other hand, gross."

Suddenly, the glamour let out a long breath, as if it were deflating just a bit. Then Karen Blaisdell smiled at Buffy, and her expression was so human it was disturbing. She rolled her eyes.

"You've got me," said the glamour.

"A little slow on the uptake, huh?"

"Tell you what, why don't I tell you what you want to know, then I'll find myself another high school to substitute teach in?" the glamour suggested. "I've got nothing to keep me here. I was a hired hand, that's all."

Buffy glared at her. "Just taking orders, huh?"

"That's exactly right," the glamour said happily.

"Let them all go," Buffy instructed her. "All of them. Giles, Snyder, Cordelia, and Xander. Do it now."

"But I already did," the glamour said, looking at Buffy as though she were a bit slow on the uptake herself. "Didn't you feel it going away? The power?"

Buffy didn't believe her for a second. But then she heard the floorboards creak in the hall behind her, and turned quickly to see Xander walk into the room, looking very penitent, and Angel behind him.

"Buff, you have no idea how sorry—" Xander started.

"Forgiven. But you don't look so hot. Why don't you lie down for a few minutes while I Andy Sipowicz our little mind-leech here?"

Xander turned a bit green and rubbed a hand over and around his mouth. "I think I've had all I can take of that bed, thanks," he said. "Maybe I should go downstairs and sit down."

"Knock yourself out," Buffy said, and turned her attention back to the matters at hand.

Xander left, but Angel stayed behind. He walked calmly to the edge of the bed and sat to watch Buffy and the glamour converse.

"So you were a hired hand," Buffy prodded. "By whom and what for?"

"Could I get up, do you think? This is sort of awkward for me," the glamour said, smiling mischievously. "I usually get the top."

Scowling, Buffy looked at Angel, who nodded to indicate that the thing wouldn't pose the two of them any real threat. Buffy backed off, standing up and wiping her hands on her pants. The glamour stood slowly, elegantly, and brushed off her nightgown with a meticulousness that seemed both ironic and somewhat absurd.

Then she sat on the bed and smiled at Angel, but she didn't make any effort to hold his gaze, or even to sit too close.

"I don't know who hired me," she said. "A vampire, though. I didn't get a good look at his face because he was wearing a sort of hood. I was already in the area. Just down from L.A., though I didn't stay long. A girl looking for emotion could starve in L.A. Anyway, he offered me a few trinkets, rather ancient little bits that I couldn't pass up. And all I had to do was feed upon a victim of his choosing, but not take enough to kill him. My bloodsucking friend was very careful about that. He didn't want Rupert dead."

"Well, there's that," Buffy said, glancing at Angel.

The glamour laughed. "You misread me, sweet girl," she said. "He plans to kill your Giles at some point. But he wanted the man to suffer first."

Buffy felt a tightening in her throat, and had to swallow before she could speak again.

"And the others?" she asked, at length.

The glamour rolled her eyes and swayed a bit on the bed, having altogether too much fun in Buffy's opinion. Buffy glared at her, then turned to Angel.

"Next time she smiles, snap her neck," Buffy told him.

This time it was Angel who smiled. The glamour looked deadly serious.

"Please," the minor demon said. "They were an annoyance. You and your little troupe of misfits trying to protect the Watcher. Laughable, really. I mesmerized Cordelia and then Xander because they were useful to me."

"And Snyder?" Buffy asked, narrowing her eyes. "Did your mysterious vampire X want you to go after him, too?"

"Not at all," the glamour explained. "I couldn't take enough of Giles's thoughts and emotions, enough of his mind, each time, to satiate me. Snyder was what you might call an appetizer. He took the edge off, and he was so easy. I barely had to manipulate his thoughts, only cover up the things he wasn't supposed to see.

"Nasty little man, your Mr. Snyder. Don't be surprised if he turns out to be a demon one of these days."

Buffy walked toward her. "But they're free?" she asked. "All of them? You could have just freed Xander."

"You mean you don't trust me?" the glamour asked, and for a moment, its lips distended again, drooping grotesquely.

Apparently, it didn't dare smile.

"Final question. Everything rides on this one. Ready?" Buffy asked. "Where's Giles?"

"I don't know," said the glamour.

Which was when Angel reached up and yanked the thing's head back by its hair. He bent over, looked it directly in the eye, and his face changed to the feral brow and yellow eyes of the vampire.

"I wonder if you'd be able to lure much by way of food with your face destroyed," he said quietly.

And the glamour begged. "Please," it whined. "I really don't know. I never saw the vampire's face. It could have been you for all I know. I don't know where he is."

"But you're certain he's free of your influence?" Angel demanded.

"Yes!" the glamour cried.

Buffy and Angel exchanged a long glance. Then Buffy gestured to the glamour.

"Lock her in the basement," she told Angel.

The sultry demon didn't even try to protest, only hung her head and sighed.

"When we find Giles, we'll let you out, and you can leave town. But go far away," Buffy advised. "You've caused me a lot of grief the past couple of days. And they do call me the Slayer, after all."

Then she turned and left the room, leaving Angel to deal with the glamour while she went down to check on Xander. It was nice to at least be able to hope that Giles had been released from the demon's influence, but that wasn't enough. Not nearly.

Between her fear for Giles's safety and the knowledge that Pike might well die if Willow couldn't help him, Buffy's mind was awhirl. She felt lost. There wasn't anything she could do for Pike at the moment, but she *could* find Giles and bring him home.

She didn't even know where to start.

When the glamour's influence was lifted, Giles came awake as though from a dream. His head hurt, and his back ached, and he felt desperately in need of a shower. It didn't help matters that there were six dead people in the large conference room with him. The stench was horrid, and he expected he'd have to burn his clothes whenever he finally was able to free himself.

And he would be free. Giles didn't allow himself to consider any other alternative.

He knew, that was the key. While much of what had happened the previous few days had been a blur, even now drifting from his mind, Giles was not soon going to forget the horror of Karen Blaisdell's terrifying and disgusting kiss. He knew what had happened to him.

But Giles also knew that Karen wasn't here. Whoever had come after him had sent vampires and even that stone demon to fetch him, and it wasn't Karen, or whatever the thing was that called itself Karen.

There was very little light in the conference room, save for the diffuse illumination that passed through the two-foot-wide floor-to-ceiling opaque windows on either side of the conference room doors. But that light was enough for Giles to see the dead men and women, and to know that his situation was dire.

Then, before he could dwell any longer on the subject, he heard footsteps in the hall outside the conference room. Not wanting his captors to realize that he had at last come to his senses, Giles lay on the conference room table, eyes slitted open just slightly, hoping that he gave the appearance of still being in a stupor.

There was the sound of a key in the lock, the tumblers turned, and then the doors were pulled open from outside. Giles saw Gunther and Jocelyn come through the door, and Jocelyn immediately looked at him and hissed her disgust.

"We should just eat and be done with it," she said.

"That kind of disrespect cost you an eye, last time," Gunther reminded her gruffly.

Jocelyn had nothing to say to that, but Giles saw her tracing her fingers over her ragged, empty eye socket. Gunther walked over to the table and slapped Giles on the head.

"Wake up, Watcher," he snarled. "You have a visitor. The master wants to speak with you now."

Giles hadn't reacted to the slap, though it had hurt, and now he ignored Gunther's words as well.

"He's still burnt out," Jocelyn said dismissively. "Rachel should punish that glamour for draining him so much. She was supposed to make him suffer, not melt his brain."

Gunther bent over and stared into Giles's slitted eyes, and for a moment, Giles wondered if he knew. But then the vampire merely shrugged and turned back toward the conference room door.

"All set, Mister Giles," Gunther said, a bit nervously.

Giles froze. Somehow Gunther had realized he had his wits back about him, that he was only pretending to be—

The thought stalled in his brain, replaced by so many others. Things half remembered from the night before, horrible ideas he tried so hard to prevent from entering his mind.

A vampire entered the room, tall and thin, with a bit of gray in his brown hair. Giles knew him. In fact, the vampire looked no different than the man had looked years earlier, before he had become a vampire. The resemblance was not merely a resemblance. It was him. It could only be him, impossible as it seemed.

He wanted to cry, to scream out in rage and grief and vengeance. But he dared not, for the vampire that had ordered his torment and abduction would then know he was aware and alert. And then the vampire might order his blood children to drain the Watcher dry.

With quiet, but growing horror, Giles stared up through his slitted eyes, and for the first time in a great many years, he found himself looking into the face of his father.

Chapter 10

"At first I thought, okay, Miss Blaisdell and Principal Snyder, major eew factor there. I'm not ashamed to confess I looked up to her a little. Trapped teaching here, of all places, with what amounts for the most part to the dregs of American teenage society—with several obvious exceptions—around her. And somehow, she still managed to seem very cutting edge. And her taste in clothing . . . demon or no, I think there are some females around here who could take some fashion tips from her."

Cordelia paused to take a breath.

"Anyway," she went on, "once I saw what her real face looked like . . . well, let's just say the whole Snyder element lost some of its repulsive charm."

Pike nodded, barely listening. His mind was on Buffy, eyes darting over to check the time yet again. He looked impatiently at Willow, who was bent over an open demonology book. She had saved Pike's life, and now she was desperately trying to find out how to destroy a stone demon. He was certainly grateful, but he was also getting pretty antsy just sitting here when they should be out doing something. There were a hundred better ways for him to use his time than listen to Cordelia go on.

Oz sat across from Willow, leaning back almost too far in his chair, practically about to topple over. Oz seemed to be nodding a bit, practically humming along to music in his head. He was a musician, so that made sense.

Then Oz noticed Pike watching him, and nodded a bit more obviously, a sort of acknowledgment of their silent communication. Oz glanced at Cordelia and took a breath, then looked back at Willow again. Pike figured that was about the most commentary he'd get from Oz, and was appreciative. Though he figured Oz had him beat hands down in the laid-back category, Pike did like the guy.

But it wasn't like they were here to socialize. He'd come here looking for Buffy to help him get a demon off his tail. Now the Watcher had been taken, he'd almost died himself, and Buffy and some of her friends were MIA for the moment. Pike wasn't going to be able to sit still much longer.

"Hello?" Cordelia said, her clipped tone revealing her obvious annoyance.

"Huh?" Pike said, focusing on her again.

"Am I talking to myself here?" she said angrily.

"Sorry, just worried about Buffy."

"Please. Worry about yourself. She obviously is. I mean, who almost got turned to stone? You. Who got brain-fried? Me. And where was Buffy? Off playing with Angel, like always. Torturing herself with her 'forbidden love.' It'd be enough to make me sick, but I'd hate to mess up this outfit."

Pike stared at her, astonished at Cordelia's total self-absorption. Nobody else seemed to notice, so maybe it was par for the course, but he thought she was a pretty extraordinary human specimen. Never mind that her comments about Buffy and Angel weren't exactly what he needed to hear at the moment. He was confused enough.

"What gets me is, why would this stone guy take Giles to begin with? I thought he came to Sunnydale after you?" she went on.

"I wish I knew," Pike replied. "That's what Willow's trying to figure out. Not much makes sense right now, though. But I guess we'll know more when Buffy comes back."

Cordelia rolled her eyes.

Pike stood up, needing to have at least a few seconds of uninterrupted silence. Cordelia was a puzzle to him. She acted like she hated them all, and couldn't bear to be in their presence more than a minute, but here she was hanging around. The only thing he could think was that maybe she really was worried—about Buffy and Giles and Angel and Xander—and that put a whole new spin on Cordelia for him. *Maybe she does care.*

"So, Willow," Cordelia said abruptly, and stood to stride over to where Willow was doing research. "Have you come up with anything, or are we just going to sit here and swap children-in-jeopardy stories? I have places to be."

Then again, Pike thought.

"Cordy," Willow said patiently, "I know you're worried about Xander, but we have to assume he's all right. Giles is our priority right now."

"Please. The only time I'd worry about Xander is if he was impeding my social progress," Cordelia scoffed.

"Seriously, though, Willow," Pike added. "Do you have any idea what we do next? I don't know how much longer I can hang out here without going nuts. If you've got nothing to go on to catch up with Giles, we should at least go after Buffy. She should have been back by now."

"She'll be here," Willow told him. "And, no, I haven't found anything else. But I can tell you how to distract a chaos demon long enough to escape," she said happily. "That could come in handy down the line, right?"

"Great," Pike said halfheartedly.

Willow looked down sheepishly, then over at Oz.

"It's a valuable job skill," Oz comforted her.

Willow perked up.

"Come on, we can't just sit here," Pike argued. "Ten minutes. Then if we don't hear from her, we're going out to that teacher's house too."

"What if Giles comes back?" Cordelia asked. "Shouldn't someone wait for him?"

Pike thought about that, then looked meaningfully at Cordelia.

"I didn't mean me," she snapped. "I was leaving, remember?"

"No, you're not," Willow said, suddenly forceful. She closed the book she'd been skimming and stood up, pushing back her chair with a screech. "Nobody's going anywhere. We'd be doing nothing but wasting our time if we went off like some . . . some posse or something."

"Posse?" Pike asked doubtfully.

"She's on a roll," Oz told him.

"Darn tootin' I'm on a roll!" Willow declared. "Waiting. Worrying. Researching. If we haven't heard anything in another forty-five minutes, then Cordelia drives Pike to Miss Blaisdell's house, and we go from there."

"Me? Why me? What would we talk about, surfing?" Cordelia rolled her eyes.

"You seem to find topics without much trouble," Pike assured her.

"Well, there's an art to conversation," she replied. "But that's not the point. Why me?"

"Angel has my van," Oz explained.

"Oh. Okay."

Willow looked at them all, then sat back down and pulled her chair up to the table. She had just opened her book again when the double doors swung open and Buffy walked in, followed by Angel and Xander. The instant she stepped into the room, her face etched with concern, her eyes lit on Pike, and her expression changed completely.

"Pike," she muttered.

Buffy met him in the middle of the room and they hugged tightly, but briefly. She stepped back from him and nodded, as if to confirm for herself that he was all right. Then Buffy turned to Willow, and smiled.

"You did it, Will."

"I managed," Willow agreed, proudly.

Oz leaned impossibly far back in his chair. "So," he said, "Miss Blaisdell. Demon?"

"Yep," Xander confirmed. "Took me over too. Possessed. Same as she did with Giles and Snyder."

"And me," Cordelia reminded them. "Could we focus on my inconvenience here for a moment?"

"Not very choosy, the glamours," Angel put in.

They all turned to look at him, Xander and Cordelia seemed offended but the others were obviously amused. This was only the second time Pike had been in the room with him, but even he knew Angel wasn't exactly known for his sense of humor. In fact, the whole group constantly surprised him. He'd had what he considered more than his share of run-ins with the forces of darkness. He'd be happy to turn around and walk away from it. In fact, he'd be happy to have all memories of vampires and demons erased from his mind. But they seemed to almost thrive on it. Sure, it was Buffy's duty. But the others seemed to think of it as some kind of calling as well.

Pike just didn't feel that way. He wondered if things would have been different for him and Buffy if he had. But it was dangerous to wonder such things, especially since he just couldn't see it. The way they joked was a wonder to him as well. With all the horror they faced, it should have been a kind of gallows humor, the laughter of those whose lives might be forfeit at any moment. But it wasn't that at all. They just weren't willing to stop living even though they might die at any time.

He admired them, but Pike knew he just wasn't built that way. He wanted the stone demon off his back, and he'd face it if he had to. He'd fight to save Buffy if she were in trouble. But saving the world from the forces of darkness?

That was somebody else's gig.

"So, what about Miss Blaisdell? Is she dead?" Willow asked, sympathetic even toward a demon.

"Nope," Xander said. "Just kind of incarcerated in the basement. She wasn't all that helpful, either. No leads on who's got it out for Giles."

They were all silent then, receding back into themselves, alone with their thoughts and fears. Even Cordelia seemed to respect that moment, and it was clear she had respect for little more than her own image.

"All right, then we go looking," Buffy said.

Everyone stood a little straighter.

"We're going to check the usual vampire spots, and we're going to do it quick and coordinated. Willow, Oz, you guys hit the other end of town—Angel's neighborhood—then out to the old drive-in, then drive by the Bronze on your way back. Xander, you and Cordelia—"

"Excuse me. I need my beauty rest. I have a presentation in class tomorrow, and I need to look sparkling for it," Cordelia cut in.

Buffy stared at her. "You have a car. You have a cell phone. You can just give them to Xander, if you want."

Cordelia smiled icily. "I suppose that was a poor excuse. Who'd believe I need beauty rest anyway, right?"

"Nobody can get that much sleep," Xander muttered, then cried out in alarm and annoyance as Cordelia batted him on the shoulder. "So, Buffy, you were saying?" he asked, wincing.

"You two go by Willy's Alibi Room, see if he's got anything. Then hit the factory, and drive by Weatherly park, but don't go in," Buffy told them.

"What about us?" Pike asked.

Buffy looked at him, about to reply, and then paused. She glanced from Pike to Angel, and back again. Everyone in the room must have seen it, and felt the tension in the air. Apparently without realizing it, Buffy had put herself in a very awkward position. Pike glanced away, scratched the back of his head. And for the very first time, he thought, *I shouldn't have come.*

Angel took a step back and slightly to the side, toward the door. "I'm going to hit the main cemeteries, the Master's old lair, see if anyone's lurking," he said.

Buffy let out a deep breath, and smiled lovingly at him. "Thanks," she said. But Pike knew that none of them thought she was thanking him for his help in the search.

He lingered in the background as they broke out stakes and other weapons. Buffy instructed everyone to be back at the library by eleven-thirty, latest. Pike figured Willow and Cordelia, at the very least, probably got into trouble on a regular basis for coming in late, but nobody complained.

Then they were all gone, and Buffy and Pike were alone again.

She stood at the study table, slipping several stakes into her bag. A cross went into her jacket, along with a bottle of holy water and extra bolts for the crossbow. As Buffy tested the trigger on the crossbow, Pike stepped up behind her.

"I'm sorry," he said softly. "About all of this. Coming here, all of it, seemed a lot simpler when it was just you and me and a demon."

Buffy turned to face him. She seemed troubled, and he could understand why. But this close to her, Pike was torn, as always, by what he felt for her and what he knew her life had to be.

"You and me and a demon," Buffy repeated. "So romantic."

"Not exactly," Pike replied. He reached out to touch her hair, and then thought better of it. It would be foolish to get too wrapped up in things with her when they both knew how all of this had to end. Instead, he pulled her to him and held her tight.

"I'm sorry," he said again. But this time, there was more than one meaning to the words.

"Hey," Buffy replied, breaking the embrace. "Your demon buddy, Grayhewn, came after Giles. You had nothing to do with that. Whoever our mystery vamp is, whoever set the glamour after him, he's the guy behind all this."

Pike smiled. "So my being here hasn't complicated your life?"

"I didn't say that."

Buffy turned back to the table, picked up the cross-bow, and slipped her bag over her shoulder. Pike stepped aside to let her pass, then followed her to the double doors of the library. Buffy flicked off the lights and then went out, walking down the school corridor in silence. They passed the locker Buffy had torn the door off of while fighting Grayhewn, and she didn't even pause to glance at it.

Outside, Pike kick-started his motorcycle, then looked to Buffy, waiting for her to get on behind him.

"Where are we going, anyway?" he asked.

"Hammersmith Park again," she replied. "If that isn't where they're hanging out, maybe we can figure out where they went."

Pike nodded. But Buffy didn't get on. He glanced over at her standing on the pavement next to the bike. There was a look in her eyes, a dangerous look that threatened to capture him forever. But there was also pain and sadness in her eyes, and Pike knew it was because she realized how impossible that was.

"I'm glad you're all right," Buffy said.

Then she stepped in close and kissed him. It was supposed to be brief, and chaste. He could sense that from the way she moved. But it was neither of those things.

When the kiss was through, Buffy wouldn't look at

him. She just climbed on the back of the motorcycle, wrapped her arms around him, and held on.

Then the wind was flying past them, and the time for talking was done.

Giles felt dead inside.

Jocelyn slapped him again, and his head rocked back. The one-eyed vampire had torn his shirt open, and now she drew her nails down his chest, drawing blood. Her grin was wide and lustful, and her face changed suddenly, revealing her vampiric nature. Her yellow eyes glowed in the half-dark room, and the way her brow contorted, protruded, it made her sunken, empty socket seem all the more revolting and obscene.

Beside her, Gunther laughed, low and guttural.

Blood began to trickle down his chest, and Jocelyn leaned forward to lick it off of him. She made little sounds of pleasure as she did so, moaning softly. Then she sat back on her haunches and slapped him again, hard enough, this time, to split his lip.

The pain was such that Giles should have shouted, roared in anger and agony. But there were no such sounds within him, nothing at all to let out. There was only cold, numb death and emptiness. He was hollow now, scraped raw and bloody and heartless at his core.

All because of the creature standing behind Jocelyn and Gunther. The thing that smiled and chuckled along with them, showing its fangs, its own yellow eyes, its feral vampire face.

His father's face.

It was impossible, of course. His mind refused to accept what his eyes were telling him. But in light of the creature itself, the vampire there before him, he could not deny the truth for long.

And the truth was agony.

The pain was good, actually. It kept him from crying. It kept him from shouting out in pain or horror. Horror. Now there was a word. Rupert Giles thought he knew about horror the day he came home to find the woman he loved draped across his bed amidst a scattering of roses, her neck broken. That emotional wound had nearly destroyed him.

But this . . .

Impossible, he thought again. His father had been a Watcher, just as his grandmother had been. But though Giles had not been at home when his father died, he had been there for the funeral. Had seen the casket lowered into the ground.

His father couldn't be a vampire.

Which was, of course, what the families of so many of the undead would say if they were to come face-to-face with their bloodthirsty loved ones. It can't be, they'd say. I saw him buried.

But that was the thing about the dead, Giles knew.

Sometimes they rise.

Amidst the horror and the hollowness, Giles could not escape the face that leered down at him. He could not fail to hear the familiar voice that spoke softly to the vampires that beat him now, warning them not to do too much damage.

No matter how often he tried to deny it to himself, there was only one possible answer. This thing had once been his father. Before a demon had occupied the shell of his father's corpse, stealing his father's mind and memories and what remained of his body—the soul was gone, of course—but no matter what he knew to be true, he also knew that this was the face of his father.

Jocelyn hit him again, and Giles did not respond. Except perhaps to bleed. She licked his mouth, and he didn't even try to stop her. *What would be the point?*

Yet there was an alternate motivation as well. They still believed that he was under the spell of the glamour. He'd figured out, not long after his mind had been released at last from the fog that had enshrouded it, that Karen Blaisdell was not human. He knew what she'd done to him, and he'd fallen for it, almost willingly. She was quite alluring, and so understanding in those quiet, painful times. He hadn't loved her. He was spared that pain, at least.

But he might have, one day.

Now it didn't matter. None of it mattered, save for making certain that the monster who now wore his father's body did not realize that he had his mind back.

"Ah, Rupert, there's a good lad," the creature sighed. "It's so nice to see you bleed. After all the trouble you gave me, you ungrateful little bastard, it's nice to be able to return the favor."

Unwilling to respond, for fear he might give himself away, Giles would have been unable to reply regardless. What could he say to this horror? In life, his father had been a stern traditionalist whose expectations of his son never seemed tempered by logic or reason. There was a distance between them that had never been bridged, not even when Giles embraced his destiny and joined the Council of Watchers.

Now he only wished he had been able to have one final conversation with his father. Before the end. Just one moment in which to have found some common ground. If that were even possible. He wasn't going to fool himself into thinking it was. For most of his life, Giles had thought his father a wretched bastard.

But he would never have wished for this.

The heat of the blood dripping on his chest reminded him how cold he felt. The pain in his face, his lips, and cheeks, the way his jaw ached . . . it was all so distant from him now.

Jocelyn slapped him again. It didn't matter. Nothing mattered. With Buffy, and before Buffy, he had gone through so very much, seen so very much, but he had always believed the fight would go on. That the battle against the darkness was worthwhile and, more important, that victory was possible.

That faith had been shattered the moment he saw his father's face, twisted into the visage of a vampire.

There was a hard rap on the conference room door, and Gunther went to open it. Light streamed from the hallway, a shaft of illumination cutting across the chairs and table, the carpet, and the corpses there in the room with them. The blond vampire girl, Rachel, entered, wrapped all in leather.

"Mister Giles, your dinner's arrived," Rachel told his father.

The vampire turned to look at her expectantly. "The olive skin. With green eyes?" he asked.

"Just as you ordered, sir," Rachel replied.

"Excellent, my dear," the elder Giles said. "You really are bloody wonderful at this, I must say."

Then he turned and approached the Watcher, who sat in one of the wooden meeting chairs that lined the table.

"Not quite sure your brain is functioning well enough to even follow this, Rupert, my boy," he said slowly. "Doesn't matter. Tomorrow we'll have our little glamour girl give you your mind back, and then the fun will really begin."

As Giles watched, eyes fluttering as he pretended to be disoriented, the creature walked out the door with Rachel. There was one final bit of conversation, however.

"So you're not going to kill him?" Rachel asked the elder Giles.

"Now? What fun would that be?" her master replied. "We're just getting started."

Then they were gone, and Gunther and Jocelyn were leaving behind them. Jocelyn blew him a good-bye kiss, but Giles barely registered it. His mind was elsewhere. On the creature's words. Specifically, *just getting started.* He had a horrible feeling about that.

Giles had reached a point where he no longer really cared about himself and his own fate. If it meant his own death, so be it. But this creature, this thing that had once been his father, seemed to have no intention of leaving Sunnydale. Which meant that Buffy would be a target. One of them would surely kill the other.

He couldn't let that happen. Giles would never stand by and allow harm to come to Buffy, no matter how crippled he felt inside.

And if anyone was going to dust the demon that now lived inside the elder Giles, it would be his son.

It was after midnight when Pike steered his Harley into Buffy's driveway. They'd had no luck locating Giles, and Buffy was tired and confused and scared that something might already have happened to him. When they'd met back at the library, everyone tried to comfort her with things she already knew. If they wanted Giles dead, they would have killed him already. But she just couldn't understand the motivation of keeping him alive if it wasn't to bait a trap for her. *And they can't expect me to walk into a trap if they don't let me know where to find the bait.*

Then there was the whole thing with Pike and Angel . . . it was all too much. She just wanted to sleep so that she could have a clear mind in the morning. They'd all agreed that school was second priority tomorrow, after finding Giles.

Buffy tried not to think about it, but couldn't get Giles out of her head. As she got out her keys and went to open the door, Pike put a hand on her shoulder.

"We'll find him tomorrow," he said.

She said nothing. They couldn't be sure if they would ever find him. Pike was trying to be supportive, but the words were empty no matter how well meant.

She turned the key, pushed the door in, and it was abruptly stopped by the chain lock.

"What the hell?" she murmured. "My mother never puts the chain on."

Alarmed, she started to bang on the door. Buffy waited a few seconds, and then banged again. Silently, she counted to ten. Then she took a step back and lifted her foot, about to kick the door in.

"Buffy, maybe you should—" Pike began.

Then from within, her mother's voice: "Just a second!"

A moment later, Buffy saw her mother's face in the small opening.

"Hang on," Joyce said, before shutting the door, sliding off the chain, and then opening it again.

Buffy was about to ask her what was going on. She wondered if there had been some sort of attack that had frightened her mother into using the chain. But then she noticed that her mother's clothes looked very rumpled. A moment later, Alan Wickstrom walked in from the living room. He looked pretty rumpled himself in jeans and a light sweatshirt.

Joyce blushed.

"Alan," Buffy said dryly.

"Hey, kids," Alan replied. "You guys are out late."

"So are you," Buffy said shortly, glaring at him.

Uncomfortably, Alan kissed Joyce's cheek, then slipped past Buffy and Pike, went out the door, and down the steps. He went to the side of the house and came back riding a bicycle. *Which explains why we didn't see a car,* Buffy thought.

"Ooh, and he's athletic, too," she said, shutting the door behind her.

"That's not fair," Joyce said.

"I'm, uh, gonna get ready for bed," Pike interrupted. "Long day."

When he was gone, Buffy looked at her mother again. "I'm sorry, Mom, but I just . . . what do you expect me to do, ask him how it went? If he got lucky?" she blurted.

Joyce stared, mouth open, then closed it quickly, and shook her head.

"Y'know, Buffy, I don't know what you want from me," she said with exasperation. "Things didn't work out with your father. I think as you're getting older, maybe you're starting to see why. Maybe your last birthday was a lesson.

"But I'm not going to give up. Mister Giles has a new girlfriend. You've got a guy sleeping on the couch out there, despite all your complaints about how being the Slayer has destroyed any chance of a social life. I don't see where you—"

Buffy held up a hand to cut her off. "Y'know what, Mom? Just don't go there. Not tonight," Buffy told her.

"It's very messy terrain, all right? And whatever may or may not be happening with me and Pike, at least he's sleeping on the couch."

Joyce flinched, sighed in anger and surrender. "You're eighteen years old, Buffy. You have all this responsibility. But sometimes I still wonder when you're going to grow up."

She turned and went up the stairs, leaving Buffy to stare after her mother wishing she could start the last few minutes, or better yet, the entire day, all over again.

Then she went one better. Buffy wished silently to herself that she could wake up in the morning and everything would be back to normal.

Whatever normal was for her.

In the corridor outside the conference room at the abandoned CRD Technology office, Gunther tossed back his long hair, and stretched lazily. He leaned against the wall, hands crossed in front of him.

He was desperately bored. Gunther didn't think he'd ever needed to kill something as badly as he did at that very moment. Never mind how hungry he was. The thirst was on him. He could practically smell the blood that Jocelyn had drawn while playing with the Watcher.

Gunther sighed, and waited for a guard to relieve him so he could go hunting.

From inside the conference room, there came a thump, and then the sound of something cracking. Splintering.

Well, well, he thought. *Maybe the meat isn't as wasted as we thought.*

Quietly, smiling broadly, body tingling at the anticipation of blood, Gunther reached out to open the door. His face contorted, brow lengthening, fangs extending.

As he flung open the door he hissed, ready to have a little fun. In the darkness of the room, he saw the Watcher, sitting lazily in the same chair he'd bled on before.

"What are you up to in here, meat?" Gunther sneered, and moved toward him.

Something moved out of the corner of his vision, and even as Gunther turned, he knew that he'd made a terrible mistake. The figure in the chair was already dead.

From the darkness, the Watcher sprang, smashing a heavy wooden chair down onto Gunther's head, driving him to the ground. He reached up and grabbed the table, trying to pull himself up.

But the Watcher was there, a splintered chair leg in his hand.

Gunther was dust.

Chapter 11

A COOL BREEZE BLEW THROUGH THE WINDOW OF Buffy's bedroom, and she turned over and snuggled more deeply under her covers. The sun shone brightly, its light and warmth splashing across the lower portion of the bed.

Half in shadow, half in light, the Slayer lay in the midst of a pleasant dream. But like all such dreams, it fled when she woke. Her waking mind tried to grasp it, to pull the shattered remnants of it together, to remember the joy it had given her. But Buffy was left with only the vague recollection of a few vital facets of the dream.

She had been old. And happy. And in love with a man who would stay.

Only a dream. And even the most pleasant of dreams could be painful under the light of the morning sun.

Three minutes before her alarm would have buzzed angrily, Buffy's eyes fluttered open and she reached out to turn it off. Stretching, yawning, the last of the bitter-

sweet dream receding now, she sat up in bed and remembered the small argument she'd had with her
mother the night before. The guilt was upon her before
she could defend herself.

Buffy sighed regretfully and crawled out of her bed.
She looked out her window at clear blue sky. Across the
street, Mrs. Karabatsos had her sprinkler on already.
Randy Porter lugged a huge bag filled with newspapers
down the street. It was a perfectly beautiful day.

But somewhere, Giles was being held against his
will. If he was even still alive. The demon Grayhewn
was still about, and if he knew Pike was still alive, he'd
be back. Thoughts of Pike made her uncomfortable,
and she knew she had to try to make sense of her feelings, maybe talk to Angel. And then there was her
mom.

Yep. Beautiful day.

It was just after eight when Buffy came down the
stairs in black jeans and a zipped sweatshirt. She had a
bag in her hand, and it was pretty clear there weren't
any books in it. Pike was still sleeping on the couch,
which was not much of a surprise. The only thing that
could get him up early was surfing, and there wouldn't
be any surfing today.

Buffy went into the kitchen. Her mother was making
scrambled eggs with cheese and Canadian bacon, and
toast for the both of them. Pike would have to fend for
himself if he didn't wake up shortly.

"Mom, listen," Buffy started, tentatively.

Joyce turned to look at her, and blinked as she took
in Buffy's outfit.

"You're not going to school," her mother said.
"What's going on? Is something wrong?"

Buffy hesitated. She considered telling her mother everything that had happened in recent days, but didn't want her to worry overmuch. Joyce knew she was always dealing with some evil or other, so Buffy decided to spare her the details. Instead, while her mother finished cooking the eggs and slid them onto two plates with fresh toast, Buffy talked about her feelings for Pike, and her fears as well. Her suspicions that she might only feel that way because he already knew her.

They sat down to breakfast together, and while her mother began to eat, Buffy talked about Angel.

"But you know you can't have any future with Angel," Joyce said gently, putting down her fork. "I'm sorry to say it so plainly, but you've told me that yourself."

Buffy was about to reply, then glanced away. What could she say to her mother? That she didn't know if she would have any future at all? That it didn't matter if she and Angel could never really be together because she was the Slayer, and the Slayer didn't have much time left by any estimate?

With a weak smile, offered only to comfort her mother, Buffy dug into her eggs. Joyce watched her doubtfully, obviously very worried about her daughter. But as Buffy ate and drank her OJ, Joyce seemed to relax. After a moment, she cleared her throat.

"Buffy, I wanted to say I was sorry about last night. Saying you needed to grow up. I guess I was just—"

"Right," Buffy finished for her. "You were absolutely right. And I should know better. You taught me to know better. I can make my own decisions, choose my own path, and so can you. We owe that to each other, at least."

Her mother blinked. "Buffy," she said, "when I said grow up, I didn't mean right away."

"Hey," Buffy said, shrugging. "I'm what my mother made me. At least partially. The sum of my experiences, all that. Just, y'know, don't tell anyone I said so."

Joyce smiled, almost embarrassed. "Don't worry. Your secret's safe with me."

Before they could continue their conversation, Pike staggered in to the kitchen, eyes barely open. He mumbled something that vaguely resembled "Good morning," and then poured himself a cup of coffee from the carafe Joyce had made. As the Summers women watched in amusement, he slid into a chair across from Buffy with all the alacrity of a sleepwalker.

"Hungry?" Buffy asked.

Pike grunted. Buffy slid her plate, her eggs only half eaten, across the table. She stood up, quickly downed the rest of her juice, then set the glass on the table. The Slayer kissed her mother on the head. Then she crouched down to try to look Pike in the eye.

"I'm going to school—to the library—to get some things. When I get back, we're searching for Giles. Nod if you understand a single word I'm saying."

Pike nodded slowly and began to eat his eggs. Buffy shook her head, wondering what sort of attraction she felt for him. This morning-Neanderthal thing might be amusing in a house pet, but not in a prospective mate.

She looked at her mother. "I'll be back."

Buffy hadn't been entirely truthful at breakfast. She was going to the library, yes. But there was another stop she wanted to make first, which meant her trip to school was going to take more time than it normally would. But there was nothing she could do about it.

It was a very long walk to Angel's.

On the front lawn of the fading mansion, Buffy paused. In the light of that perfect day, the house looked even older and more dilapidated than usual. Used up, almost. Abandoned. And she had to wonder if one day she'd come here looking for Angel and find that he'd gone. For good. The idea wounded her more than she would admit to herself. Not now, at least. In the midst of all this confusion.

When she let herself in the back, light splashed into the shadowy recesses of the house. It was a bit dusty, but quite orderly. Despite the once-upon-a-time ostentatious atmosphere of the house, Angel led a Spartan existence there. He slept very little, roaming Sunnydale at night and haunting his own corridors by day, avoiding what sunlight might somehow pass through the heavy drapes that covered the deep-set windows.

In the vast room that led into the gardens, Buffy paused a moment, blinking to allow her eyes time to adjust to the darkness within. She thought about turning around, wondered if it was really fair for her to be here, to even talk to Angel about what was haunting her. For just a moment, she started to turn to go.

Something stopped her. Words. Her memory of the conversation she'd had with her mother earlier that morning. She had to be responsible for her choices. That meant doing the hard things, facing the hard decisions because they affected others who deserved that courtesy.

Buffy loved Angel. No matter what else was in her heart or her head, that was the one thing that would not change, would not be blinded by the confusion she felt.

But love wasn't always good for you. She'd learned that the hardest possible way.

"Hello."

With a gasp, Buffy spun to see Angel emerging from the shadows of a side corridor.

"I was just coming to find you," she said.

"Why?"

Hurt, Buffy winced and looked away a moment. He hadn't said it cruelly, hadn't even looked sad or angry, but Buffy knew the depths of Angel's soul. She knew what he felt. She also knew—and nothing was more important than this at that moment—that Angel understood everything she was going through.

"Sorry," he said softly. "That wasn't fair. Any word on Giles?"

"Nothing," Buffy said. "I'm going hunting for him today. If I haven't found anything by sundown—"

"I'll try the 'underground' again. See if there's any word at all," Angel confirmed.

An awkward silence developed between them. A couple of times, Buffy began to say something, only to find herself unable to put her feelings into words. It happened to her more often than she wanted to admit.

Finally, it was Angel who broke their silence.

"So," he said, "Pike's hunting with you today?"

Buffy looked at him. Her nod was barely perceptible, but it was enough.

"Do you love him?" Angel asked her.

"Not like I love you."

He stared. She looked away.

"That's not what I asked you," Angel said.

"I don't know how to answer that question," Buffy said at last. "It's just . . . none of it makes sense to me now. And this is . . . Pike couldn't have come here at a worse time with all that's happening. It's hard enough to concentrate without feeling this. Part of me wishes he would just go away!"

Buffy turned, threw her arms up in frustration. "I'm sorry," she added. "Maybe I should go."

"What does the other part wish?" Angel asked quietly.

Buffy froze, turned to face him again. She met his gaze this time, tried to communicate in just that look how much she loved him, how deeply he moved her every time his eyes found hers.

"He'll never stay, you know," she told Angel.

Angel smiled painfully. "But what if he does?"

"He won't," Buffy said confidently. Then, after a long pause, she went on. "And maybe that's okay," she said. "It all hurts so much, Angel. I know you know. I know it hurts you as much. Sometimes. But maybe that's okay, too."

"Maybe what you need isn't me or Pike," Angel said, though it was clear what it cost him emotionally to speak those words. "You could have a real love, Buffy. With someone who has no idea what the darkness holds. Someone who didn't cause you so much pain."

Buffy turned, railed at him.

"Don't do that," she snapped. "Don't pretend you don't know what's in my heart. A real love? What's that? It tears at me to love you, Angel. But any time I start to fantasize about the kind of life other girls have, the kind of love they find, I think that maybe the pain of loving you is better than starting a relationship with a guy who has no idea what he's getting himself into, no idea that his girlfriend could bite the dust at any given moment. God, how unfair would that be, if I let someone fall in love with me, not even knowing what would happen?"

She swallowed, felt the guilt sweeping over her again, and looked down.

"And maybe that's why Pike gets to me. He knows what I am, and what the future might hold. A guy like that . . . I wouldn't be making empty promises to him," she said. Then she paused again, looked up, took a breath, and started to nod to herself. "And maybe that's why Pike would never let himself stay so long that he wouldn't be able to leave me behind. Not when he knows how it has to end."

"I know," Angel said softly. "And I stay."

Buffy bit her lip. Then she strode over to Angel and stood on her toes to kiss him softly. Her smile was filled with pain.

"I know," she said. "And I'm not sure which hurts more."

The perfect day seemed to taunt Buffy as she walked toward Sunnydale High. It was just wrong. She wanted clouds, even rain. Something miserable to match her mood. But she knew that was selfish. The good weather would help with her search for Giles. A search that she had already put off long enough. Stopping by Angel's had been horribly selfish of her, but it was something that she had known she had to do. The fact that they hadn't talked had been haunting her.

She was still haunted. But she had found the confirmation and support she had needed. The love she had known would be there, but needed to feel anyway. Buffy knew that she would have to work out her feelings on her own. But she also knew that Angel would love her no matter what.

All of that was secondary now, however. Pushed aside indefinitely until she had either found Giles alive, or, if the worst had happened, destroyed whatever had killed him.

It was with a head filled with such sobering thoughts that Buffy walked into the school as the bell rang ending second period. She merged effortlessly with the flow of other students in the halls and made her way directly to the library. There was no time to even think about what classes or assignments she was missing. Willow had already promised to cover for her as best she could.

No, Buffy was single-minded as she walked through those halls. In the library, among the cache of weapons Giles had secreted away there, was an ancient, long-handled war hammer. Buffy had forgotten all about it until the night before. She had stakes and a crossbow at home, not to mention crosses and holy water. Those would do for the vampires who'd taken Giles the night before.

But the stone demon was another thing.

When she'd thought of the war hammer the night before, pictured Grayhewn's face shattering under her blows, Buffy had smiled thinly, dangerously. Anger and determination created that smile, not amusement. And it was with that same smile on her face that she pushed into the library now.

Buffy paused just inside the doors. Xander, Willow, Oz, and Cordelia were hanging around the study table. Oz sat on the steps going up to the stacks. Cordelia sat on the edge of the table showing much too much leg in a very expensive skirt that had no place within the walls of a high school. Willow and Xander sat across from one another, a stack of books between them.

Everyone looked content. Comfortable.

Xander saw her and smiled. "Hey, Buff. Where'd

you get off to?" he asked happily. "You and Pike got that randy morning smoochies thing going on?"

Buffy blinked.

"Living vicariously through others as always," Cordelia sighed. "The sad story of Xander Harris."

Only Willow noticed the look of surprise, even sadness, on Buffy's face. She frowned.

"Buffy?"

It was too much for Buffy. They were acting like nothing was wrong, like nothing at all had happened and everything was back to normal, when, in truth, nothing had been normal for weeks. And the past forty-eight hours had been nothing but pain and chaos.

Which was when Giles stepped out of his office, a book in one hand, adjusting his glasses with the other.

"Now then," he said, "I believe I've found a most effective way to rid Buffy's young man of this stone demon."

When nobody responded, Giles looked up at them, saw them all looking toward the doors, and turned to see Buffy standing there staring back, her mind awhirl.

"Ah, Buffy, excellent," Giles said. "I called your mother when you hadn't appeared this morning, but she said you were on your way. I was beginning to grow concerned."

"Giles?" Buffy finally managed.

He raised his eyebrows, waiting for her to continue. But Buffy didn't know what else to say. After a moment, Giles gave a slight tilt of his head.

"Well, then," he said. "All of you run along to your classes. Come back after school. We ought to have a game plan by then, yes? If we can find this beast quickly, perhaps we can all enjoy a quiet weekend."

He turned to go back into his office as if nothing at all had happened.

"Giles?" Buffy said again.

The Watcher paused and turned to look at her impatiently, as if something far more important awaited him in his office. The others all looked on in silence.

"I don't understand," she said. "What about last night?" she asked. "The vampires and Grayhewn and Miss Blaisdell. How did you—"

Giles softened. "I'm quite well, Buffy. As you can see. As to Miss Blaisdell, I'd prefer not to discuss it, as I'm sure you'll understand. We'll do our best to track down this Grayhewn creature, and as for the vampires . . . there are always more, aren't there?"

Then he went into his office and closed the door. Buffy stared anxiously at the closed door. Giles wasn't just preoccupied. There was something going on that he was definitely not telling her. He had his mind back, finally, but he still wasn't quite all there. And Buffy wasn't the only one who noticed.

"*He's* acting weird. What's going on with him now?" Cordelia asked, as if the Watcher's behavior had been a personal offense to her.

"Maybe he's just upset that Miss Blaisdell turned out to be, y'know, something else. That she wasn't interested in him romantically," Willow suggested.

"Demons," Oz muttered sadly.

"Yeah. Story of my life," Xander said. "Maybe I should try to talk to him. Y'know, commiserate."

"Oh, that'll help," Cordelia sniffed.

"Did he say anything?" Buffy asked. They all looked at her. "This morning, I mean," she went on. "Did he say where he'd been, how he'd gotten away? When you told him about Miss Blaisdell . . . I mean, what did he *say?*"

They all looked blank. Finally, Willow spoke up.

"Well, it was sort of business as usual," she said. "He seemed to know about the Miss Blaisdell thing, and then he started in on helping Pike, and it was like he was the same old Giles."

"More fun than a barrel o' monkeys," Xander clarified. "Even sea monkeys."

"Sea monkeys don't come in barrels," Oz reminded him.

"See, now that's a gap in their marketing strategy."

"Guys!" Buffy snapped.

They looked at her guiltily.

"Buffy," Xander said in his what-a-reasonable-and-perceptive-guy-I-am voice, which rarely fooled anyone. "Maybe he's just tired. If I had a night like that, I'd be tired too. But he's our funky party weasel again. The G-man. And not, and I repeat, not the space cadet he was when the sultry Miss Blaisdell was using her femininely demonic wiles to suck his brain dry."

Which gave Buffy pause because, for once, Xander's reasoning seemed sound, even perceptive.

"All right," she said. "Maybe he's back among the boring. But I'm not taking that for granted. I left Pike back at my house. I'm going back there, and we're going out looking for the demon. I'll check in when school's over. In the meantime, I want you guys coming by here between classes to check on Giles. Something's still not right here, and I want to know what it is."

"We can do that," Willow said helpfully.

Xander saluted. Oz nodded. Cordelia rolled her eyes and mumbled something about a manicure.

Buffy thanked them, then walked across the room to open the cabinet where Giles stashed the weaponry. In a false-backed compartment in the back she found the hammer. Its handle was long and thick, wrapped in aged leather that also wound around the center of the hammer itself, which was a thick block of metal that had been forged by hand centuries before and inscribed with protective runes which made it unbreakable.

"Whoa," Xander said appreciatively. "Where you going with that?"

"To kill something," Buffy replied.

"That oughta take care of it," Oz said.

"Beats a spear and magic helmet," Xander added.

Then Buffy was gone, her mind preoccupied again. Old questions had not been answered, but instead replaced with new ones, equally troubling. There was no question in her mind that there was more going on with Giles than he was letting on, and she had no intention of letting him off the hook that easily. Something had to have happened the night before. There were too many vampires, not to mention Grayhewn.

All of this, the chaos of the past two days, was far from over. She was sure of that.

But if Giles was going to be uncooperative, there were other ways for Buffy to get answers. Maybe before she shattered Grayhewn into rubble she'd ask him exactly what this was all about.

Chapter 12

By the time Buffy got back to her house, her mother was long gone to work. When she opened the front door, Pike was sitting on the couch in the living room watching the Cartoon Network. He'd showered and dressed, but hadn't bothered shaving, and there was stubble on his cheeks that Buffy would have found ridiculous on most guys. On Pike . . . well, the boy had Grrr. No doubt about that.

"Hey. Everything all right? You were gone a while."

"Well, let's see," Buffy said, plopping down on the sofa next to him. "Giles called my mom earlier, so you already know he's back and alive—"

"Yeah. Very cool."

"—but the nasty is still happening. He's in pretend-happy mode, but I know Giles. There's major bad mojo coming, and he's doing a poor job of trying to hide it." Buffy finished.

"Not cool," Pike added grimly. "What's with the secrecy? He's not the most laid-back player, but he's usually pretty much on the team, no?"

"Yeah. I have no idea what Mister Covert is up to, but I'm gonna find out. In the meantime, I figured I already missed most of the morning, so I thought we'd do a little rockhead hunting while the sun's still out, maybe get to him when he doesn't have reinforcements."

Pike nodded. "Not like he needs reinforcements, but yeah, good idea. On the other hand, he thinks I'm dead, right? Maybe he'll just leave town."

Buffy frowned. "Grayhewn's not going anywhere, Pike. Okay, he had a mad-on for you, but now that he's here, he figures Sunnydale's home sweet home. He's got gainful employment now, and you know how that demon job market is. So he's staying. And if he stays, eventually, he'll figure out you're still among the breathing."

Despite the lightness of her tone, Buffy couldn't even manage a smile. She was making jokes, but inside she was filled with dread at what Pike would say next. She could almost hear him: *Not if I leave.* And in a way, he'd be right. If Pike left, he'd be out of danger, and Grayhewn would have less interest in sticking around. They had no way of knowing what the vampires had offered Grayhewn for his help, or how long he would really stay.

Buffy was torn. She enjoyed being around Pike, enjoyed having him with her on patrol. But if he was going to leave, maybe sooner would be better. She couldn't help remembering what she'd said to Angel: *"And maybe it* would've *been better if he'd never come."*

Pike looked at her thoughtfully, then shrugged. "You're probably right," he said. "Guess we should go out and punch the dude's ticket, huh?"

With a soft chuckle, Buffy rolled her eyes. "You watch too much TV."

"What?" Pike asked, offended. "You making fun of the way I talk? Buff, take a look around. You and your buds aren't exactly speaking the Queen's English."

She couldn't argue with that, and really, Buffy didn't want to argue. Pike was staying, at least for the moment. As much as that complicated her life, she figured she could live with it. He was going to stay.

"So," Pike said as they went out the front door, "did Giles figure out how to destroy my stoner friend?"

"He's working on it," Buffy told Pike. "But till he comes up with something, I'm not completely idea deficient."

Pike blinked. "Yeah? What've you got?"

Buffy walked over to where Pike's Harley stood at the edge of the driveway. On the ground next to it she picked up the heavy bag she'd carried back from school. From within, she drew the massive war hammer and slung it over her shoulder. Pike smiled and shook his head.

"Hell," Pike laughed, "if it ain't the Mighty Thor."

"As solutions go, it's of the primitive," Buffy admitted. "But sometimes primitive's the only way to get things done."

She bent to slide the hammer back into her bag, and when she stood, Pike was beside her, still smiling slightly. He put a hand on her hip and moved closer, bent to kiss her.

"Primitive," Pike said softly. "Kinda like the sound of that."

Buffy stiffened and withdrew. Pike stood looking at her awkwardly, trying to understand. But Buffy couldn't help him. She was trying to understand herself.

"Buffy?"

"Sorry," she said. "Just, all this . . . I can't take the time to figure this out right now. Later, when it's done, then I'll make the effort. But Giles needs help, and so do you, and whatever's in that kiss is going to have to wait."

Pike sighed and slipped a leg over the Harley, climbing aboard. "I think I liked primitive better," he said, pulling on his helmet.

Buffy didn't say it, but she thought it: *me too*. But primitive wasn't fair to anybody.

The big problem with looking for Grayhewn was that they didn't have any real clue where to start looking. Sure, he'd been in Hammersmith Park at one point, but they had no way of knowing if he'd ever gone back. Newspaper reports about a couple of broken statues that had been found with large pieces missing began to make sense when coupled with other items. For instance, no museums had been broken into. Nobody knew where the statues had come from.

And there had been a lot of disappearances in the past forty-eight hours in Sunnydale.

Nothing all that unusual about people turning up missing in town. It was the Hellmouth, after all. But Buffy figured it wasn't just vampires. Grayhewn was eating.

So they checked the three sites where the half-eaten statues had been found, and looked around for any sign of a place where a huge stone demon could hide out and hope to go unnoticed. They tried to map out the places where the demon had been, wondering if his bolt-hole would be somewhere central to all of them.

They rode the Harley around Sunnydale for hours,

until Buffy's ears felt numb from the roar of the engine, and her thighs were sore from the hard leather of the seat. When two o'clock finally rolled around and she knew they had to start heading back to the school, Buffy was relieved rather than disappointed. They hadn't found Grayhewn, but she didn't think they were going to have any more luck than they already had. Without some kind of lead, it seemed like they were going to have to wait for him to come to them.

Not a happy thought.

A short while later, when Pike pulled the Harley up in front of the school and killed the engine, the parking lot was already filled with students fleeing madly from their academic prison. Over the time they'd spent on the bike, Buffy and Pike had talked less and less. Though it seemed now that he might stay in Sunnydale for a time, she dared not think too much about it. Buffy found herself almost perversely grateful for Giles's mysterious trouble and Grayhewn's vendetta against Pike. Bizarre as that was, at least it gave her something else to focus on.

Side by side, Buffy and Pike pushed the library doors open and went in. They were the last to arrive. Oz, Willow, Xander, and Cordelia sat around the study table, much as they had that morning. But there was more of an edge about them now. All of them seemed nervous, the very atmosphere in the library uncomfortable. Buffy had a sick feeling in the pit of her stomach, wondering what had happened now. Before she could ask, however, Giles appeared from the stacks and came to stand at the top of the steps that led down into the study area.

"Ah, you're all here. Excellent," Giles said idly. Then he paused, and looked directly at Buffy, and offered a weary smile. "I appreciate your concern. All of you. You've been quite dutiful in looking out for my well-being. But as you all know, I am no longer under the influence of the glamour. As such, I would appreciate having my privacy back. It's quite disturbing to be under constant surveillance."

"We're worried about you Giles," Willow said gently.

Giles directed his stern gaze at Buffy. "Needlessly, I assure you. We all have a great deal to do if we're to destroy the stone demon. I'm also involved in some research of my own."

Buffy started to ask about that research, but Giles interrupted.

"Which is purely academic, and no one's business but my own," he finished meaningfully.

"Giles, listen," Buffy said, imploringly. "It's obvious something's bugging you—besides us, I mean. You look like a rabbit in the headlights or something. You're spooked. Whatever's going on, we want to help."

For a moment, Buffy thought he was actually going to spill, to share his concerns. But then the Watcher shook his head.

"I'm fine, Buffy," Giles said. "Please concern yourselves with the business at hand."

Then he started down the stairs, a pair of thick books under his arm. At the bottom, he stopped to glance at Pike.

"Almost forgot," he said. "If you can get in close enough to destroy Grayhewn, he's only going to reform his body, either from its original components or from some other source of stone. If you can stay alive long enough, get his head and hands and put them in a wooden box with a lock. He should be relatively harmless after that."

Then Giles went into his office and shut the door, making it clear he didn't intend to discuss Buffy's concerns any further.

"Well, that was weird," Pike said.

"Yeah," Buffy agreed. Beyond that, she just didn't know what to say.

Outside, standing on the lush lawn beneath a perfect blue sky, Buffy looked around at her friends and was saddened by the fact that none of them were smiling. Obviously, she wasn't the only one unconvinced by Giles's evasive answers. But before she could put her thoughts into words, Xander spoke up.

"Okay, is it me, or is Giles getting all Mysterio on us?" he asked.

"For once, it isn't you," Oz assured him.

Xander pointed at him. "There you go. Not me."

"It isn't you," Buffy confirmed. "He's not himself, but this isn't like before. This isn't somebody playing with his head. That's all Giles in there, weird as it is. Obviously he escaped last night, but something tells me he didn't dust the whole bunch on his way out. Something's going on with this particular pack of vampires, and he's trying his best to hide it, or protect us from it or something. But this group is pretty nasty, and, hello, Slayer?"

"So what now?" Oz asked.

"I guess we start looking," she replied. "Pike and I haven't had much luck, but if Giles isn't going to tell us what's going on, the only way we're going to get answers is to beat them out of something evil.

"Those vampires from last night. I think the one-eyed Amazon's name is Jocelyn. The blond is Rachel. We find them, or one of their buddies, or even that stone demon—who I'm beginning to think may have skipped town already. We figure out who they're working for. Track the boss down and kick *his* ass.

"Giles may not want our help," Buffy added, "but he's going to get it."

Pike cleared his throat. Buffy turned to look at him. He had a sort of dubious, questioning look on his face.

"Pike?"

"There's a little hole in your plan," he told her, absently scratching at his ragged hair and running a hand over the stubble on his chin.

"You've got a better one?" Xander asked defensively.

"Down, boy," Willow said.

"Let Buffy do her own macho posturing," Cordelia told him.

"Which might be less macho. More macha," Oz added quietly.

But Buffy ignored them all, her eyes still on Pike. "What's up?"

"This town isn't that big, but it's big enough," Pike said. "We all searched around last night and came up with nada. Me and Buffy spent most of the day cruising Sunnydale's danger zones. Not a fang out of place. I don't know where these dudes went to, and I don't know if we can find them. But if they've got it out for Giles, chances are they're not gonna be happy that he's back playing librarian."

Buffy blinked. Pike was right. She'd been so hurt and angered by Giles's behavior that she hadn't even seen it.

"Okay," Xander said sheepishly. "Surfer boy catches a wave."

"Anyone have any plans for later?" Buffy asked.

"Hello?" Cordelia replied instantly. "Mall? New

shoes?" When they all glared at her again, Cordelia rolled her eyes. "All right," she said. "I guess I can get to the mall and back by sundown. Just make sure we don't have much running to do. If I run in new shoes I'll get a blister."

"I think there's something in the Bible about that. Right after the apocalypse and the number of the beast," Xander teased.

Cordelia seared him with her heat vision. Xander smiled helpfully.

"Dusk then," Buffy said. "Right here. But try to stay close to the school and out of sight of the library. I'd rather not let Giles know we're doing this."

"He'll appreciate it later, Buffy, when he realizes we were only looking out for him," Willow reassured her.

"Oh, yeah, he'll just kill us with thanks. He'll be even more grateful than *this* time," Xander said.

"Don't see how that's possible," Pike muttered.

"With ya," Oz told him.

Then they all went their separate ways, off to spend a few hours pretending they were normal American teens in a normal American town. Buffy and Pike watched them go, and then she looked at him.

"I have a need for mocha," she said.

"We're on it," Pike promised.

They took off on his bike, and under Buffy's strict navigation, were soon parked in front of the Espresso Pump. For two hours, they just talked. About their time together at Hemery, and about their lives now. Pike spoke lovingly about surfing, and Buffy fondly described getting to know Willow and Xander. They talked about the coming of nightfall, and what they might do if their stakeout was for nothing, and nobody came looking for Giles. They talked about everything but what Buffy knew was on both their minds.

Then it was time to go.

The horizon was an angry red on one end and a deep indigo on the other. The ghost of the moon hovered above, gradually solidifying as the sun slipped away. A cool breeze brushed lightly through the trees on the campus of Sunnydale High, but the air still had a warm tang to it from the pleasant heat of the day.

On the back of Pike's Harley, Buffy held on tight and resisted the urge to lay her head on Pike's back. Now wasn't the time.

They passed Oz's van and Cordelia's car parked on the street across from the school. No reason to get Giles all worked up if nothing happened and he ended up leaving before them. If he came out to the lot and saw all their vehicles parked there, in his current state of mind he'd be apoplectic. Pike pulled the bike to the curb in front of Cordy's car, and they both climbed off. Buffy had the hammer in its long cloth bag across the seat in front of her, and she hefted it to her shoulder now. Pike threw her other bag, in which she had stakes and other vampire-hunting accoutrements, over his own shoulder, and they headed across the street to the school.

Under the trees, they found the others waiting for them. Willow sat on the ground next to a large wooden box Buffy had asked her to round up just in case they ran into the stone demon.

"Could you two try to be on time?" Cordelia said snippily. "Talk about a lack of courtesy."

"It's young love," Willow said happily, grasping Oz's hand.

Buffy shot her an urgent look, and Willow blinked.

"Um, just in the air this time of year," she added.

Buffy put down the hammer and handed each of them a stake from her other bag. She doled out small bottles of holy water and several crosses. Xander produced a crossbow that Buffy had stashed in the back of Oz's van for emergencies a few weeks earlier. When she got to Cordelia, Buffy looked down at the ground.

"Nice shoes," she said.

Cordelia beamed.

They took their places in the shadows around the school, and they waited.

Alone in the library, Giles sat at the desk in his office, poring through his father's journals. It was all he really had of the man, his records of his time as a Watcher. That, and memories of the many clashes they had had, the bitter recriminations, the disappointments. They'd made their peace, of a sort, eventually. When his son had finally toed the line, accepted his role with the Council of Watchers, the elder Giles had been pleased. He'd even done his best to hide the self-satisfaction that his apparent victory over his rebellious son had given him.

He'd done a bloody awful job of it.

Still and all, Giles had loved his father. Blood was still blood.

But this ... this was unthinkable. The previous night, he'd been weak, exhausted, his mind still reeling from Karen Blaisdell's manipulation. He wasn't willing to completely trust his senses, not given the state he'd been in. As the Watcher, he knew what could be done with illusion and magick.

But it had seemed so real, only inches from him.

Every detail, there in the cold, dead flesh. The voice, the inflection, the disdain . . . yet in spite of it all, Giles refused to submit completely to what he'd seen. He knew it might be little more than denial, wishful thinking, and he didn't care.

For if it were true . . . the very idea tore at him. That a demon might live within his father's corpse, might have assimilated much of his father's knowledge and memories, it sickened him to consider it. He would not accept it without further proof, and he refused to involve Buffy and the others until he knew that truth.

If that creature had once been his father, he would destroy it himself. It would be about family, then. It was . . .

No. He wouldn't accept it until he knew for certain.

Unable to read the words on the page now, Giles lowered his head. He removed his glasses and ran his fingers through his hair, then just sat there for a few moments doing nothing but breathing. Breathing, and trying to remember that he was alive. He had been allowed to live. If the creature wearing his father's face had wanted him dead, he wouldn't . . .

. . . *if the creature wearing his father's face had wanted him dead* . . .

"Good Lord," Giles whispered to himself, shaking his head.

He felt cold suddenly. Cold and lonely and devoid of hope.

What if it's true?

Sucking in a deep breath, he sat up, jaw set with determination. He slipped his glasses back on and picked up the book to skim its pages again. No matter what had gone before, if this vampire had once truly been his father, when the time came for a stake to be driven into its heart, it would be Rupert Giles who performed the act. It wouldn't be for Buffy or Angel or any of the others to do this. He had never felt anything so strongly.

Though the mere possibility that it might be true was maddening, though his heart felt cold and silent and dead, though he found himself unable to speak without anger or bitter sadness . . . despite it all, Giles would not allow this burden to be lifted from him.

If nothing else, he could do that for his father, in memory of the man who had drilled into his mind the importance of the Council of Watchers.

Out of respect for his father's memory, Giles knew that if this monster had once been his father, he would have to destroy the monster the man had become.

And it was killing him.

At the southwest corner of the school, Xander stood gazing alertly around him. If he looked along one wall, he could see Cordelia standing around pretending to be bored when she was probably just as scared as he was. Looking the other way, he saw Oz sort of half crouched, leaning against the wall and scanning the trees. He had to wonder if Oz's werewolf gig made his senses better attuned to the things that went bump in the night.

"Huh?" Xander mumbled, turning back to look down to where Cordelia was standing.

He'd heard something rustle close by, but Cordelia hadn't so much as moved. Xander looked around, stepped out onto the lawn, and glanced into the trees, then at the windows, and finally, up at the roof.

Nothing.

But he'd been sure he'd heard something go bump in the night.

"Gremlins," he told himself, walking back to his post. Then, on second thought, "Let's hope not."

"Do you always work this late?"

Giles spun, knocking books from his desk at the sound of that voice. He grabbed up a cross as he turned, and held it up in front of him even before he met the creature's gaze.

The man, the thing, the vampire, stood there, leaning against the doorjamb with a smug little grin on his face. So familiar, that look. Giles wanted to hit him, and the urge had nothing to do with him being a vampire.

In that moment, he knew.

His mind was clear, alert. The thing that stood mere feet away was a creature fully formed, not some illusion rising out of his fevered mind, not some magick trick. It was every inch his father, right down to the arrogance in its voice.

But it wasn't. It was a corpse with a demon inside.

"Get out," Giles ordered, his voice an acid growl, his heart growing numb.

"Oh, really," the creature said, rolling its eyes as it turned to stroll back out into the library proper. "Must you be so dramatic? I'm not going to kill you, Rupert. Not yet, at least. If that was all I wanted, would I have made such a bloody production out of all of this? Could've done that myself, couldn't I, old boy? Not a damn thing you could've done about it, either."

Giles sneered. "You say that as though you let me escape last night."

The vampire nodded appreciatively. "That was unexpected, and well done. I raised you right, lad, that I'll give you. But snatching you up in the first place was just another way to play about a bit. You must realize that. I thought it was time you learned who'd been fiddling with your life. And now you know."

"Yes, now I know," Giles replied, moving out of his office after his father. He began to work his way to one side, toward the cabinet where the weapons were kept. "I'm glad you showed up, really."

"Indeed?" the elder Giles asked. "How so? I would've thought you'd be happy to be rid of me last night. Although perhaps a bit on edge, knowing that I was still lingering about, reveling in your anxiety and fear of what might lurk in the shadows. Perhaps I'm extrapolating a bit too much, eh?"

"You always did tend to run on," Giles told him.

Buffy had left the cabinet unlocked. Giles grabbed the handle and ripped the door open, reaching inside.

The vampire's iron grip clasped his shoulder, fingers digging in. He spun his son around and glared into Giles's face, eyes yellow now, features twisted into the true countenance of his nightmarish race.

"Do you take me for a fool?" he demanded angrily.

"Always did," Giles replied coldly.

The creature threw him onto the study table. Giles rolled off and landed painfully on one of the chairs. It stormed after him, hauled him up by the shirtfront and slapped him across the face with a savage backhand. Blood sprayed from the Watcher's nose, spattering his shirt.

With a fingertip, his father dabbed at the blood, then licked it off.

"You were always an insolent little bastard," the vampire said, voice deep and raspy with fury and bloodlust. "Almost makes me willing to change my mind and just kill you now. But I know I'd regret it quicker than you can say 'Bob's yer uncle.' "

It smiled broadly and let him go. "Not much as Watchers go, are you?" he asked.

Torn inside, every bit of light in him shattered into jagged fragments, Giles steeled himself from the pain and the aching bitterness and the abyss of despair before him. He would not give this creature the satisfaction of seeing those things on his face. He turned his back and began to walk toward his office. The vampire reached out and grabbed him by the hair, yanked him off his feet, and Giles landed painfully on his back on the ground, the wind knocked out of him.

"Where the bloody hell do you think you're going, you little git?" the vampire roared.

"You're not going to kill me," Giles told him. "I thought I'd go back to my research."

The elder Giles only smiled. "Ah, well, please do. Go on, then. About your business."

Giles blinked, began to get up. He stood staring at the thing in his father's body. It grinned, fangs bared grotesquely.

"But this is just starting, Rupert. You're going to love what's next."

Outside, Buffy turned at a sound behind her and saw the one-eyed Jocelyn emerging from the shadows, reaching for Willow.

All around her, Buffy's friends began to shout.

The vampires had come, and they were many.

Chapter 13

ANGEL WALKED WITH PURPOSE, HIS DUSTER FLAPPING and swaying behind him as he moved quickly along the sidewalk. With all that had been going on between himself and Buffy, he'd made less of an effort than he might have to find out who was behind these attacks on Giles. Tonight, that had changed. He'd gone the extra mile. He'd hurt people to get the answers he needed.

For Buffy. And for Giles. Angel owed Giles more than he could ever possibly repay. But this was a start. He'd been able to narrow down the general vicinity of the lair of these new arrivals, and he was certain that between Giles, Buffy, and Willow, they'd be able to pin it down.

If she asked for his help, he would give it, as always. If she didn't, he'd just go home. Angel didn't want to get in the way, to muddle her thinking. He had no right. He'd told himself that time and time again. With what little he could offer Buffy, he had no right to speak up for himself. For his love.

But it was becoming harder and harder for Angel to believe that. He was beginning to think that love gave him the right. And maybe it did.

As he passed from one splash of light from a streetlamp above and made his way toward the next, Angel heard an urgent shout. The voice was familiar.

"Buffy . . ."

He ran across the street, unmindful of the car that had to swerve, honking, to avoid hitting him. Up onto the opposite curb, he sprinted onto the lawn in front of the school, running for the front door. Then he saw her.

Buffy was under attack, three vampires trying their best to take her down. Even as Angel rushed toward her, she leaped into the air and spun around to kick one of the vamps in the head. The creature's neck snapped, and it went down hard on the ground, twitching, but alive. Angel had never seen such a thing happen to a vampire before.

But Buffy was the Slayer. The children of the night were no match for her.

One of the other vamps lunged for her from behind, and Buffy shot an elbow into his chest, then belted him away. The third was on her, though, throwing her off balance, driving her down.

Then Angel was there. With a grunt, he gave the vampire on Buffy a swift, vicious kick to the side, hard enough to flip the thing off of her and onto the ground. It started to rise, and Angel moved to meet it. Before he could even get there, Buffy swung her legs around, dropped the vampire off its feet again, and sprang up to stake it with a crunch as wood met bone and flesh and muscle.

"Good timing," Buffy told him.

"Sometimes," he replied gravely.

The dust whirled away in the wind. Already, though, the other two were coming at her again. Even the one with the broken neck, whose head hung at an odd angle.

Angel stood next to her.

Buffy spared him a quick glance. "I'm set. Go help the others."

"But—"

"Go!" the Slayer snapped. "We have to regroup. They'll pick us off one by one if we stay spread out like this!"

With a final look at Buffy, who lunged out to stake the vampire with the drooping head, Angel turned and ran along the side of the school. He knew she was right. Though every part of him screamed to stay behind, to make sure Buffy was safe, she was the Slayer. The others were nowhere near as able to defend themselves.

He knew where he was needed.

"Take them."

Willow's eyes went wide as she stared at Rachel. The vamp-chick grinned at her, then merely stood there as a pair of savage-looking vampires moved in on Willow and Oz. The creatures looked as though they hadn't fed in weeks.

But oddly, Willow wasn't afraid.

The first vampire lunged for her, and Willow splashed holy water across its face. The thing hissed in pain, then let out a cry as the water dripped into its eyes. Fluid erupted from its eye sockets as the holy water melted them. Willow moved in quickly and staked it.

She turned around, heart thumping wildly with excitement. Oz was using a cross to fend off the other, but it had batted the stake from his hand. She was about to shout to him, to throw her stake over, when Rachel grabbed her by the hair and yanked back hard.

"Aaahh," Willow cried, eyes wide. "That hurts."

Rachel smiled. "You should be more afraid," she said grimly.

Which was when Willow lifted her cross to Rachel's face, and the vampire girl shrieked and drew back, forehead smoldering where the cross had touched it.

"I should be," she admitted. "But it's you're fault I'm not. You kinda let the cat out of the bag."

Hissing, the vampire circled, trying to find an angle to attack Willow. "What are you babbling about?" Rachel demanded.

"I do that, don't I? Babble. I'm just a babbler. Kinda like, oh, you? You said 'take them.' Not 'kill them.' 'Take them.' Which means you're trying to keep us alive. Which gives us the advantage."

Rachel offered a fang-filled smile. Then she whipped a hand out, almost faster than Willow could see, and slapped the cross from her hand.

"My master won't mind it if *one* of you doesn't make it," she sneered, advancing on Willow.

Willow's eyes widened, but she didn't even glance to see where the cross had fallen. *Too late now.*

She held her stake in her right hand and stood with her legs apart in the fighting stance Buffy and Giles had taught her. From there, she didn't think there was much she could do, but she wasn't about to let this blood-sucking bitch take her out without a fight. She put on her *mean-Willow* face, and tried to pretend she could back it up.

Oz nurtured a little fantasy in his heart. Well, more than one. But this one didn't involve Willow. In this fantasy, he could use the fact that he was a werewolf to help Willow and Buffy and the others when things got nasty. Problem was, it was only a fantasy. Three nights a month he became little more than a bloodthirsty animal. No mind. Nothing. Fate had changed him, the supernatural had claimed him, and there was not a single benefit he could think of.

Except maybe a familiarity with manacles.

The vampire he was up against gave him a savage backhand, and Oz hit the ground, rolled, and came back up to his feet.

"You were drifting," it said amiably.

"I'm a pensive guy. Happens." Oz had no stake—the vampire had knocked it from his hand—but he still had his bottle of holy water. Holding his cross up to ward off the vampire, he reached inside his coat and pulled it out, flipped the cap off.

The vampire kicked him. It was a good kick, practiced and precise. It nearly broke his wrist, and knocked the bottle of holy water out of his hand, spilling half of it onto his coat and shirt as it fell.

"Butterfingers," the vampire said. "You should try to hold onto things a little tighter."

Oz shrugged. "I'm a guitarist," he said. "No one ever said that had to mean manual dexterity. But I can hold on as well as the next guy. . . ."

He lunged forward. The vampire tried to grab him, but Oz was too quick. He wrapped his arms around the creature in a tight embrace. For a moment, the vampire seemed to hesitate, then it realized how close he was, that his bare neck was right there, and it started to bend, fangs bared.

Which was when it felt the holy water on Oz's shirt and jacket seeping through the thin shirt it wore. It screamed, staggered back, and beat at its steaming chest. Oz winced at the shrieking, and then the furious growl, but he knew from growling. He dove for his stake, came up fast, and turned in time to protect himself and then to strike.

The vampire turned to dust.

Oz nodded solemnly, flipped the stake confidently in his hand, and nearly bobbled it. Then he rolled his eyes . . . and remembered Willow. He cursed himself in a low voice, and turned to run to her aid. When he saw her facing off against Rachel, hand to hand, he almost yelled.

He ran at them, holding the cross in one hand and stake in the other. Rachel saw him coming and lunged for Willow, but Oz was there, shoving the cross in her face.

"Come on, then," he said.

"Odds look bad for you," Willow told her.

"Worse than bad," said a voice behind them.

Oz glanced over his shoulder to see Angel moving in. Rachel tried to reach for Willow again, and Oz was too late with the cross. Willow went down. Oz grabbed Rachel by the hair and slapped the cross to her cheek. But it was Angel who pulled her off. He threw her, hard, into the stucco wall of the school. When she looked up, there was fear in her vampire eyes.

Then they heard Cordelia scream.

"You have this under control?" Angel asked.

"Go," Willow told him.

He took off. Willow and Oz moved in on Rachel. But now the fear was gone from her face. In fact, she was smiling. Oz didn't like that look. Not at all.

"Are we missing something?" Willow demanded.

Rachel nodded. "It's a big joke, actually. See, the

reason you can never win this battle is that I have more friends than you do."

Oz heard something, and spun to find Jocelyn and three other vampires moving in on them. Willow swore softly next to him, a word he'd never heard her use before. In a twisted way, he was proud. But now wasn't the time.

"And even better," Rachel added, getting up and moving toward them again. "I can always make more."

When Angel rounded the corner, he saw Xander and Cordelia standing side by side beneath a tall shade tree. Xander held a small crossbow in front of him with a wooden bolt set to fire while Cordy waved a cross back and forth in front of her. A pair of female vampires— sultry, slender girls who looked similar enough to have been sisters when they were alive—were moving about warily, trying to find an opening to attack.

Xander fired a bolt from the crossbow. Much to Angel's surprise, it found its mark. One of the two girls went up in a cloud of dust.

Angel moved up behind the other.

"Well, thank God," Cordelia sighed, lowering the cross. "It's about time."

Tipped off to his presence, the vampire girl whipped around to face Angel, then attacked, claws raking his cheek as she tried to force him to the ground. Angel managed to pull a stake out from inside his jacket, and slammed it into her chest.

She joined her sister on the wind.

As he rose, Angel brushed off his jacket. Cordelia and Xander walked over.

"You two all right?" he asked.

"We were doing just fine, thanks," Xander said, nodding.

"Oh, please, Xander, rein in the faux-macho vogueing," Cordelia sighed. "Unless, of course, you mean to be amusing. Then by all means—"

"We're fine. Thanks for the assist," Xander said flatly.

"No problem," Angel replied. "Why don't you guys hook up with Willow and Oz, then get back around front with Buffy."

"Good plan. Strength in numbers," Xander agreed.

Angel ignored him. He was looking into the darkness behind the school.

"Where's—"

"Pike?" Cordelia finished. "He's back there somewhere. We were pretty spread out when they attacked. If he hasn't shown up now, gotta figure he's dinner."

"Damn!" Angel snapped.

He turned and ran around behind the school. The last thing he heard was Xander's voice.

"Gotta admit," Xander said. "Dead Boy's a good sport."

Yeah, wonderful, he thought. *A good sport. Save the life of the guy trying to take Buffy away from me.* But none of that mattered now. If Pike died, it would hurt Buffy deeply. Angel wasn't going to let that happen.

"So, a kiss for the hero of the day?" Xander suggested.

Cordelia smirked. "Happy to. Only he just left." She turned and started off to find Willow and Oz.

"Wait up . . . and hey!" Xander protested. "I did pretty well there with the whole Robin Hood thing." Even as he walked, he fit another bolt into the crossbow.

"Robin Hood never used a—" Cordelia began, but then her words were cut off by a gasp.

"Never used a what?" Xander asked, looking up.

More vampires were coming across the lawn toward them. He whipped up the crossbow and fired the bolt. It missed by yards. Then he and Cordelia turned to run. At the tree, Cordelia stopped, grabbed a thick branch, and started climbing.

"Where are you going?" Xander said angrily.

"They can't fly!" Cordelia snapped.

"Doesn't mean they can't climb," he said in exasperation. But Xander climbed anyway. He couldn't leave Cordelia to the vampires. Though he had a perverse little happy moment at the thought of it.

They climbed up as high as they could. Xander looked down and saw the vampires arriving at the base of the tree. They were silent, staring up. One of them was laughing.

"Lots of vampires," Cordelia whispered.

"I count five."

"Sort of overkill, don't you think?" Cordelia said disapprovingly.

Xander raised an eyebrow. "Vampires, Cor," he reminded her. "I'm thinking overkill probably a foreign concept to them."

One of the vampires began to climb.

Pike grabbed a beefy, bearded vampire by his dirty, matted hair, and slammed him face first into the rear wall of the school. Another, a short, matronly-looking female, grabbed his right arm. Pike spun and shot her a hard left to the face, then followed it with another. She staggered, and he staked her.

Dusted.

The hairy, hulking one grabbed him in a tight bear hug from behind. Pike grunted in pain, all the breath going out of him. He felt like his ribs were about to break.

Tensing his muscles, he threw his head back as hard as he could, the back of his skull shattering the vampire's nose. The big guy dropped him, and Pike was up in a second. He threw his entire weight into ramming the guy back against the stucco again.

"Buddy, I'd wring your neck if you had any neck to speak of," he said furiously.

Then he rammed the stake home.

The hairy dude made a large cloud of dust.

"Well done."

Pike turned at the voice, saw several more vampires moving toward him. He was growing tired. There were too many of them. He had no idea how any one vamp had gathered so many of the others around to follow him. From what he'd heard from Buffy and the others, it wasn't common for them to gather in these kinds of numbers . . . especially when Buffy was there for bloodsucker population control.

They had to be out-of-town talent. An army of them. Not good.

Pike was starting to think there was only one way this night was going to end. And that was badly.

"Wanna see my muscles?" he asked the vampires.

In his peripheral vision, something moved. Before Pike could turn, Angel moved to stand beside him.

"More your veins they're interested in, I think," he said.

"Yeah. Hey."

"You need a shave," Angel told him.

Pike blinked, looked away from the vampires that

were even now spreading out to encircle them. "Could we stay on topic, please?" Pike suggested.

"Sure." Angel nodded. Held up a stake.

"So you're gonna watch my back, huh, dude?"

Angel said nothing. Which was good enough for Pike. Why speak when there wasn't really anything more to say. They stood side by side, waiting for the vampires to make their move.

But they didn't move.

"Away!" commanded a deep, imperious voice. A voice like the rasp of stone on stone.

"Aw, man," Pike sighed.

"What is it?" Angel asked.

"Total drag."

Grayhewn stepped from the darkness, striding toward the gathered vampires. For a moment, they did not move from his path. He paused and glared at the one immediately in front of him, red eyes blazing.

"They're ours," the vampire said. "We answer to the same master, demon. Back off."

"I have no master, leech. Move aside."

"You can't harm me," said the vampire. "Don't try to intimidate me."

"What, because I cannot turn you to stone?" the demon said, and laughed heartily.

The laughing stopped abruptly. Grayhewn reached out with both hands, grabbed either side of the vampire's face, and with a profound growl, tore the creature's head from its shoulders. What remained of the vampire exploded into dust, and the others scattered out of Grayhewn's path and ran off to find someone easier to kill.

"Okay, that's bad," Pike whispered. He glanced over at Angel to see that even he seemed stunned.

"Yup," Angel said at length.

Grayhewn stood only a few yards away, facing them as though a duel were in the offing. But there would be no duel. Only slaughter.

"You may go, vampire," Grayhewn told Angel. "My vendetta need not concern you. Only this one. Pike. Who killed my mate."

Though he had never been so frightened, never felt such a chill fall over him and run through him like he was freezing up inside, Pike managed to laugh.

"Her?" Pike said, standing up straighter and licking his lips. "That's what this is about? Man, you should thank me for offing that beast. I mean, you could totally do better."

Grayhewn stared in astonishment, a low growl building up inside him.

"What the hell was—" Angel began.

"I have a strategy," Pike whispered.

Angel turned slightly and whispered in return. "If you're pissing him off so he'll kill you quick and painless, I'm not sure that could actually be considered a strategy."

"I want him off guard," Pike replied. But inside, he didn't know what he wanted. Except to live.

Angel sighed. "Ah, hell," he said. "Go get Buffy, will you?"

"What about—"

But then Grayhewn was charging, fury boiling over, hands raised as if he might tear Pike's head off as he'd done the vampire's. Which was a definite possibility.

Angel ran at the demon, pulling his jacket off. As Grayhewn tried to get past him at Pike, Angel threw the long duster over the demon's head, and then drove him on, using his own momentum against him. Grayhewn slammed into the outer wall of the school, his head actually cracking the wall.

He went down hard. For half a second, Pike felt hopeful. Then the demon began to rise.

"Pike—" Angel started.

"I'm going!" he snapped. Then he ran to find Buffy, hating himself for it.

If anything happened to Angel because he'd led Grayhewn to Sunnydale, Buffy would never forgive him.

Giles heard glass shatter somewhere. Shortly after that, he heard a scream. He turned at the sound, then looked back at the vampire, the creature that had arranged all of the torture he had suffered in recent days.

"What's happening?" he demanded. "What have you done?"

"It's a little vengeance, Rupert," the vampire said, smiling broadly. "You spurned your father, don't you remember? Gathered around yourself another family, one not bound by blood. Those idiots you called friends. And now you have these . . . children. They're hardly more than that, are they? Almost as if they were your children.

"Your family." The creature paused. "And now," he added, "I'm taking them away."

Giles's eyes went wide. He lunged for the wall and grabbed the crucifix that hung there. The vampire tensed, waiting for an attack. But Giles had no more time for him. Instead, he ran for the double library doors, mind reeling as he attempted to push from his imagination the images of what might even now be happening to Buffy and the others.

But he never reached the door. A powerful hand landed on his shoulder, pulled him back. The vampire threw him across the room, and Giles slammed into the door to his office, shattering the glass. For a moment, he was disoriented. When he shook it off, he saw the grinning face above him again.

"You bloody bastard," Giles spat, rising again. "I swear to God if you so much as—"

"Please, son. Call me Daddy."

"You're not my father."

"Oh, Rupert, you cut me to the quick," the creature simpered. Then it grabbed the Watcher by the throat, choking him, driving him to the ground. "You're going to stay right here while your little family out there is removed."

Giles raged inside, but he felt powerless.

And he hated himself for it.

The vampires swarmed over Willow, lifting her up. She screamed. Screamed for Oz to help her. To stop them. To save her.

Oz tried.

He ran at them and drove a stake through Jocelyn's back. But it didn't go in far enough. The one-eyed Amazon roared with pain and anger, and turned on Oz. She reached out quickly, empowered by her pain, and grabbed Oz, lifting him off the ground.

"No, Jocelyn, stop!" Rachel snarled. "Just bring him with—"

But Jocelyn didn't listen. The vampire ran forward a few steps, muscles tensing, and Oz knew what was about to happen. The creature would use every ounce of strength to throw him against the wall, breaking some bones. Maybe his skull. Maybe it was about to be all over for him.

Oz closed his eyes.

Jocelyn threw him.

Oz crashed through a long row of windows and into a corridor of the school, hitting the floor hard and rolling to slam against a row of lockers. He hit his head on the metal, and for a second, he was out.

Then he shook it off as best he could, and tried to lift his head. A needle of pain poked into his eyes, but he forced himself up. Dragged himself to stand, so as not to crawl over broken glass. He practically fell out onto the grass.

But the vampires were gone.

And Willow with them.

"Would you just stop!" Xander shouted.

The vampire below ignored him, reached for his leg again. It recoiled as Cordelia flashed her cross again. But Xander had nothing else to fight them with. No more bolts for the crossbow, even if he hadn't dropped it.

"How 'bout this?" Cordy asked.

Xander glanced at her, at the bottle of holy water in her hand, and grabbed it greedily.

"Yeah, that might help," he said. Then he dumped the contents of the bottle onto the vampire, who shouted and let go, then fell steaming to the ground. Xander shot an annoyed look at Cordy. "It would've helped a couple of minutes ago, too."

"That's the last time I give you anything," she snapped.

"You said that in the fourth grade when I lost your fuzzy pencil," Xander reminded her.

"I forgot all about that. I loved that pencil." She hit him in the shoulder. "Jerk."

"Okay, sticks and stones may hurt but, remember the vampires?"

Two more were climbing to replace the one who'd fallen. Cordelia held the cross low, hoping to keep them from climbing any farther. Xander reached out and tried to snap a thick branch off the tree. It wouldn't break easily, and he had to put some effort into it.

The nearest vampire grabbed his leg and pulled.

Xander lost his balance and fell from the tree, crashing through the branches and taking the vampires down with him.

Cordelia screamed as all three hit the ground.

The vampires rose, shakily, muttering curses.

Xander didn't rise at all.

The vamps looked up at Cordelia, and she held the cross down again, even as she watched Xander for some sign that he was all right. But still he didn't move, even as they lifted him up and started to carry him away.

"What about her?" asked the one Xander had burned with holy water.

"Leave her," said another. "She isn't as important as the others. And if we took her and didn't kill her . . . I think she might annoy me to death."

Too frightened to be insulted, Cordelia watched them move away. Then she started to scream. First Xander's name.

And then Buffy's.

Angel felt he was doing pretty well just staying alive as long as he had against the stone demon. But he was growing tired of dodging, tired of ducking. His fists were bleeding from hitting the thing's rock flesh, and his blows hadn't seemed to have any real effect.

Grayhewn came after him again. Angel ducked the thunderous right cross that came at him, and tried to come up with both hands to knock the demon's arm away, maybe get a decent shot at its face.

But Grayhewn had suckered him in. Even as Angel rose up, the stone demon's left hand crashed into the side of Angel's head. Angel staggered back and fell hard, ears ringing, eyes glazing over. He couldn't see straight. There was blood in his eyes. His brain was barely able to recognize the demon looming over him.

"You invited this, vampire. It wasn't your fight," Grayhewn said. "It makes me angry. But I don't have the time I'd like to take for you to die. I have to get after the other. Pike. That means you'll die fast.

"You're lucky."

Grayhewn lifted Angel up by the front of his torn shirt, and raised his stone hand over Angel's face.

In the library, the elder Giles looked down at the Watcher, tilted his head to one side, and sighed. Then he looked up at the clock on the wall.

"Well, that ought to do it," it said pleasantly. "Ta-ta, Rupert. It's been so nice spending time with you again. Family means everything, doesn't it, lad?"

Then it walked up the stairs into the library stacks, and headed out the back. The moment he heard the rear door shut, Giles ran for the corridor, silent prayers running through his head.

Buffy saw the stone demon about to kill Angel, and her heart froze. In that moment, she had the answer to all the questions that had been haunting her. Her love was for him and only for him, until the day he willingly gave it up. If that doomed her to bitterness and robbed her life of intimacy, so be it.

She loved Angel. More than life.

"Nooo!" she screamed.

Grayhewn looked up as she ran toward him. He barely had time to notice the long war hammer slung over her shoulder before she swung it around in a deadly arc. It struck home with perfect accuracy, crashing into the back of the demon's neck.

Shattering it.

Grayhewn's head tumbled to the grass in a shower of crushed stone. Immediately, the demon's body began to move, blindly, hands searching, reaching for the head. It could easily put itself back together.

And if those hands touched Buffy, she would turn to stone.

The Slayer kicked the stone demon's body over, then moved in and kicked the head across the grass.

"Ow!" she cried.

Angel struggled to stand up next to her. "You're hurt?" he asked.

"Stubbed my toe," she replied, watching the demon body searching for its head. Then she glanced at him. "Oh, and why aren't you stone?"

"Doesn't work on vampires," he said, and shrugged. "Apparently it's a living flesh thing."

"So there are advantages to being dead," Buffy said in wonder.

Grayhewn moved closer to the head. It must have been able to sense it somehow. Buffy wasn't about to let it get itself back together. She moved in with the war hammer, and brought it down on Grayhewn's left arm, which snapped off. She broke the right hand off at the wrist.

Then she moved on to the rest of the body.

"Should it be this easy?" Angel asked.

"Without the head and hands, it's not much more than stone," Buffy explained, staring down at large chunks of living rock.

The hands were still moving about, trying to find other bits of stone to merge with, to reform the body. The left hand crawled over the head, and Grayhewn's eyes opened.

"Slayer!" the demon growled. "I'll kill you. There is rock in this earth. Stone everywhere. I will grow again, and destroy you."

Already, the right hand was crawling away, looking for something to attach itself to.

"No," Buffy told Grayhewn. "You won't. Pike, bring me the box." There was no response. She turned around to look past Angel, toward the school. "Pike?"

"Where is he?" Angel asked, glancing around.

"He was right here," Buffy said frantically. Then she shouted his name. "Pike!"

She ran toward the school. "Don't let him reform," she told Angel. But before she had gotten very far, she found the wooden box, lying on the lawn as though someone had simply dumped it there.

Pike was nowhere to be found.

Then she heard her name called, weakly, painfully.

Buffy spun and saw Cordelia coming toward her, supporting Oz, who looked pretty banged up. His blond-dyed hair had blood spattered in it, and from the looks of things, Buffy guessed it was his own.

"What happened?" Buffy demanded.

"They took Willow," Oz said weakly.

"Xander, too," Cordelia said.

Buffy turned slowly in a circle, looking out across

the darkened school grounds. Xander, Willow, Pike—all gone.

A sudden fury overtook her. For she knew who had the answers. Answers he had refused to give.

"Giles," she said, through gritted teeth, and started for the school.

Chapter 14

As Giles ran down the corridor, the slap of his shoes on the floor echoed back off the lockers with a hollow sound. The school had never felt more empty. All the rage and pain within him at the memory of his father and the knowledge of what he had become had been overwhelmed by pure, unreasoning fear.

The creature had been right. Giles cared greatly for Buffy. For all of them: Willow, Xander, Oz, even Cordelia. They were his only concern in those horrible moments as he sprinted headlong for the front door to the school. When he slammed against the door, it swung wide, and he barely slowed as he ran out and started down the front steps, glancing around wildly.

Two steps from the bottom, he faltered, then stopped altogether. He stared, heart pounding, trying to catch his breath, as Buffy came across the front of the school toward him. She looked haggard, but nowhere near as bad as Oz, who was bleeding and limping. Cordelia only looked scared. Behind them all came Angel, carrying a heavy wooden box. Giles felt certain he knew what was in that box.

For a moment, his knees felt weak. *She's all right. They're all right.* He nearly sat down on the stairs, but then Buffy was coming up, moving toward him, and Giles's relief kept him standing.

"Buffy," he said. "I was . . . I'm so . . . you're all right, then?"

"We're alive," she said coldly.

Giles head snapped back at the sound of her voice. He looked at her without comprehension. He didn't know if he had ever seen her look so angry.

"Well, thank the Lord for that," he replied. He was surprised the others hadn't appeared as well. For about a full minute. Then he blinked, the fear sliding over him again.

"Where are the others?" he asked at length. "Willow, Xander—"

"And Pike," Buffy said flatly, glaring at him. "They're gone."

For a moment, he couldn't breathe. Then Giles swallowed and took a long breath, fury and remorse battling for mastery of his spirit in that moment.

Fury was the victor.

"That's Grayhewn, then," he said grimly, nodding at the box in Angel's hands.

Buffy frowned. "What's wrong with you? Didn't you hear me? Whoever's been stomping all over your life lately has taken them away, Giles! They are *gone!* Are you missing that?"

"Hardly." Giles buried his guilt as best he could and met Buffy's hard look with one of his own. "I understand your concerns, Buffy, and *I* will deal with them. I have to be the one to deal with them."

He turned to Angel. "There'll be a shovel in the groundskeeper's shed. Go bury that damn thing back beyond the fence. Deep."

"I'd like to know what's going on here," Angel replied. "What are you hiding, Giles?"

For a moment, Giles felt the urge to scream. His left eyelid twitched, and he reached up and rubbed it harder than was necessary. Then he tried desperately to get himself under control.

"You want to help, Angel, then please just go bury that bloody thing. When you come back, there'll be plenty for you to do, don't worry about that."

Then Giles turned and walked back into the school. Buffy, Oz, and Cordelia hurried after him. Angel paused a moment, but then he went in search of the groundskeeper's shed.

"For the record?" Cordelia said. "This boogedy-boogedy mystery crap is getting pretty tiresome. I don't know why Buffy isn't calling you on it, but I, for one, think we should be trying to find Xander and Willow."

"They're alive," Oz said quietly.

That gave them all pause.

"How do you know?" Buffy asked.

"It was pretty clear," Oz replied. "The way they talked. They wanted us all alive. But they were happy to take just Willow and Xander. Pretty sure they've got something planned."

"Maybe torture," Cordelia suggested.

"And helpful of you to suggest it," Buffy said, teeth clenched.

"Yes, well, torture is better than death," Giles put in. "Though I must say from firsthand experience, not by much."

They pushed into the library. The doors swung shut. Giles went over toward his office.

"Stop."

He turned to face Buffy, who stood in the center of the room, arms crossed expectantly.

"Buffy, I think it's best if we—"

"I don't care what you think," she fumed.

Buffy walked toward him, the anger, the energy of her pique nearly steaming off her. She stepped right up to Giles and stared him in the eye. He couldn't help it. He looked away.

"This is your fault," she told him. "If you'd been up front with us after the whole thing with Miss Blaisdell, we could have prepared. But you had to have your secrets. And I let you, so in that way, I guess it's my fault too. But you were storming around here in a snit, and I figured, give him time.

"But whatever's going on with you, it isn't just about you anymore. Maybe you thought it was personal—"

"It is *very* bloody personal," Giles replied harshly.

"That's not an excuse," Buffy snapped. "Open your eyes, Giles. Look around. You've gone turtle on us, pulling so far into your shell you can't see anything but whatever all this is about. Maybe you're reverting to type, huh? The teen rebel. Old Ripper Giles? But you're not that guy anymore. Teen rebels usually end up alone. You told me that, Giles. You *taught* me that. Well look around you, James Dean.

"You're not alone. You have people that care about you. And because you've been behaving like such a butthead, some of them are in very serious trouble," Buffy said, her voice going gradually from bitter to tender.

Giles opened his mouth to retaliate, then snapped

it shut. He hung his head, lifted his hands in surrender.

"Do you think I don't know that?" he asked, heart aching. "Do you think it hasn't occurred to me? You . . ." He looked up, glanced at Oz and Cordelia and then back at Buffy. "All of you. You mean a great deal to me. And that is very specifically why Willow and Xander and Pike have been taken."

"Now I'm missing something," Cordelia said. "What do they have to do with any of this?"

Oz took a step toward Giles. "How 'bout just getting to the *why* part?"

Giles nodded slowly. The doors to the library swung wide and Angel stepped in. There was a moment's pause, and they all looked back to the Watcher.

"He took them because he sees you all as my family," Giles said softly. "All of this, with the glamour, and the vampires . . . it's been to torment me, not to kill me. Even when they had me, they weren't about to kill me. He wanted me to suffer. And now he wants to hurt me by hurting all of you. It *is* personal. I wanted to deal with him myself, to find the courage to kill him before it could get any worse. It's up to me, you see. Killing him is the least I could do to make things right.

"Also, I think I may have been a bit ashamed."

All the anger drained from Buffy's face. Eyes wide, she moved closer to Giles until they stood face-to-face.

"Who is he, Giles? Who's doing all of this?"

Giles lifted his chin.

"It's my father," he said, voice unwavering. "He's a vampire."

Then he turned and walked into his office.

* * *

Buffy blinked several times before she realized she wasn't breathing. Then she sucked in air, and looked around at Oz and Cordelia and Angel, all of whom seemed to be in a similar state of shock.

"Did anybody else know his father was a vampire?" Cordelia asked, confused.

"Doesn't sound like *Giles* knew," Angel said.

Oz let out a long breath and leaned on the study table. "Drag."

Buffy didn't say a thing. She couldn't think of anything she *could* say. But then Angel was there with his hand on her shoulder, and she turned and pulled him to her. His arms slipped around her, and they stood like that a moment, and she knew it was right. Times like this, she needed him to be there to hold her.

And then to let her go.

With a glance at Oz and Cordy, Buffy pushed away from Angel and turned toward Giles's door.

"Buffy," Angel said.

She glanced back at him.

"There is one piece of good news. I think I know where they are."

A tiny spark of hope ignited within her. Hope that this nightmare, for all of them but especially for Giles, could be put to an end soon. She nodded at Angel, then turned and went into Giles's office. She shut the door behind her.

The Watcher was standing behind his desk, holding a tiny silver frame in his hands. Buffy went to him, glanced at the picture. He didn't try to hide it from her. It was Giles as a young man in his more rebellious days. He stood with an older, very proper couple whom Buffy assumed to be his parents.

"I've never seen that picture before," she said softly.

"I keep it in a drawer," he said distractedly, as though he were speaking more to himself than to Buffy. "I hate it, really. None of us look very happy, do we?"

Buffy hated to lie to him. "No."

"Perhaps because we weren't. Not really. He could be a self-righteous bastard, Buffy. Never was there a more stubborn man. But I'm sure he had his own opinions of my behavior as well. And Mother? She didn't like to get between us. Not that I could blame her."

Giles paused. In the confines of the office, just the two of them there to share his pain, it felt like a very long pause.

"He had such hopes for me, you see. All parents do, I suppose. But the Council of Watchers was the world to him. The only worthy pursuit imaginable. What use is an archaeologist or an architect or a rock and roll star in a world with horrors such as we have in ours, hmm? That was the way he thought.

"Bollocks.

"The world needs protection, mind. But it also needs people to just be people, to go about the business of burning the candle of civilization at both ends. One day perhaps it will all be gone, but we've got to fight for the right to destroy human society ourselves, haven't we?

"There was never a time when I didn't understand the need for the Council. It was the idea that I had some destiny predetermined by my father that drove me to fight it the way I did. Rebel? Bloody well right. Hooked up with that silly sod, Ethan Rayne, didn't I? And a bunch of other wankers besides. There was that whole mess with Eyghon, not to mention all kinds of other things I never should have gotten myself into."

Giles smiled a little then, dropped his head.

"Drove my father mad, and I had a wonderful time

doing it," he said. "But eventually I came 'round. The world needed more Watchers a good deal more than it did another museum curator or archaeologist. And they let me dabble in my other interests, of course."

Buffy had a small smile on her face, and Giles blinked in surprise as he noticed it.

"What is it?" he asked.

"You're speaking in tongues."

"Hmm?" He thought about it. "Ah, yes, well, when I dwell on it, I suppose I do sort of revert to a more, ah, colloquial speech."

They fell into mutual silence again. After a moment, it was Buffy who spoke up.

"I guess I never realized how much of that we have in common," she said. "The whole unwanted destiny schtick. I did a little Jane Dean rebellion myself, too, didn't I?"

"But you came back," Giles told her.

"So did you."

"Yes," he agreed. "My father got precisely what he wanted in the end. A proper Watcher. A proper Englishman. I suppose our parents really do shape the people we become as adults, whether we want them to or not."

"You weren't all that proper," Buffy scoffed. "Okay, when I first got here, you were of the rigid. All right, you were a total sconehead. But I think you're only half right about the whole parent deal."

Giles had seemed lost in thought, back in time even, while he talked about his father. Now he looked at Buffy more closely, back in the real world again.

"It isn't our parents who make us what we become," she said. "It's our relationships with them. It's what we take away from that. Okay, my dad hasn't exactly been a major inspiration. It's not . . . I don't have to tell you it isn't something I like to talk about. It hurts. But I learned something from that.

"And look at my mother. I mean, think about what she's been through. Forget divorce and starting over as a single mom. How 'bout finding out your daughter spends her nights battling the forces of darkness. She's still living in mom universe, which means we have the stupidest disagreements, but she's the strongest woman I know. I learn from her every day."

"And I learn from you," Buffy added. She blinked. "Not that you're . . . what I meant was . . ."

"Got it. Thanks," Giles said, then glanced awkwardly away.

"When you came here," Buffy went on, "I didn't want to even think about vampires. Slaying was a no-go. Priority zero. But I knew what had to be done, and realized I had to do it. Sound familiar?"

"Indeed. Like me, you wanted to do it on your own terms. You wanted guidance instead of instruction." Giles looked down at the picture in his hands, then put it on his desk. "Unfortunately, my father never understood that."

"Once again, you beat me to the point," Buffy told him.

Giles only looked confused.

"That's what you learned, Giles. Okay, maybe he was a jerk, maybe his methods were harsh, but he wasn't a bad guy, right? He knew what had to be done, but didn't know how to just trust you to do it. That's what you got from him."

Buffy went over and picked up the small frame and handed it back to him.

"You knew I needed the space to figure things out for myself, but that I wouldn't even bother if you didn't at least show me the way. You gave me a little shove now and then, but you knew what would happen if you pushed too hard. You knew from experience."

Giles had a small smile on his face then, and Buffy looked at him oddly.

"Don't know if this is a happy conversation," she reminded him.

"You're not a child anymore, are you?" he asked.

"Nope."

He looked at her warmly. "Yes, well, don't expect me to get used to it right away, all right?"

"Actually, I think you figured it out even before I did," Buffy told him. "Now let's go get our friends."

The smile disappeared from Giles's face, to be replaced by a flicker of guilt—maybe for having strayed from that purpose—and then a grim look of determination.

"Yes," he said. "Let's."

"Angel knows where they've been taken."

Giles glanced away. "I know where they are. Couldn't very well escape from the damned place and not know how to get back there, could I? I was just set on doing it all myself."

Buffy looked at him sadly. "Well, so much for that plan," she said. Then she turned to the door, reached for the handle.

Giles stopped her with a gentle touch on her arm. "The thing that haunts my father's corpse?" he said, jaw set.

Buffy met his fierce gaze. "Yeah?"

"Nobody kills it but me."

Willow was jolted awake as the truck rumbled over a bump in the road. Her eyelids fluttered, she blinked a couple of times and felt the sharp pain in her head, the burning of a deep cut across her back. She didn't remember how she got it, but the how didn't matter, only the pain. The temptation to slide back down into unconsciousness was almost too much to resist.

"I'm thinkin' big vampire barbecue, roasted on a spit, apple in my mouth," Xander said suddenly, his voice barely a groan in comparison to his usual sardonic tones. "Pike, what about you?"

"No idea. But you gotta figure, still alive is good. We're still drawing breath in an hour, *then* I'll start worrying about why," Pike replied.

Willow sighed.

"Hey, Will, you awake? Wanna play the how-are-we-gonna-die game?" Xander asked, more than a little manic.

Slowly, painfully, she sat up. They truck went over a speed bump, and Willow groaned.

"I don't think I'm any good at that game," she said timidly. "In fact, I'm sort of thinking anything more than 'go fish' is kinda beyond me right now."

"I guess you can't magick us out of here?" Pike asked hopefully, scratching his chin.

Willow glanced around the truck, looking for anything that might be useful. There were no windows. The truck was moving. The back door was probably locked, but—

"Checked the doors," Xander said.

"I knew that," Willow said. Then she looked at Pike. "I can make pencils fly," she said helpfully.

Pike didn't seem terribly impressed. Willow thought about it. Just about the only other thing she could think to do was set the truck on fire, but that took concentration—something hard to manage when she was in pain—and she didn't know if turning their mode of transport into an inferno of death would be the guys' idea of help.

"If it's any consolation, I'm pretty sure they're using us as bait," she said hopefully. "Which, okay, might not be great news, but at least they need to keep us alive until Giles and Buffy show up."

Pike and Xander were both staring at her. After a moment's pause, Xander shrugged.

"Nope," he said. "No consolation."

"I don't think we should rely on Buffy coming after us," Pike said. "Not that I don't think she will. But we don't even know what might still be going down back at the school. Hell, for all we do know, she could be in a truck right behind us. If they haven't—"

"Stop right there, mister," Willow said huffily. "They haven't. Trust me, they haven't."

Xander was glaring at Pike. "Yup. Surfer boy comes to town, and suddenly every night's a party."

Pike just rolled his eyes.

The truck slowed, turned, and then they were bumping over several additional speed bumps, each punctuated by an *"Ow!"* from Willow. After a moment, the brakes squeaked, and the truck rolled to a stop. Doors slammed, and then the rear of the truck was unlocked, the doors flung open to reveal Rachel and Jocelyn glaring at them expectantly.

"Well?" Rachel asked, amused.

"Would you mind closing the door?" Xander asked politely. "It's a little drafty in here, and—"

"Come on, meat," Jocelyn snarled. "I'm getting too hungry to stay patient very long."

"Coming," Xander replied quickly. He got up and started shuffling toward the back of the truck, hunched over. "Have you thought about Fig Newtons as a snack food? Pretty healthy, and they really take the edge off if you're hungry and—"

Jocelyn reached up into the truck and yanked Xander out by the hair. He let out a yowl and crashed down on the pavement hard, letting out a curse and then cradling his elbow as he began to sit up.

"Don't you ever shut up?" Rachel asked him.

"Not generally, no," he answered truthfully.

Rachel slapped him.

"No, stop, please!" Willow cried.

The two vampire women turned to scowl at her, but she jumped down from the truck and moved to help Xander.

"It's true. He really can't control himself. Y'know, kinda like Rain Man. Don't know if you saw that movie. Tom Cruise and . . . I'm doing it too, aren't I? Don't slap me."

Rachel and Jocelyn looked up at the sound of engines. Several cars rolled slowly into the parking lot around the truck with their lights off. One of them was a long black limousine. In the moment before they came to a stop, Willow looked around and realized that she recognized their surroundings. It was the abandoned headquarters of CRD Corp., where she'd once faced a computerized demon who wanted her for his bride.

What she felt was more nausea than nostalgia.

"Seen that limo before," Pike whispered as he came up beside Willow. "Outside Giles's house."

Vampires began to emerge from the various cars. A lot of vampires. Willow was waiting for Xander to make some smart remark about clown cars at the circus of the undead, but he kept his mouth shut for the moment.

Then the rear door of the limousine opened and a tall, thin man with graying hair appeared from the backseat. He looked very proper, very British in his choice of fashion.

"Who's the butler?" Pike whispered again.

Jocclyn strode over to glare into his eyes with her single remaining orb, and the dark, ravaged hole where the other one had been.

"That's Malthus," she said intimidatingly. "But you might call him Mister Giles. At least for a short while before he feeds me your heart."

They all gawked.

"Did you say—" Xander began.

Willow finished. "Mister Giles?"

In the lot, the vampire Jocelyn had called Giles turned to face those gathered around him.

"An excellent night's work my friends," Malthus said happily. "In order to celebrate, I give each of you an hour to go and hunt. To feed to your heart's content. Then be back here to prepare, for the Watcher and his Slayer will most certainly be coming. I want something lovely prepared for them when they arrive."

The vampires turned and fled out into the night, a scything breeze of death sweeping across Sunnydale. Malthus watched them go. When the last had disappeared in the dark, the vampire turned and strode to where Rachel and Jocelyn stood guarding Willow, Xander, and Pike.

"Ah, yes," he said, walking in front of them, examining them like a drill sergeant. "Friends of the Slayer. And children of the Watcher in a way, aren't you? This ought to be a great deal of fun."

"You're not Rupert Giles," Willow said defiantly.

"Of course, not my dear," the vampire replied. "Perish the thought. But family ties are such strong bonds, don't you think?"

"You're a virus, moron," Pike said grimly, stepping forward. "You don't have a family."

Jocelyn and Rachel stiffened, but their master laughed amiably. He walked over to Pike and slapped him hard across the face. His smile had disappeared.

"I was wondering which of you I should have torn apart completely, and I think now I know," said Malthus. Then he paused to consider his words. "You know," he said, turning to Jocelyn and Rachel. "Perhaps I'm being rash. Why don't you put all three of them in the conference room for now. If any of them survives, we'll give them the gift of eternal life, yes?"

Jocelyn and Rachel grinned and reached for Willow and Xander. Pike hung back a second, but Malthus moved forward, glaring at him dementedly.

"This should be a delicious little experiment," the vampire said.

"Why do I think *experiment* is such a bad word?" Willow said softly.

Xander was the last one shoved through the door into the conference room. Jocelyn and Rachel smiled, then turned and left them, locking the door as they went out.

Willow went to the wall and flicked on the lights, and gasped to see the corpses that lay all about the room, on the floor, on chairs, and even one on the table itself. She counted six in all.

"Well," Xander said, glancing around. "Other than the dead guys, this isn't so bad. No real torture devices. Nice comfy spot to plot our escape, right—"

"Uh, guys, we may have a problem," Pike noted, crouching over one of the corpses.

"Nah, it's kind of cool in here. The bodies shouldn't really start to get ripe for another day or so," Xander replied, sitting in one of the high-backed, old-fashioned wooden chairs around the mahogany table.

"I don't think we have another day," Pike said.

And the first of the newborn vampires began to rise.

Chapter 15

Oz RAISED AN EYEBROW AND TILTED HIS HEAD ALMOST whimsically to one side. Beyond that, there was no more expression than usual on his face. But there was steel in his voice.

"Maybe I didn't say this clearly enough," he said, glancing from Buffy to Giles and Angel, and then back again. "I'm going."

"So am I," Cordelia added quickly. "Not that I don't have ten million better things to do, but I'm not going to let Xander die because he was trying to save me. I'd never hear the end of it from you guys."

"You're all heart, Cordelia," Buffy said coldly. "But I'm sorry. You've both been up against vampires before, and smoked your fair share, no question. But this is going to be fast and messy, and in that kind of fight, there's just too much room for mistakes."

Angel could stand so still at times that he seemed almost a statue. He shifted now, and they all looked over at him.

"The goal here is to keep everyone alive," he said. "If we get the others back and lose one of you in the process . . . that's just not acceptable."

Oz only stared at him a moment and then looked back at Buffy. She glanced away.

"They have Willow," Oz said. "I'm going after them. Want to keep us all alive, then we have to work together."

Buffy contemplated this. She glanced at Giles. Normally, at a time like this, he'd say something like, "This is an exceedingly poor idea." But nothing about this was normal. It was very nasty and very personal for him, and he had a lot more on his mind than what their attack protocol should be. Angel also kept silent, now that he'd had his say. The decision was hers, and hers alone.

"All right," she said. "We all go. But we have to keep some things straight. It's going to be all *Pulp Fiction*— quick and violent. That means whatever weapons we can carry. It means fast work and forethought and maximum damage. Once we get to the others, just trash the place. If we can blow it up or burn it down or whatever we have to do, just do it.

"I have a few ideas about things we can use to get an advantage. They won't take us far, but they'll throw the damned bloodsuckers into chaos for a bit. Hopefully long enough for us to get Willow and Xander and Pike out of there."

"Let's do it," Oz said grimly.

"One more thing," Buffy added, looking from Oz to Cordelia and finally to Angel. "The vampire behind all of this? Giles wasn't kidding, and he's not crazy. It's his father. None of us have seen him so far except Giles, but he's the one Rachel and Jocelyn are working for. If you run across him, give us a shout, but do not attack.

"It's for Giles to finish," she told them.

No one argued.

"Good. Any questions?"

"I have one," Angel said, and turned to regard Giles. "Buffy says these vampires had access to your apartment. I know the Blaisdell woman turned out to be a glamour, but that doesn't explain how the vampires could get into your place without an invitation. Do you have any idea what happened?"

Giles thought about that a moment, and then he managed a thin, sad smile of realization.

"We were going to have a small dinner party," he replied, understanding it all for the first time. "It was supposed to have been an informal thing, my friends and hers, to get to know one another better. I told her to invite whoever she wanted. That was my permission."

He hung his head. "I was a fool."

"No man can resist a glamour if he's unaware that he's become a target of one," Angel reassured him.

"Hello?" Cordelia said. "A glamour? No man can resist an attractive woman. Period."

"Yes, well, you are the expert," Giles said, though not unkindly. "We shall have to take your word for it. Now, can we please move along? If we're not swift in our pursuit, my father may decide that our friends are not valuable as bait."

That quieted them all.

In the corridor outside the conference room, Jocelyn stood with a smile on her savage face, and listened to the shouts and the sounds of battle that erupted suddenly from within. Rachel stood several feet away, glancing nervously at the door to the room where the Slayer's friends were captive. And now, apparently, under attack.

"The master will be furious if we allow them to die," she told Jocelyn.

Jocelyn's smile disappeared. "Don't presume to instruct me, girl. I accept your place at the master's side only for his sake."

Rachel stiffened and seemed suddenly nervous. Jocelyn knew the other vampire was frightened of her, as well she should be. She would not hesitate to tear the cold, dead heart from Rachel's chest if she were driven to it.

"Merely a reminder that Malthus has plans for them," Rachel told her.

"The Slayer will come whether they live or die. She has no way to know if they still draw breath. And if our new friends in there feed on them, we must only be certain that they are turned. The Slayer may arrive and discover that those she has come to save are now out for *her* blood."

Rachel still looked quite uncertain about that course of action. Jocelyn went to her, smiling, and nuzzled against her cheek and her hair and the crook of her neck.

"Relax," she whispered. "If you're so nervous, I'll go and speak to him myself."

"That would make me feel better," Rachel admitted. "I would hate to anger him."

Jocelyn kissed her forehead, then turned and walked off, leaving Rachel standing nervously outside the conference room, listening to the thump of something within. The girl—Willow—shouted. Jocelyn smiled.

* * *

"Pike, watch it!" Xander shouted.

Too late. A second vampire had risen up behind Pike, insane with blood lust, as newborn vampires almost always were. The vampire grabbed Pike by the throat and slammed him against the wall, choking him. Pike's feet dangled above the carpet.

Xander tried to go to his aid, but the first vamp to have risen was there to block his way. He had an old-fashioned wooden chair in his hands, holding the vampire off like a lion-tamer, but it only smiled at him and hissed a little.

"Have you thought about Listerine?" Xander asked anxiously.

"Xander?" Willow asked, panicked. She stood behind him, and pointed across the room to where Pike was flailing helplessly, trying to beat the vampire off him. She thought his face was turning a little blue.

"Go help him!" Xander snapped.

Then he ran at the vampire with the chair, trying to buy Willow the time and space to help Pike. Xander drove the vampire back toward the wall, its arms momentarily restricted by the legs of the chair. The creature snarled, yellow eyes blazing, and went berserk, arms flailing, snapping the legs off the chair and reaching for Xander.

But Willow couldn't help him. At the moment, Pike was in a lot more dire need. She ran two steps forward and launched herself onto the conference table on her stomach. She slid across the table and went rolling off the other side. Fast as she was able, Willow leaped to her feet. Pike's eyes were bulging in his head, and the vampire who held him by the throat was already leaning in, fangs bared, to tear into his veins and feed.

Willow lifted one of the chairs over her head, muscles straining, and with every ounce of her strength, she brought it down with a crash onto the vampire's back and head. The thing staggered and dropped Pike, almost went to its knees. Then it looked up at Willow, enraged, and leaped on her.

There was nothing she could do. No way to defend herself. The bloodsucker drove her to the ground. It grabbed her by the hair and slammed her head against the carpet several times, and then it grinned hideously at her and bent to take her blood.

"Please . . . no . . . ," she whispered.

The vampire exploded into a cloud of dust that spattered her face and drifted down to the carpet. Willow shuddered, shaking the dust off, and looked up at Pike, who stood over her with a broken chair leg in his hands. His face was red and there were angry welts on his neck where he would undoubtedly have bruises, but he was alive.

"Pike," she said breathlessly, as he helped her up. "You're okay."

"Not everyone's okay!" Xander cried in alarm.

Pike and Willow turned to see him dive under the conference table, trying to escape the other vampire, which went under the table after him.

"We can fix that," Willow said earnestly.

"Yup," Pike agreed.

They ran to meet Xander as he crawled out from under the table. Pike grabbed his hand and yanked him past them. Then he turned toward Willow, smiled, gestured for her to step back a bit. The vampire scrabbled across the carpet, and began to emerge.

Pike kicked it hard in the side of the head. Willow thought she heard the crunch of its skull giving way. The vamp went over onto its side, and its arms came up to defend itself as Pike dropped down hard on its chest with both knees, then brought the stake down hard, burying it in vampire flesh. The thing exploded into dust, and Pike dropped the last six inches to the ash-covered carpet.

"Whoa," Xander said admiringly. "Did you learn that move when you and Buffy were doing the dynamic duo bit back in L.A.?"

Pike laughed and shook his head. "Don't you ever watch wrestling?" he croaked, rubbing his aching neck. "And Buffy and I were never the dynamic duo."

That comment lingered in the air a moment, and then Xander shrugged. "So," he said, "I guess we should do a little chair-leg acupuncture on the rest of these sleeping beauties, huh?"

Willow glanced around for another shattered piece of wood, and then she stiffened.

"We'd better hurry," she said.

The guys turned to look, and they all watched as two more of the corpses in the room began to rise.

Oz turned off the van's headlights just before he turned into Technology Park. All of the buildings still had at least a few lights on inside them, but Buffy didn't think it very likely that there were many employees about. This late, she figured there might be some deadline-crunchers and maybe maintenance personnel, but that was about it.

"So where do you want me to park the battle wagon?" Oz asked as he guided the van silently along the road that ran past the various corporate structures.

There was a broad lawn and an expanse of trees on the left, and then they were passing Lorrin Software. CRD was just around the next bend on the right.

"Pull up here," she said. "We'll walk the rest of the way."

Oz did as she'd asked. They quickly unloaded everything they'd brought, and even as she surveyed the weapons, Buffy hoped it would be enough. Cordelia carried a huge, industrial flashlight they'd just loaded with new batteries, as well as a stake she'd shoved through her belt. Giles had a large crossbow, good for both distance and short work, with a rack of bolts strapped to his left arm. Oz had a stake strapped to his leg with electrical tape, and a paper bag.

Buffy didn't have anything but a stake in her hand, and two more in the special pocket her mother had sewn inside her sweatshirt. Angel had stakes as well, but he also had a long sword which he wore in a scabbard slung across his back. That was the sort of thing Buffy had been talking about when she said things might get messy.

In silence, the five of them walked across the grass and into a stand of trees that Buffy gauged would bring them out right behind CRD. Giles was in the lead, with Cordelia and Oz behind him. Buffy and Angel brought up the rear, and she scanned the trees ahead and all around them to be certain they would not be ambushed before they even reached the building.

"They'll wait until we reach them," Angel said, his voice low.

"How can you be sure?" Buffy asked, stepping over a thick root.

"They have what we want," he said gravely.

Buffy drew a measured breath, nodding grimly.

"We'll get them out," Angel assured her. "All of them."

She didn't miss the implication of his words. He was

dedicated to rescuing all three of them, including Pike, despite what he must still have thought was the competition between them. Buffy was a bit surprised. Angel ought to have known better than that. Certainly, she knew *him* well enough to know without him saying so that he would never have allowed his personal feelings to keep him from doing the right thing.

"Thanks," she said. "But I want you to know something, Angel. Whatever's between Pike and me . . . it isn't what I thought it might have been. He's a friend. We've shared enough together that he'll always be that to me. I care about him. But he's also been a distraction, and I'm sorry if—"

"I'm glad he came," Angel said quickly. "You've had this experience now. You know how it turns out."

Buffy's dark expression softened. "I guess." Then her gaze turned hard again, and grave. "I just wish I knew how *this part* turned out."

"Soon enough," he whispered.

Angel reached out and grasped her hand, and they moved on like that, fingers intertwined, as they forged on toward blood and death and the unknown outcome of a battle against a very personal evil. But the future was always unknown, Buffy knew. And suddenly she felt very guilty for having been so concerned about herself and her own problems, when Giles faced what was likely the most difficult moment of his life.

They reached the edge of the woods and found themselves, as she'd expected, behind CRD. The building was perhaps fifty yards away across a parking lot. There were lights on there as well, and she marveled that nobody had reported it, drawing the police out to investigate. Then she reminded herself that it was Sunnydale, and the police often weren't very cooperative when it came to looking into anything out of the ordinary. Obvious crime, sure. But anything odd, they ignored or did their best to make disappear.

Home sweet home, Buffy thought.

Oz started forward, and Giles slapped a hand across his chest to stop him. He held a finger to his mouth. Buffy looked into his face and saw that though his expression was grim and determined, his eyes were sad.

"There," Giles whispered, and pointed across the lot to several cars that were parked in the darkness.

For a moment, Buffy saw nothing. Then something shifted in the night, and she could make out a vampire standing sentry beyond the cars, watching for them.

"Angel," the Watcher whispered. "The perimeter."

With a nod, Angel set off through the trees. He could move faster and more silently than any of them, except perhaps Buffy, and she knew that Giles wanted her there with the rest of them. As the Slayer, she was less expendable. It disturbed her to realize that this was Giles's thought process, but she understood it.

So they stayed there, at the edge of the woods, trying to remain as quiet as possible while Angel moved around the perimeter of the building, remaining at a safe distance. It wasn't very long before he returned, but to Buffy, it felt eternal.

"Only four," Angel whispered as he slipped up to them through the trees again. "One on each side."

"Fortunate," Giles said thoughtfully. "Their numbers are apparently not as limitless as we had thought."

"Or we put a real hurtin' on them earlier," Oz offered.

Nobody argued with that. Buffy only hoped it was true.

"So what now?" Cordelia asked impatiently.

Giles had been taking the lead thus far, but now he looked at Buffy. They conferred silently, without any exchange of gesture or word. But they had worked together long enough that this was possible.

"Do it," she said.

The Watcher lifted the crossbow and set its stock against his armpit. He sighted along the bolt, and waited for the vampire in the shadows to move.

"Hey guys, sorry to interrupt," Cordelia whispered, "but the sanity train has apparently left the station. If Giles misses this guy, we'll be as conspicuous as Xander in a frat house."

"He won't miss," Buffy said flatly.

Angel glanced at Buffy, frowning. "What if he does?"

Buffy turned to Giles. "Take the shot."

He sighted along the bolt again, and waited. After a moment, they all saw the vampire move beyond the car. Giles fingered the trigger, and the bow snapped. The bolt whispered through the air and found its target.

From that distance, they could not be sure how well Giles had aimed. They heard a grunt, and Buffy held her breath a moment. Then the vampire disappeared in a cloud of ash.

Buffy smiled thinly. Oz, Angel, and Cordelia all seemed a bit stunned.

"He's been trained to be a Watcher almost his entire life," she told them. "The crossbow was his favorite. Trophies. Medals. All that."

"Nice shootin', Tex," Cordelia said admiringly.

"We should hurry," Oz said quietly. "Can't be long before they notice they're one man down."

Buffy nodded, and turned to study the building again.

"Oz, go with Giles. Take the west side," she said. "I've got the east. Cordelia, you go with Angel. We'll all meet around front, and go right in through the lobby."

"Y'know," Cordelia said, her voice high and stressed, "I realize I keep interrupting, but does that sound like a good plan to the rest of you? Not that anyone would ask me—and I know you all think of me as just an extraordinarily beautiful face, not to mention having impeccable taste in fashion and hairstyles—but to me a good plan has always meant the best way to do something, instead of the most idiotic, stupid, sure-to-get-us-all-killed way."

Buffy raised her eyebrows. She looked over at Giles, who stared back impassively. Angel said nothing. Oz reached into the paper bag he'd been carrying and pulled out a huge, dark blue, heavy plastic Big Squirt with a gallon tank. He ratcheted the pump to bring water up into the barrel, and then looked at Buffy.

"I've kind of made it a point in our relationship not to keep Willow waiting," he said.

"Let's go," Buffy replied.

They started out across the parking lot moving as swiftly as they could without making a sound. Though Buffy did hear one thing. A whisper from Cordelia.

"God help me, they're all on crack."

The conference room was silent. Rachel stood just outside the door, anxious and uncertain what to do. She was a bit hungry herself, and wouldn't have minded a little nip out of the throat of the scruffy one, Pike. There was something about him that got to her.

But Jocelyn had not returned, and Rachel did not dare make a move without the consent of her master.

He was more powerful than any of them had imagined. Jocelyn herself was much older than Malthus, but he had easily bested her in combat. It had been the master who had taken her eye, gouged it from her skull.

Then he'd eaten it.

Rachel shuddered at the memory. No, she wasn't going to go against the master's wishes. But he had been the one to give the order to place the prisoners in the conference room with the freshly dead. There was no way to know how soon they would rise

The sounds of the fight inside had been brutal and loud. Splintering wood and cries of pain and fear. But now there was only silence. They must be dead, she reasoned, or they would at least be speaking to one another.

Rachel knew she had to check it out. If they were dead, and the master was displeased, she would need to put the blame on Jocelyn to save herself. To do that, she would have to give the information to the master first.

Her course decided, Rachel used her key to unlock the door. She turned the knob and with a click, the door opened just a crack. There was no light inside. Without entering, she shoved the door open.

In the light that spilled into the conference room from the corridor, she could see the sprawled form of the one called Xander. He lay on the carpet, eyes unseeing. Dead. Beyond him, she saw the legs and lower torso of the girl, though she could not remember the girl's name.

In the shadowy recesses of the room, a figure stirred and growled low, recoiling from the light.

Damn, Rachel thought, praying the master would not punish her for what had happened.

"You can come out now," she said tiredly.

But even as she said it, she stepped into the room. The corpses were still warm. She had not done the killing herself, but that did not mean she should not partake of the spoils. They were already dead, after all. And Jocelyn had been right. If they were turned, they could still be of use in baiting the Slayer.

Rachel bent over Xander. Just as she started to reach for him, a thought crossed her mind.

Where's the other?

Which was when Xander reached up and grabbed her, swung his feet over to sweep her legs out from under her, and slammed her to the ground. Before she could even begin to respond, she heard someone shout "Now!" and then looked up to see the huge, heavy conference room table tipping over, coming down on her.

It slammed into her chest, breaking several ribs and pinning her to the carpet. As best she could, with the stabbing pain in her chest from those broken ribs, Rachel struggled to free herself.

But then Pike was there. It had been him, lurking in the shadows, not a newborn vampire. He came at her with a stake.

Rachel closed her eyes as she died.

Xander looked over at Pike. "Good job," he said. "I don't like letting toothy women get that close. Even the cute ones. Thanks for the save."

"No sweat," Pike replied.

"Can we go?" Willow interrupted. "I'm thinking it would be nice to be far from here."

"We're already gone," Pike replied.

* * *

It took less than four minutes. Buffy took out a large, dangerous-looking vampire simply by sneaking up and taking him by surprise. If their boss had spent any time analyzing her, she knew, he wouldn't expect stealth from her. They would expect directness and irreverence, but not stealth. Buffy knew, though, that there were times when sarcasm and swaggering were inappropriate.

Even when he died, the vampire didn't make a sound.

Buffy moved around to the front of the building. Giles and Oz were coming around the other side at almost the same time. Just beyond the dim light emanating from the glass-fronted lobby, Cordelia and Angel stood waiting for them. There was no sign of the sentry who'd been posted out front. Angel had done his work as quickly as the others.

They drifted together, still in silence. There was a moment when they paused, and glanced at Buffy. She only nodded.

Giles nocked a bolt into the crossbow, aimed it at the glass of the double doors into the lobby, and let fly. The bolt punched a hole through the glass and kept going through the lighted lobby and into the darkness beyond. The glass splintered around the hole.

Angel kicked the frame, and the glass shattered. One by one, they stepped through the door frame, shoes crunching on broken glass. Oz held his Big Squirt at the ready. Giles nocked another bolt into his crossbow. Buffy and Angel held stakes and stood in a battle stance.

Cordelia brandished her flashlight.

"Luuu-cy, you got some 'splainin' to do," Buffy called. Perhaps there was always room for a little sarcasm.

For a moment too long, nothing happened.

Then *everything* happened.

The dim secondary lights that had illuminated the lobby wcrc switched off, plunging the wide expanse of marble floor into darkness. A moment later, the orange emergency lights clicked on, casting a hellish glow across the lobby, capturing the vampires already on thc move.

Attacking.

"Dust 'em!" Buffy snapped, even as one of them came at her, slavering as though it had never tasted human blood before. Buffy staked it in midair, then spun out of the way of flying dust, ready for another.

Cordelia screamed as a skeletally thin female vamp came at her laughing. She switched on her flashlight and shined it in the vampire's face. The thing shrieked and shied away in fear.

Giles had painted the symbol of the cross on the lens of the flashlight. They hadn't even really known it would work, but Buffy hadn't been about to tell Cordelia that.

Buffy lunged in and staked the vampire, and Cordelia turned the painful beam on another.

Oz pumped a stream of holy water, strafing a pair of stocky male vamps who were circling, trying to get past the burning fluid. Oz aimed for their faces. For their eyes. He blinded them both.

They had Willow, the bastards. They deserved nothing less.

As Giles moved in to stake those two, Oz backed up against the reception desk in the lobby, swinging the barrel of the Big Squirt around, looking for another monster he could hurt. He almost didn't hear the thing behind him, but it scraped against the desk as it came up out of its hiding place.

He spun. It lunged for him, mouth open, fangs flashing. Oz fired point-blank right into the vampire's throat. It screamed raw and ragged and clutched its throat, falling to the ground and shuddering as though it were having a fit. It tried to spit but the holy water was burning it like acid.

Then Angel was there, dropping down with a stake, and the thing's suffering was over.

There was a huge roar behind Angel, and he turned to see a hulking vampire with rippling musculature who must have weighed more than three hundred pounds, hurtling at him with impossible speed.

He brought the stake up, and it was batted from his hand. The hulk grabbed him by the hair and slammed his head twice against the desk. Angel was disoriented as the creature wrapped a thick arm around his neck, and he knew the thing had the strength to decapitate him with its bare hands.

Then the massive beast screamed in fury, and Angel cried out in pain as well as holy water spattered his back, soaking into his shirt. Oz had sprayed the huge vampire, and hit Angel as well. Not that Angel minded. He was free.

Angel lifted a leg and kicked the huge vamp as hard as he could, sending him falling back against the reception desk.

"Spray him again!" Angel roared.

Oz strafed him, the huge vampire screamed and covered his eyes. So he didn't see Angel pull the long sword from its scabbard on his back. Its honed edges whispered a metallic hush as it cleared its housing, and he swung it around in a long arc through the air hacking the massive beast's head off with one slice.

The head bounced once on the reception desk, and then head and body both exploded into dust.

Still there were more. Cordelia screamed, and Angel and Oz turned to her defense.

Giles fired a bolt into the chest of a dark-skinned man he thought had once waited on him at his bank. The vampire's eyes widened with surprise before he was blasted to ash. The Watcher spun, nocking another bolt, and glanced around the lobby. There were still more vampires coming, but their approach had been correct, he knew. Fast and hard and merciless. It was the only way they were going to survive.

Off in the shadows of the elevator banks to his left, something moved. Giles spun and fired the crossbow even before he saw what he was firing at. Whom he was firing at.

His father.

Hatred and bitterness surged up within him at the demon that now inhabited his father's corpse.

Malthus whipped one hand down, and the bolt passed through his palm, embedded itself there, half on one side of the hand, half on the other. If he had not been so fast, the bolt would have been on target, right through the heart.

"You're really very talented, son," said the vampire.

"Don't call me that!" Giles snapped, moving into the elevator bank after his father.

A vampire grabbed the back of his coat. Giles hadn't

had time to nock another bolt, but he turned quickly and used the crossbow as a club. The wood splintered and shattered across the creature's head, and Giles drove it down, using the broken weapon to stake it through the heart. It fell away to dust.

Giles was very aware of the danger behind him, but when he spun and stood again, his father, or the demon within his flesh, had not moved.

"Come and get me, then, Rupert," he said happily, spreading his arms out, crossbow bolt still jutting from his right hand. "You know you want to."

Giles reached into his jacket and withdrew one of the stakes he'd brought. He moved slowly toward this creature with his father's face.

"You're not my father," he said.

"Ah, but you know better than that, don't you?" the thing said, its voice almost a whisper. "You know better than most what really happens when a vampire is sired. The human soul moves on, yes. But every little bit, every memory and every bit of knowledge, every habit or gesture, is still a part of the newborn creature.

"I *am* your father, Rupert. We both know that. I remember the day you were born. I remember the way you cried when Peter Morgan didn't come to your fourth birthday. I remember the sting on my palm and the fury on your face that one and only time that I slapped you. And you deserved it, didn't you? That kind of disrespect haunts us when our parents are gone, doesn't it?"

Giles felt cold revulsion working its way through him. He felt hot tears beginning to well up in his eyes. His anger had disappeared, replaced only by pain and growing numbness and regret.

The rest of the battle raged on out in the lobby. But here, off to one side, the man he had become fought a private war with the rebellious child he had once been. And both of them suffered.

"Come on," his father whispered. "Kill me. Show me what kind of man you've become. If you were half the Watcher I was, I'd already be dust."

"Shut your gob, you bloody bastard!" Giles roared.

He ran at his father, but the vampire put up very little fight. Giles batted his arms away, used his left hand to slam him up against the wall, and then drove the stake into his father's heart with an awful sucking sound.

For only an eyeblink, all of Giles's emotions prepared to overwhelm him. The pain and regret, yes. But the relief, and the pride that he'd been able to do what he knew his father would have wanted. What he knew, despite their differences, that his father deserved. His memory could be at rest once more.

Then Giles blinked. Backed up, staring in horror and astonishment.

For the vampire had not exploded into dust. He had not died. He merely stood there, looking rather amused, with a stake through his heart. Then he smiled broadly at Giles and reached up and pulled the wooden shaft from his chest.

"Bravo," he said. "I honestly didn't think you had it in you. Truly. Bravo."

Then the face changed. To Buffy's. To Angel's. To his grandmother's. And finally, to his own face. Rupert Giles's own features, own eyes, stared back at him.

Once more, the flesh melted, molded into new features.

But this new face, this last face—this true face—wasn't human. Not at all. And yet, it was a face he knew. A face that rose now out of distant memory, long forgotten but now returned to haunt him, torment him, perhaps even kill him.

"No," Giles whispered.

Chapter 16

Xander threw his arms up. "You're not the boss of me, Pike. We don't have time to argue about this."

"That's what I'm tellin' ya, dude," Pike agreed.

They'd come out into the corridor and almost immediately been set upon by a pair of vampires who'd been walking down the hall toward them, maybe to relieve Rachel of her sentry duty. But Rachel wasn't ever going to be doing sentry duty again.

Willow had a long scratch on her arm, and Pike had said his left wrist felt sprained, but they'd managed to dust the vamps anyway. That was the important thing, Xander knew. *Well, that and getting out alive.*

"I'm telling you, the straightest route, y'know? We go down the elevator, they don't know it's us coming down, we come out swinging and go right out through the front," Xander insisted. "Call me brain damaged, but this is a retreat, right?"

Pike sighed. "So that's your plan? You think that's sneaky, huh? On the elevator, which could stop at any

271

floor, which you can see is moving by looking at the numbers over the door *on any floor,* which open up right in the middle of the lobby, which could be filled with vampires as far as you know."

"We have weapons," Xander said. "All we want is out of here. If we go down by the stairs, there's an even better chance they could do a little monkey-in-the-middle. I've had plenty of dreams, asleep and awake, that involve sandwiches. But the sandwiches are never garnished with vampires."

Pike scratched his chin, staring at the elevator banks. Then he looked at Willow. He raised his eyebrows.

"Don't look at me," she said. "I'm choking on so much testosterone, I can barely breathe. My vote is jumping out the window, 'cause, y'know, fastest way out of here."

"Pike, I'm telling you—" Xander began, but was interrupted.

"Look at it this way," Pike said quickly. "You're braver than I am."

"I'm sorry, which of you is brain damaged again?" Willow asked.

"Hey!" Xander protested. "But okay."

"Seriously," Pike went on. "Okay, maybe I'm better at this than you. Scratch maybe. I'm better. But I don't want to be here. If I felt like I had a choice, I wouldn't ever have come here to begin with. I was running away, bringing all my troubles down on Buffy and you guys. I'm not gonna choose this life.

"But you're here, man. Both of you. All of you. You fight the good fight *just because,* and I could never do that. If my ass isn't on the line, I'm gonna close my eyes and pretend I don't see, just like the rest of this damned town."

Xander looked at him thoughtfully. After a moment, he shrugged. "What's your point?"

Pike smiled then. "Well, hell, Xander, who you wanna follow? The guy trying to vanquish evil, or the guy out to save his bacon?"

Xander's eyes went wide. After a moment, he nodded once. "After you," he said, letting Pike and Willow lead the way. To the stairs.

Sometimes Jocelyn almost thought she could see with her missing eye. It was ridiculous, of course. Even if that eye could see, the only image it would receive would be the inside of the master's gullet. Still, it was almost as though her brain held a phantom image, as though it were attempting to fill in the missing half of the picture supplied by her good eye.

Then something would happen to remind her. The wind would blow, and she would feel it in the empty orbit of her eye socket. Or an insect would alight there, looking for somewhere to lay its eggs.

But for the most part, the gouged socket didn't hurt her, unless she was hungry. At the moment she was ravenous, and the empty orbit throbbed with an ache that was almost enough to distract her from her purpose.

She'd asked the master about the prisoners, and he had given his leave for her to kill them, to drink from them, to turn them. She would bring that news to Rachel, and it would be a small victory for Jocelyn in the competition between them.

As she rode the elevator up to the third floor, her eye socket ached even more, and a feeling of great restlessness settled over her. For no reason she could have explained, she moved back slightly in the elevator and tensed, ready to spring should the need arise. When the door slid open onto a silent corridor, she paused, blinked the one eye still capable of the act, and stepped out of the elevator.

All was silent.

But down the hall to her right, in the opposite direction from the conference room, the door to the stairwell clicked quietly shut. Jocelyn turned abruptly and stared at the now tightly closed door.

Too quiet.

If it had been some of the master's other servants, they would have heard the elevator opening and stopped to see who was coming up. Which left only one possibility.

"Damn," she grunted, and ran for the door.

"Go," Willow said in a hushed voice, urging Pike down the stairs ahead of her.

"Someone came up the elevator," Xander whispered. "Guess I gotta look into that brain damage thing."

Willow shushed him, and the three of them hurried down the stairs as quietly as possible. Whoever it had been hadn't seen them, which was a relief. But in a minute, their escape would be discovered, and that would be that. In a minute—

Upstairs, the fire door to the third floor slammed open, metal banging against concrete.

Willow swore. "Run!"

Pike leaped down to the second floor landing, momentum carrying him forward to crash into the wall. He rebounded just as Willow rounded the corner behind him, and Xander muttered little prayers or curses, Willow wasn't sure which, as he pounded down the steps behind her.

"Run fast, children!" Jocelyn cried above them.

"Run far. I'll still catch you. I'm hungry, and hunger lends me speed."

They were at the landing halfway down to the first floor when the door into the lobby banged open, and a pair of vampires started for the stairs.

"Xander!" Pike snapped.

The two vampires looked up, and froze a moment. Then both of them grinned and started up. Xander pushed past Willow, and stood beside Pike, the two of them brandishing their makeshift stakes.

"Guys, we don't have time for this," Willow said, moving down the stairs after them, holding her own splintered chair leg in her hand, to use as club or stake, whichever was required.

From above them came Jocelyn's high, insane laughter, mixed with a kind of bestial snarl. Willow glanced up, halfway down the stairs, and was horrified at what she saw.

Jocelyn threw herself over the metal railing into a free fall, arms and legs out, ready to crush Willow beneath her like some guerilla warrior. In that heartbeat of a moment, every ounce of energy in Willow came together in a concentrated mix of fear and anger, all of it focused on Jocelyn. Almost without realizing it, Willow released the broken chair leg from her grip, and it spun there in the air, for a millisecond.

Then it flew straight up as though shot from a bow and impaled Jocelyn through her heart. Willow was watching her face in that moment, and she could see in the vampire's single good eye that she knew what was coming, saw that she'd been bested. She started to scream in fury, then the wood thunked into her chest, and she disintegrated into a shower of dust that fell all over the stairs.

"Whoa, me," Willow whispered.

She had never moved something so large. Only pencils and stuff. But in that moment, she'd never needed the power of magick more.

The chair leg clattered to the stairs next to her. She grabbed it up, and went down the stairs to help the guys.

Bathed in the sickly orange illumination of the emergency lights, the lobby was in chaos. Buffy was starting to worry. There were just so many of them, and if they couldn't even get past the lobby, they'd never get the others free. Her chest hurt as though she'd been holding her breath. She thought of Willow's sort of lopsided grin, the who-me? look that was so often on Xander's face . . . and she thought about Pike. His scraggly chin and ragged haircut and the scar she'd given him, the way his eyes always seemed to say he knew much more than he'd let on, the fact that he'd come to her for help.

He'd been there for her when all of this insanity was first taking her life over. He'd wanted desperately to run away, but he hadn't. He'd stayed and seen it through when she needed him.

If they were still alive, Buffy was going to keep them that way.

A dark-skinned, bald-headed vamp snarled and leaped at her. Buffy's only weapon was her stake. But that didn't include her hands and feet. She kicked up hard, and her foot connected with his jaw, brought him up short. Then she moved in with a devastating fist to his throat, spun and brought her elbow around to thunk against his chest. He was so off balance by her attack that he didn't even see the stake coming.

"Buffy!" Cordelia shouted.

The Slayer turned to see another vampire, a woman with close shorn red hair, trying a sneak attack. Cordelia brought the beam of her flashlight to bear, and the vamp-girl shied away, moving right into Oz's path. He pumped holy water into her face.

Then he brought the stake down.

A thick hand landed on Buffy's shoulder. She grabbed it and spun, breaking the vampire's arm. She staked him from behind, his broken arm dangling uselessly.

There were just so many of them.

Buffy looked around, trying to see if they'd made any progress. It seemed they had. Not so many new creatures had joined the fray. A pair of gothic-looking girls backed Angel into a corner, but Buffy knew from the look on his face he wasn't worried. A moment later, she knew why. He was drawing them in close on purpose.

Angel thrust his sword forward, impaling one of the goth chicks. The steel wouldn't kill her, but he used it to keep her out of reach as he staked the other one with the wooden shaft in his left hand. Then he brought his leg up, kicked the first one off his blade, and swung it around to cleave her head from her neck.

The two dusted within seconds of each other.

Buffy fended off a pair of vamps who looked like they were probably junkie runaways before this life. She thought even then that they were likely better off.

"Damn!" Oz swore, off to her right. "A little help here!"

He'd run out of holy water, and the vampires were closing in. Oz threw the Big Squirt at the three who advanced on him, but they only laughed. Buffy knew she had to go to him, but there were just too many.

Suddenly, Cordelia was there. She shone the flashlight beam on the vamps attacking Buffy, giving her the seconds she needed to stake two of them, then run to help Oz. It was no coincidence, either. Buffy could see in Cordelia's eyes that she had chosen her moment carefully. For once, there was no need for them to pretend that Cordelia was anything other than what she was: a mostly unlikable but brave and good-hearted girl. Sure, she had a stake, but Cordy was mainly using a weapon that didn't do anything but spook the bloodsuckers, buying the others precious moments. That took guts.

Buffy ran to help Oz. She staked one vamp from behind, and as it dusted, she turned to check up on Cordelia. She needn't have worried, Angel was there to help her, his sword flying.

"Go get Jocelyn!" one of the vampires snapped, and two others withdrew immediately and headed for the stairwell door.

Oz staked a vamp in front of him, and Buffy brushed its ash from her face. They were taking on the third together when she saw Oz's eyes widen as something over her shoulder caught his attention.

Buffy staked the third vamp, then turned around and stared across the lobby. In the infernal light of the emergency lamps, back in the elevator banks, Giles stood face-to-face with a demon.

"Malthus," Giles said, his voice filled with bilious hatred.

The demon laughed, its crimson lips pulled back to reveal black gums and gore-encrusted razor teeth. Its eyes were a putrid green with tiny yellow embers as pupils, and where certain breeds of demons had horns, this creature had weird contorted antlers that curled under and back as though the thing had brushed them there. Its body was the color of a bone-deep bruise, its feet more like those of a wolf than a man.

"Ah, excellent," the monstrosity said pleasantly. "My reputation precedes me."

"It does indeed," Giles replied coldly. "My grandmother went more than a quarter century without a decent night's sleep thanks to you. Sketches of your face litter her journals. I'd almost forgotten you. My mistake."

The demon sneered, smile disappearing from its face, eyes narrowing to their burning centers. Giles moved slightly back and to the left, taking the demon's measure. He slipped his jacket off quickly.

"Oh, really, Rupert, what must you be thinking? Are we to resort to simple fisticuffs like a pair of back-alley brawlers?"

"Oh, yes," Giles whispered.

He leaped forward. The demon changed, growing larger, more muscular, more human. But he'd misjudged. Giles wasn't about to fight him fairly. Malthus was a demon, after all. Instead, the Watcher whipped his jacket over the demon's head, swung behind him, pulled the sleeves taught around his neck, and yanked him down hard. With all his strength, he slammed the demon's covered head into the metal elevator doors, over and over.

Malthus shrank. In a moment, he was a small, lithe girl child, who slipped easily from Giles's grasp. When he stood up, he was already changing again.

Into Buffy.

When Buffy glanced over at Giles again, she froze. The demon had changed its shape instantaneously. One second, hellspawn, the next . . . the next.

"You've gotta be kidding me," Buffy whispered.

Then it attacked Giles. She wanted to go to him, but two more vampires moved in, and she had to defend herself. The odds weren't looking great. She and Oz and Cordelia and Angel were running out of weapons, and they were still badly outnumbered.

"Relax, ladies and gents," a familiar voice said behind her. "The cavalry's here."

Buffy staked a vamp, then turned to see Pike, Willow, and Xander standing just inside the stairwell door, all armed with sharp bits of wood. Her heart rose. Her friends were alive and, even better, they were armed.

"The cavalry's bloody and exhausted," Pike added, "but it's here."

Willow stepped forward, and Buffy thought she looked pretty confident for a girl who'd been a captive earlier in the evening. She slapped a thick, sharp stick against her hand and looked at the vampires who had turned to stalk the new arrivals.

"What we have here," Willow said, with a long, poorly executed southern drawl, "is a failure to communicate."

Buffy nodded.

"Angel!" she shouted, and ran toward him, slamming a vampire out of her way without even bothering to kill it.

Pike glanced over at her, hearing her shout Angel's name. She looked at him, their eyes met, and then she was at Angel's side, his hands reaching for her shoulders, steadying her, comforting her just by his presence. Once more, she glanced at Pike, and saw that he understood. He knew just as well as she did that things could only end up one way.

Pike offered a painful grin. Buffy smiled in return.

"We've got them now," Angel told her.

Buffy looked up at him, smile disappearing. "Maybe. But it isn't over yet. I need something from you."

"Anything," he said.

Giles winced in pain both physical and emotional as he heard the voice of Malthus spilling from the lips of his Slayer.

"Don't speak to me of that woman, boy," the demon-Buffy growled. "Your dear old granny is the only human ever to hurt me. And she did it twice. Long before you were born she poisoned me, Watcher. And I punished her. Oh, didn't I. And your dear old da as well."

Giles lifted the last stake, which he had drawn from within his coat, and lunged at the demon. Malthus knocked the stake from his hand, and it clacked against the wall and then rolled out into the lobby. Then, mimicking Buffy's fighting style, it leaped into the air and spun into a kick. Giles knew it was coming, had defended against it while sparring thousands of times. But he was astonished to find he could not defend himself in time.

He thought he felt his cheekbone crack as its foot connected, and he was thrown off his feet to land hard on the marble floor. His mouth was bleeding as he tried to drag himself up again. When he looked up, Malthus was merely Malthus once more, horrid as that was. The demon reached down and grabbed him, hauled him up, and slammed him against the wall.

Its breath was rancid.

"Ah, yes. Lovely old Granny Giles. That diseased old hag trapped me in the form of a crippled old crone. I couldn't walk, could barely speak, and her spell lasted more than fifteen years. You could say I have a bit of a grudge against the Giles clan."

It slapped Giles hard, and he went down again. From the floor, the Watcher glared at the creature before him. Malthus the Unformed. Deadly shapeshifter, trickster, and the bane of his family for more than half a century.

"How dare you?" Giles snapped. "After all you've done, *you* have a grudge? Well, let us end it here and now, then."

"By all means," the demon agreed amiably. "I mean, what more can I do to you now, hmm? I've broken your heart, broken your spirit, made you question all that you believe in. And now I'm killing the little family that you've gathered around you. Probably what your father really would have done, actually, if he'd been a vampire.

"That's how I know so much about you, by the way. His private journals made very entertaining reading. The things I could tell you about your mother would—"

With a roar of pain and sorrow and fury, Giles launched himself at the demon again. Malthus stood confidently, ready to hurt him some more. But Giles only feinted toward the demon, then lunged past him at the rectangular glass window on the wall. With his elbow, he shattered the glass, then reached in and grabbed hold of the fire extinguisher.

"Come now, Rupert. Do you really think I'll—"

Giles turned and sprayed the demon's face with the foam from the metal canister. Malthus snarled, not in pain or anger, but annoyance. That's all he was to the demon now, Giles knew.

But it underestimated him.

The Watcher ran at it, lifted the metal extinguisher,

and swung at the demon's head. With a clang, the metal slammed into the side of Malthus's face, snapping off the lower part of one of its horns. The demon started to stumble back, falling hard onto the tile. Giles went down with it, on top of it. Then he was straddling the demon, lifting the extinguisher over his head and bringing it down again and again, splintering horns, breaking teeth, crushing the demon's face to an oozing, pustulant pulp.

Malthus the Unformed fell still.

Giles slammed the heavy metal against its skull one final time, and then he slid off the demon's body. He shuddered, let the extinguisher clunk to the marble, cracking a tile, and it rolled away. The Watcher stood slowly, shakily, and only then did he realize that at some point he'd lost his glasses. He glanced around, vision a bit blurry, and spotted them just in front of one of the elevators.

When he bent to pick them up, he swayed a little. He stood, took a deep breath, and slipped them on. Then he bent his head to his hands, fingers steepled on his forehead, and whispered into the cup of his palms.

"Rest in peace, old man. Thank the Lord you still rest in peace."

Then from behind him there came a sudden wet tearing sound.

Giles spun to see Malthus changing, undergoing yet another metamorphosis. The demon's gut was tearing open, forced apart by what was rising from within. Yet another face, perhaps its true face at last. If it could have been compared to anything, Giles would have said it was insectoid. But he'd never seen an insect with teeth like that.

Malthus opened pincers that passed for its mouth,

and a stream of stinking black fluid sprayed across the marble floor, nearly splattering his shoes. Where it hit the ground, the thing's spit ate through the tile like acid.

"Once again," it said, in a voice like the buzzing of a million mosquitoes. "Once again a Giles has hurt me. But I promise you, Watcher, it's for the last time."

Giles took one step back and looked at the thing coldly, tiredly.

"Yes, well, I don't doubt that at all, you silly sod," he said, and crossed his arms in defiance.

The demon hesitated, startled by his response. It took Malthus a moment to understand. Even then, the demon was too late. Buffy was there. The Slayer swung the gleaming steel sword in a diagonal arc, and it sliced through the insectoid head at that angle, sending a cascade of black ichor flowing onto the floor. The top half of its head hit the tile near Giles's feet, and he kicked it away.

Beyond her, Giles saw the others dusting the last two vampires, then moving to Buffy's aid. But Buffy didn't need their help. She kept hacking furiously, angrily, perhaps in some way punishing the demon for having hurt Giles so.

For his part, though, Giles felt oddly calm.

It was over.

Epilogue

THREE NIGHTS LATER, BUFFY STOOD AT THE LONG BANK of windows in the main airport terminal, and watched as Giles's plane lumbered across the sky. He'd suffered a great deal of emotional pain in the past week or so, and it had stayed with him. Now he was headed to the only place he felt he'd be able to let it go, to put it behind him.

Rupert Giles was going home.

Of course, other than the Council of Watchers, there was very little home for him to go back to. But as Giles himself had explained, "There are streets to walk, memories to savor, both good and bad. And there are some lingering little hauntings I'd like to finally lay to rest."

In spite of all he'd suffered, Buffy was happy for him. He'd finally realized that, for better or worse, he owed a great deal of what and who he'd become to his parents, mother *and* father. And while her Watcher was busy figuring all that out, the Slayer had come to almost exactly the same realization.

Despite their difference in age, they were both still learning. And this time, the lesson was the same.

"Freaky-deaky," Buffy whispered.

Then she couldn't see the plane anymore, and she turned around to walk back down the concourse. Outside, Oz, Willow, and Xander were waiting in the van. Cordelia had declined to come along. She'd hyperventilated for about twenty-four hours after the melee at CRD, and now she was off getting her manicure repaired. She'd threatened to send Buffy the bill.

"He got off okay?" Willow asked tentatively, eyebrows raised.

"Yeah," Buffy confirmed. "He'll be fine."

"Okay, no sad face, Summers," Xander ordered. "I might have to do the whole happy feet thing, and you know how ugly that can get. C'mon, you vanquished the evil, crushed the stone guy to gravel, and ran the lovely but nasty demon harlot out of town. You're like the John Wayne of the supernatural."

Buffy raised an eyebrow and looked at him.

"Only lots prettier," Xander said, blinking. "And, um, blond, and, right, whole girl thing."

"Is that helping?" Willow asked him. " 'Cause to most people, it would seem to be just babbling. And I know babbling. I'm an expert."

The van pulled up to a red light, and Oz glanced back at Buffy. He smiled that sort of knowing, lazy smile of his, and nodded slightly.

"Hey, Rock," Oz said. "Watch me pull a rabbit out of my hat."

Buffy laughed, her eyes narrowing, nose crinkling up. She shook her head. "Again?" she said in reply. "That trick never works."

Willow smiled at her guy, realizing that he'd just accomplished what Buffy's two best friends hadn't been able to do: he'd cheered her up. Only for a moment, but it was a start.

Buffy wondered if Willow really knew how lucky she was. Oz might not exactly be normal—the whole werewolf thing pretty much shot that to hell—but what they had together . . . Buffy could only dream about it.

When she turned the key and pushed open the front door, Buffy was trying to be quiet. Pike had opted out of the airport trip. He was still pretty banged up from the whole mess. But her mother was having Alan over for dinner again, and she didn't want to interrupt them. Everyone else was going down to the Bronze, and she'd told them to go on without her. She figured she and Pike could ride down on the Harley, give her mom some space.

"Buffy?" Joyce called, coming out of the kitchen.

"Sorry, Mom. I was trying to be quiet."

"That's all right," Joyce said, smiling wistfully. "Do you want something to eat?"

"I don't want to interrupt."

"Nothing to interrupt, actually. Alan left an hour ago."

Buffy stared at her mother. "I'm sorry," she said, after a moment's pause. "What happened?"

Joyce walked over to Buffy and kissed her on the head. "It isn't important."

"Sure it is," Buffy insisted, drawing her mother over to sit next to her on the couch.

"Well, he asked where you were, and I told him," Joyce explained. "Then he asked me if I thought a girl your age ought to be out so late, and suggested I keep a closer eye on you. I asked him if he thought he could find his own way out."

Buffy sighed. "I don't know what to say."

"You don't have to say anything," Joyce said, smiling. "And I know what you're thinking. It has nothing to do with you being the Slayer. It has to do with you being a teenager, and me being your mother. You're my daughter, dammit, and nobody but nobody is going to tell me how to raise you."

"I think you've done just fine on your own," Buffy told her.

"Darn tootin'," Joyce said firmly.

"Darn tootin'?" Buffy asked, dubious.

"Well," Joyce replied, a coy expression on her face, "I wouldn't want to set a bad example with foul language, would I?"

"Oh, of course not," Buffy agreed, chuckling. "You'd never do that."

They were interrupted by the sound of footfalls on the stairs, and Buffy turned to see Pike coming down. He had his duffel over his shoulder. But then, somehow she'd known he would. She looked at him, and smiled sadly.

"Why don't I leave you two alone?" Joyce said quickly.

Buffy didn't reply.

When her mother was gone, she stood up and went to the door. She opened it, let Pike pass, and then followed him out to the Harley in silence. He stowed his gear on the bike and then turned to face her.

Pike put out a hand and stroked her face so gently with his fingers. Buffy reached up and traced his scar, still not quite able to believe it had been she who had put it there.

"You're always leaving," she said quietly.

"It's what I do," he agreed. "But I always come back."

"Until you don't," Buffy said.

Pike nodded once. "Until I don't."

About the Author

CHRISTOPHER GOLDEN is the award-winning, *L.A. Times* best-selling author of such novels as *Strangewood* and *Of Saints and Shadows,* among others. He has written eight *Buffy the Vampire Slayer* novels (seven with Nancy Holder), including the recent hardcover *Immortal.*

Golden's comic book work includes the Marvel Knights restart of *The Punisher,* as well as *Wolverine/Punisher: Revelation* (both with Tom Sniegoski), *The Crow: Waking Nightmares,* and issues of *Spider-Man Unlimited, Wolverine,* and *X-Man.* He has also written a number of *Buffy*-related comics projects.

The editor of the Bram Stoker Award–winning book of criticism, *CUT!: Horror Writers on Horror Film,* he is the co-author of *The Watcher's Guide: The Official Companion to Buffy the Vampire Slayer* and *The Sunnydale High Yearbook.*

Golden was born and raised in Massachusetts, where he still lives with his family. He graduated from Tufts University. Please visit him at http://www.christophergolden.com.

Bullying.
Threats.
Bullets.

Locker searches? Metal detectors?

Fight back without fists.

fight for your rights:
take a stand against violence

BUFFY

THE VAMPIRE

SLAYER™

IMMORTAL

She cannot die.
Strike her down, but like the night she will always
come again.
And she will bring forth the end of Man....

Has Buffy met her match in an
immortal vampire?

The first Buffy hardcover
by Christopher Golden and Nancy Holder

Available from Pocket Books

Buffy: "Willow, why don't you compile a list of kids who've died here who might have turned into ghosts."

Xander: "We're on a Hellmouth. It's gonna be long list."

Willow: "Have you seen the 'In Memorium' section in the yearbook?"

BUFFY
THE VAMPIRE
SLAYER™

How *does* the Sunnydale yearbook staff memorialize all the less fortunate classmates?

Get your very own copy of the Slayer's Sunnydale High School yearbook, full of cast photos, school event wrap-ups, and personal notes from Buffy's best buds.

By Christopher Golden and Nancy Holder

Available Fall 1999

Published by Pocket Books